WE
REGRET
TO
INFORM
YOU

ARIEL KAPLAN

EMBER

Text copyright © 2018 by Ariel Kaplan
Cover art copyright © 2018 by Maggie Edkins

All rights reserved. Published in the United States by Ember,
an imprint of Random House Children's Books, a division of Penguin Random
House LLC, New York. Originally published in hardcover in the United States by
Alfred A. Knopf, an imprint of Random House Children's Books, a division of
Penguin Random House LLC, New York, in 2018.

Ember and the E colophon are registered trademarks
of Penguin Random House LLC.

Visit us on the Web! GetUnderlined.com

Educators and librarians, for a variety of teaching tools,
visit us at RHTeachersLibrarians.com

Library of Congress Cataloging-in-Publication Data is available upon request.

ISBN 978-1-5247-7373-1 (pbk.)

Printed in the United States of America
10 9 8 7 6 5 4 3 2 1
First Ember Edition 2020

FOR MY PARENTS

CHAPTER ½

IN THE BEGINNING, THERE IS A FORMULA.

Actually, there are several formulas. You start learning them in algebra and then keep going, because you need them to pass your classes and eventually graduate. You memorize formulas to get through geometry, through science and SATs and AP exams. You fill your brain with exponents and derivatives, wondering *When am I ever going to use this?* and the answer for most people is probably "never," but learn them you do, because the alternative is a lifetime of misery and poverty and unemployment. Learn them or you will not pass GO. You will not collect two hundred dollars. Your life, it seems, will be ruined in some strange, horrible, undefinable way. You imagine yourself on your deathbed, reaching out a withered hand to future grandchildren, beckoning them closer, closer, to impart the wisdom you wish you had possessed in your youth,

1

before your life was derailed, misspent. "If only," your aged self says, "I had remembered the quadratic reciprocity theorem." And then: death.

So you learn your formulas: the Pythagorean theorem, the quadratic equation, $E=mc^2$, and all that. And then, just when you're approaching the finish line, when high school seems so, so close to being over, you have to learn the biggest, ugliest formula of them all.

The college admissions formula.

This is the formula that hangs over you from the first day of high school until the day you walk out again, mortarboard atop your head, diploma in your hand, as your mother cries and takes way too many pictures. It's the formula you parse out in dreams, pick at while eating pizza during student government meetings or studying for finals that account for precisely 20% of your grade. The one you wake up thinking about every morning, the one you breathe in and out like heavy oxygen, filling your lungs with it as you walk from class to class, as you grip your pencil while you scribble on pop quizzes, as you flex your tired fingers while you hammer out essays on keyboards. It lingers behind your eyes as you drift off to sleep, dreaming of that single "YES" that will be the key to unlocking four years of learning and networking, and a lifetime of success to follow.

It looks like this:

$$\frac{\left(11 \int_{2014}^{2018} (\mathfrak{gpa}) \, dt + \frac{\mathcal{SAT}_{\text{math}} + \mathcal{SAT}_{\text{verb}} + \frac{\mathcal{SAT}_{\text{essay}}}{3}}{4\pi} + 27\left(\chi_{leg} + \chi_{aff} + \chi_{ath}\right) + \epsilon_{curricular}^{extra}\right)}{\prod_{j=1}^{n}\left(\text{Recommendation}_j * \Re\left(e^{2\pi i} * \frac{4+2i}{7-2i}\right)\right)}$$

Like I said, it isn't pretty. It's also unofficial, since every college has its own secret formula, but this is as close as the administration at Blanchard High has been able to approximate. This formula is on a poster in Ms. Pendleton's college counseling office, and we've all worked it out for ourselves, inputting our GPAs and SAT scores to figure out our college admissions number. Mine, for example, is 812. The higher your score, the more likely you are to get in wherever you're applying.

The upshot is that it's pretty easy to predict whether you'll be accepted at most schools. (I say most because at schools like Harvard or Stanford that reject almost everyone it's a total crapshoot, even if the formula shows that you ought to get in. It's just that hard.)

So I knew what my chances were when I sat down during the spring of my junior year and assembled a list of reach schools, middle-of-the-road schools, and a safety. Seven schools total. I was confident. I was prepared. I was a college admissions machine.

Once my applications were signed, sealed, and delivered, there was nothing to do but sit back and wait for the acceptance letters to roll in.

CHAPTER ONE

THE MORNING I STARTED TO SUSPECT THAT MS. PENDLETON'S equation had some holes in it, I was late for school. Mom and I were on the way to the Metro; we share a car, and on the days I have stuff to do after school I drop her off to take the train into Arlington. We're a well-oiled machine in the morning; to get both of us where we need to be on time, we have to go out the front door by 7:10. This gives us fifteen extra minutes of wiggle room in case we hit traffic, or someone spills coffee on themselves and has to change again, or whatever.

Mom was driving so I'd have time to eat a bagel before I had to switch seats at the station, and with my free hand I was fiddling with the radio, bouncing back and forth between the morning news, which my mom wanted to listen to, and the music I was listening to during the commercials. I wasn't really 100% awake yet; I hoped she was, because she was driving, and then there was a huge *clunk* followed by *rattle-rattle-rattle,* and then my mother looked in the rearview mirror and said, "Holy crap." I turned and looked, and there were sparks coming from the back of the car.

"Pull over," I said, dropping my bagel. "Pull over, pull over, WE ARE ON FIRE."

"I'm working on it," she said through gritted teeth. "It's not on fire. Yet."

"There are sparks!"

"I'm aware of the sparks! Can I get to the right?"

My mom is always doing this thing where I have to copilot and tell her if she can merge. I have no idea what she does when I'm not in the car. "It's fine," I said. "Just go. Go. Go like you mean it. No, wait. Wait!" This last bit was because she'd waited too long, and there was a truck bearing down on us from the right lane.

"You said I could go!" she shouted, jerking back into her lane.

"You could have, when I actually said it!"

"I was merging!"

"You flinched! You can't flinch on 95!"

"I think there might be fire now," she said. "Do you smell that?"

"Get over," I said. "Get over get over get over."

She merged and pulled over to the shoulder. The car made an ungodly scraping sound as it came to a stop.

Both of us turned to look out the back window. I couldn't see any flames, but there was smoke, and something smelled like burnt motor oil.

"What happened?" I said, still looking out the rear window, hoping that nothing was getting ready to explode back there.

5

"Muffler, I think," she said. She got out of the car and went around to the back, and I followed. "Oof," she said. The muffler had indeed detached itself from the bottom of the car and was being dragged on the asphalt by whatever it was attached to on the other end. A bolt? I have no idea what holds mufflers on.

"I'm thinking that's bad?" I said.

"It's bad."

"Can you, like, put it back? Maybe with duct tape?"

"Duct tape," she said, mulling it over. "No, we'll have to get it towed."

"Great," I said. "I'm supposed to be in calculus in half an hour." I pulled out my phone and started texting to see if anyone could come and pick me up, but it was still early, and nobody answered.

"Nate?" Mom said. "Caroline?"

"Still asleep," I said. "They're not answering."

"Well, you'll just have to go in a cab," she said.

"Mom," I said. "I don't think—"

"It's fine."

"A Lyft would be cheaper," I said.

"I'm not putting my eighteen-year-old in a Lyft," she said. "Anybody could be driving it."

"Do you know how much a cab is going to cost?"

Stupid question. She knew exactly how much it would cost.

"Here's what's happening," she said. "You're going to school in a cab. I'm going to wait here for the tow truck." She rubbed her face with her hand. "I had a nine o'clock meeting today."

We stared at the dead car. I don't usually think about how much depends on a big chunk of metal and an internal combustion engine, but one sheared-off bolt was all it took to set us scrambling. The car repair and the cab would both end up on the credit card, my mom would miss her meeting, and if I was very lucky, I wouldn't miss a pop quiz in calculus.

Ten minutes later my cab showed up. I gave the driver directions to my school and then sat back to listen to twenty minutes of the second act of *Hamilton,* plus three different cell phone conversations in Amharic. Then Hamilton died (both literally and metaphorically) and the music ended, and then the driver was singing along with *Evita,* and I guess the driver had watched too much *Phantom of the Opera* because he kept saying "Sing! SING!" and seemed annoyed that all I knew was the chorus, and also that I really don't sing all that well.

I got out after the second verse of "Don't Cry for Me, Argentina," shutting the door as the driver belted out, *They are illooooooosions* ... and wondering if this guy had had theatrical aspirations before settling down as a cabdriver, because he sang like a dream but did not seem to know how to, like, parallel park.

The forty-dollar cab got me to school ten minutes past the bell, and I had to sprint through the building, racing past Mr. Pelletier, the assistant head, who looked like he would really have liked to give me service hours, except he was already in the middle of giving service hours to someone else.

The rest of my calculus class was still half-asleep as I slid into my chair, sweaty and panting, but Mr. Bronstein frowned at me as I pulled out my notebook. "Miss Abramavicius," he said. "You are aware that your grades this quarter will be sent to your college?"

"Yes, sir," I said, still puffing.

"And we still have the AP exam coming up," he went on.

"Unless you are looking forward to repeating this class in college with a less understanding instructor." He pointed at me with his dry-erase pen. "One who locks the latecomers out of the classroom."

I wondered if that was an actual thing that happened. "I'm sorry," I said. "My mom's car died."

He nodded thoughtfully. I was a "special case" at Blanchard because I was a senior and I didn't have my own car. I wasn't the only person there on a scholarship, not by a long shot, but I spent less time trying to pretend than the others. We aren't poor, but the tuition at Blanchard is almost as much as my mother makes in a year, and I don't think it's particularly shameful not to have a cool forty thousand dollars a year sitting around collecting dust. The school fronted me three-quarters of my tuition, and my mother went broke paying the last bit.

"This is the best education you can get," Mom said when we went without things like vacations or new shoes or takeout. "You know, we live in a global economy. You're competing against people from all over the world. That's how things are now."

It was a speech I heard often. It wasn't enough to compete against the kids from my school, or the mid-Atlantic, or the US. I was competing against people from China and Germany and Brazil, and would be for the rest of my life. How many people are there these days? Seven billion? The idea of all those people fighting for all the same things I wanted weighed on me. It was like circling the parking lot at the mall on Christmas Eve and discovering that there was one spot left—and several million people were already there, lined up to snatch it. If I thought about it too much, it made my head hurt.

Mr. Bronstein turned back toward the board and started

discussing derivatives, which I already knew how to do, and I absentmindedly took some notes on what he was saying. My phone buzzed in my purse, and after deciding that no one was paying attention, I fished it out of my bag and stashed it on my knee.

It was a text from Caroline Black, who was sitting two rows behind me on the other side of the room.

Did you hear? she texted.

Hear what?

Oh my God, it's Admissions Day. You did NOT forget.

But I had. A day so significant I had not even bothered to write it down. I'd been waiting for it forever, but with the car situation it had slipped out of my mind, and I hadn't thought about it since breakfast. Not every college sends out emails on Admissions Day: it's only for the Ivies and some of the other top schools, which have some kind of agreement to tell everyone on the same day, aside from the early-decision folks. At Blanchard it's become like a party day for the super-high achievers, the day we've been waiting for since we enrolled (or, in some cases, since preschool). Parents wait on standby to throw impromptu dinner parties for kids who get into Haverford, or set up emergency therapy sessions for kids who don't. It's like having a stripper pop out of a cake and declare the direction of the rest of your life, with all the awkwardness that implies. I'd made a point of not telling my mom about it, because it would have made her nuts, and the last thing she needs is more stress.

It's also the last thing I need, but I'm younger and more durable. I think.

I turned around and glanced at Caroline. She raised her eyebrows at me.

I texted, *AND?*

I totally got into Dartmouth, beyotch.

!!! I typed, which looked dumb, but it's hard to text enthusiasm. Dartmouth, I knew, was Caroline's first choice. *I'll get you a cookie at lunch!*

YES YOU WILL.

I slid my phone into my purse and went back to half paying attention to calculus. I hadn't gotten any emails yet, but I knew other people were hearing as responses trickled in and people would let out stifled little shrieks in the middle of class. After calculus, I saw girls standing puffy-eyed in the bathroom, staring unmoving at their own reflections, and I wondered who'd turned them down. I checked my phone after I washed my hands, but so far I'd heard nothing. I sent myself a test email, just to make sure it was working, and it popped right back up in my inbox, and because I'm an idiot, I still jumped a little when it showed up.

The girl at the sink next to me—an underclassman I didn't know—said, "Well?"

"It was no one," I said. "No one yet."

During third period I squeezed into my seat between Nate Miller and Jim Wei; Nate had his laptop out and was working on a paper, and Jim was obsessively hitting refresh on the email app on his phone.

"What are you working on?" I asked Nate, who was in this pattern where he would type three or four words, swear, hit the delete key, and then start over again.

"Eh," he said. His hair had fallen into his eyes, and he brushed it out of the way. "Leave me alone. This is due in an hour."

I leaned sideways for a look at the screen and saw that the title was "*Heart of Darkness:* A Literary Analysis," which I'm pretty sure was due a couple of days ago. "How much you got?"

"Three paragraphs. This book *sucks.*"

"You could have watched *Apocalypse Now.* It's basically the same thing."

"I hated that, too." He pushed the computer away and tapped my hand. "I just got your text, by the way, about needing a ride. Call the house next time and tell my mom to wake me up."

I shrugged.

"No, I mean it. I don't hear my phone if I'm asleep, but Mom'll wake me up if you tell her to."

I pulled out my own phone and refreshed my email a few times to end the conversation. It's kind of awkward being Nate's "poor" friend sometimes, especially since no one in the real world thinks I'm poor. But the first time Nate came to visit me at my townhouse, he'd thought we owned the whole block, that it was one big house, not five houses pushed together.

"So what are you going to tell Ms. Parker?" I asked when it was obvious no college emails were forthcoming.

"I don't know." He rubbed his temple. "I think I feel a migraine coming on."

"You look a little sick," I said, which was totally not true.

"Maybe I should go to the nurse."

Nate had faked so many migraines over the last six months that his parents had taken him to a specialist, who prescribed him some very expensive pills that he never took. As far as coping mechanisms go, I guess it wasn't a bad one.

He closed his computer and looked across me at Jim,

who was still hitting refresh, refresh, refresh on his email. "A watched pot never boils, dude."

"Actually," Jim said without looking up, "it does. The watching has no effect on the temperature."

"Okay," Nate said. "Make yourself nuts if you need to."

Jim rolled his eyes and stowed his phone. "So did you hear? Meredith Dorsay got into Harvard, Yale, *and* Princeton."

"Whoa," I said. "All of them?"

"I'm surprised you didn't hear her screaming. She sounded like the freaking fire alarm."

"Huh," I said, because all I could think was Meredith Dorsay heard back from Harvard and Princeton, and I had not, and what did that mean?

"Yeah, her mom picked her up from school. In a limo."

Nate made a face. "What for? She has a car."

"Caitlin Mayfair said they were on their way to the airport. They're going to Paris for the weekend."

"Caitlin Mayfair is full of it."

"Yeah, well, I know she left, though, because she was supposed to be in calculus with me last period and she wasn't there."

I shrugged. I, for one, hoped that Meredith actually *had* gone to Paris. Maybe she'd stay there until graduation.

"Hey," Jim said. "Maybe if you get into Harvard, too, you guys can be roomies."

I gave him my best death glare, which lacked the desired effect, since it made him crack up. "Don't worry, Vicious," he said. "You've got everything Meredith's got. You're a shoo-in."

I nodded, because it was true. I had the grades, the scores, the extracurriculars. Not the internships, maybe, but that was because I had an actual paying job in the summer. Not the random trips to Paris, either. Or the limo. Probably mufflers don't fall off limos, or if they do, the people riding in them don't trouble themselves over it.

Mrs. Freeport started class, and I was taking some half-hearted notes on the failure of the Bohr model to accurately describe the atom when my phone beeped with a new email. I slipped it under the lab table, just long enough to see if it was from a college.

It was from Princeton.

Princeton, like most of the other Ivies, has an admissions website; you log in with your student PIN, and a message pops up to tell you whether you got in or not. Nate peered over my shoulder to see what I was doing, and I shut my phone off and stuck it into the pocket of my jeans. Then I put my hand in the air and asked to go to the bathroom.

Two minutes later I locked myself in a stall and clicked through to the Princeton website. I imagined going back into the room to tell Nate and Jim I'd gotten in. Maybe someone would get *me* a cookie at lunch.

The website popped up, and I entered my PIN, drew in a triumphant breath, and clicked NEXT.

Status, it said. *Not accepted.*

"WHAT?" I said too loudly, and the girl in the stall next to me said, "What is your *problem*?"

"Sorry," I said.

I stared at the screen. I refreshed the screen. Nope. Nope.

Maybe, I thought, I'd entered the wrong PIN. But there was my name, Mischa Abramavicius, and my birth date, and it said, NO NO NO.

"No way," I whispered.

I banged my head against the stall door.

"Are you taking a pregnancy test in there?" the girl said.

"No," I said. "No. Everything's fine."

"'Cause I'm trying to *PEE* here."

"And no one's stopping you."

"I have a shy bladder and you're being seriously intrusive."

"Just go to the bathroom. Jesus."

"Maybe you could have your breakdown somewhere else?"

"I'm not having a breakdown!"

"Well, whatever. Go away."

I looked at the shoes of the girl next to me. Black lug-soled Mary Janes with lace tights. Probably they belonged to Shira Gastman, which meant that she was waiting for me to leave so she could smoke a joint in the stall. "Nice shoes," I said.

"Would you *go*?"

"I'm going," I said. Just not to Princeton, apparently. Crap.

I stared down at my phone one last time, reminding myself that Princeton was one of those schools the formula didn't exactly apply to, because there were just more qualified applicants than spots. I could have lost out to the entire Olympic gymnastics team, or to that girl I read about who published her first novel at sixteen. People with that crazy "it" factor that most of us have no shot at getting. It was fine. It was fine. It was fine. I shut off my phone and went to tuck it into my pocket and

fumbled

it

into

the

toilet.

I stared down at it for a minute. It had already sunk to the bottom of the bowl. I said, "Damn it."

"*Really?*" said Shira.

Then, because there was nothing else to do, I picked my phone up out of the toilet, dried it off with some toilet paper, and stuck it back in my pocket, knowing full well it would probably never work again.

I slumped back to class, where Nate looked at me expectantly. "So?" he whispered.

"So what?" I asked, still contemplating the replacement cost of my phone. It hadn't been an expensive one, at least.

"Princeton?"

"You are so nosy!"

"Like you wouldn't ask."

"Mischa," Mrs. Freeport said. "Nate. Please."

"Sorry," I said. Nate smiled and ducked his head. He leaned over and wrote *PRINCETON?* on my notes.

I stared forward. I shook my head the barest amount possible.

NO WAY, he wrote.

I was a little touched that he thought I'd be such a shoo-in. But it didn't exactly make me feel better. I kept thinking, though, that I couldn't imagine how I hadn't even ended up on the wait list.

From my other side, Jim wrote, *I heard that some schools make deals with each other, like if you apply to both only one will take you. It keeps their acceptance numbers low.*

Who told you that?

My aunt's friend is in the admissions office at Cornell.

So how do they decide which school takes you?

Not sure about that part. But maybe this means you're in at Harvard?

This sounded like wishful thinking to me.

All through the rest of the day, I watched as people's phones pinged, and their owners either whooped or burst into tears. A few hardier souls turned their phones off, because they didn't want to have to get the news in front of everyone else. I didn't want to tell anyone about my phone's potty adventures, so I claimed to be doing the same. "I'm waiting until the end of the day," I said. "I'm not really worried about it." Ha. Ha. Ha.

So I didn't get my email from Harvard until I went home and fired up my mom's ancient laptop.

I copied my PIN into Harvard's website and closed my eyes. I counted to ten. I opened them again.

I hadn't gotten in there, either.

CHAPTER TWO

IT WAS OKAY, I TOLD MYSELF AS I LAY ON MY BED WITH MY calculus notes. Harvard and Princeton are long shots for everyone, and both had been contingent on my getting big bucks in financial aid anyway, so there'd always been a chance that I might not have been able to go even if I had gotten in. And I still had five schools left. It was too bad, but it was okay. I was okay. I just had to wait for the others, and those should be coming in any time now. Any time now.

Any. Time.

My mother came home from work an hour later. She was a lawyer with Legal Helpline, which means that she spent the day working with people who needed lawyers but couldn't afford them, and she didn't know what to expect from day to day. Sometimes she got some really sad cases: parents trying to get custody arrangements changed, people with immigration status problems, all kinds of things. That day, she looked particularly tired.

"Hey, Mischa," she said. "Good news: the car's fixed. I think. How was school?"

"It was fine," I said. "Nate got sick, though. I need to take him my government notes later." Nate had gone AWOL right after physics, probably with the expected migraine. He'd called my landline after school.

"You aren't answering my texts," he'd said. "Are you dead?"

"I'm not," I'd said. "But my phone might be. What's up?"

"Wait list at Northwestern," he'd said. "I'm on it."

"Oh. Sorry."

"It's okay. I'm still holding out for Emory anyway. Chicago's too cold in the winter."

"Yeah," I'd said, because Chicago *is* cold in the winter. Emory, I knew, was Nate's first choice and had been for years. "So did you finish your *Heart of Darkness* paper?"

"Gaaaaah . . . don't ask me that. I'm going to have to ask for another extension."

"Another one? How do you keep getting these?"

"My eyes," he'd said, "are very blue."

"Ha."

"If you bring me your government notes later, I'll love you forever."

I'd known Nate long enough to know that he was not going to love me forever, government notes or not, but I'd said, "Yeah, fine."

"You're the best."

"I know."

• • •

"Again?" my mother said. "That kid." Which meant either *Poor Nate, he's sick all the time* or *That kid is going to be living in his parents' basement until he's forty if he doesn't get it together.* Or possibly both. My mother liked Nate, but when she looked at him, she saw a bona fide parental nightmare. Success was defined in a limited way for Norah Abramavicius: it meant college ⟶ graduate school ⟶ job. Or possibly, college ⟶ medical school ⟶ job. Actually, she would probably be okay with just college ⟶ job, too, if it came right down to it. But anything that didn't involve higher education and employment (and me living someplace that was not with her) was a disaster too horrible to contemplate.

Nate and I had been lab partners in biology freshman year; I'd come in from public school, and it seemed like everyone else at Blanchard had known each other from kindergarten, which made making friends kind of a problem, and I had to remind myself on the regular that I was there for the education—for the diploma—and not for the companionship. But then I went to Nate's house after school one day, and we ended up spending four hours watching *Gilmore Girls* reruns on Netflix, and I'd really wanted to kiss him, but he was dating Pete Neilson, so I figured he was gay, and by the time I realized he was bi, I was pretty much in the friend zone, which is fine, because Nate's great, and this way I get to be with him with no drama or breakups.

There's no making out, either, which is kind of unfortunate, but oh well.

I probably should have told Mom right then about Princeton and Harvard, and I took a deep breath to do it, too, but then it occurred to me that there was absolutely no point in telling her at that exact moment. If I waited a few days, or maybe a week, I'd hear back from my other schools. Telling her I'd been rejected from Harvard and Princeton wouldn't matter so much if I was telling her that I'd gotten in a bunch of other places at the same time, and there was no point in making her feel bad for no reason. The only people who knew were Jim and Nate, and they and my mother did not, so far as I knew, attend the same coffee klatches, so it wasn't like she was going to hear it from either of them.

So instead of saying, *I have wasted three and a half years of effort and a very expensive private school education!* I said, "What's for dinner?"

"Oh," she said. "Shoot. I was supposed to stop at the store on my way home from the garage. I was going to make tacos. I don't have the shells."

"We could just do them like burritos," I said, which is what we'd done the last time we'd been out of shells on Taco Night.

"No tortillas."

"Um. Nachos?"

"No chips."

"Taco salad?"

"No lettuce."

"Erm. Taco sandwiches?"

She rolled her eyes. "Now that's just sad."

But no one wanted to go back out, and we needed to use up the ground beef, so we had taco sandwiches on soggy white bread, which had been on sale the week before. They weren't terrible, actually. That's a lie. They were super bad. Anyway, afterward, I went to see Nate.

He'd gotten into Emory, and his mother had come home with a cake.

・・・

That night, while my mom was in the shower, I snuck back into her room and checked my email again. I hadn't told her about my phone. It was currently stashed in a box of rice, which I hoped would dry it out enough to make it usable again, but that meant I couldn't even try to turn it back on for three days, which was a huge pain.

I had trouble looking at the screen when my email opened up, but I could still see right away that I'd gotten a bunch of new messages. College messages.

I took a deep breath, in and out. This was it. The moment I'd been anticipating for four years. Longer, even. Since I was old enough to know what college was. Maybe first grade? I dimly remembered a trip Mom and I had taken into DC; I'm not sure why we'd gone, maybe we were having lunch with one of her friends, but afterward she'd taken me through the Georgetown campus. I remembered all the students, who looked like real grown-ups to me, since I'd only been seven or so. They were so beautiful, I thought, talking and laughing and swinging their arms, carelessly brilliant as they made their way to class, carrying stacks of books under their arms or stuffed into messenger bags. The buildings looked to me like they were a thousand years old. "If you work very, very hard at school," my mother had said, "maybe you can go here someday, too."

I'd looked up at her. I was a pretty good kid, I thought. I usually did my homework, and when I didn't, I'd get a lecture and then feel bad. My grandmother had escaped from life behind the Iron Curtain at the age of five; she and her own mother—who had survived the Shoah and avoided the camps by the skin of her teeth—had fled through East Berlin before the wall was built. "Grandma didn't escape from Communism," my mom would say, when tiny Mischa would balk at writing out her spelling words, "so you could mess around." The lecture worked: I seldom messed around. I thought I was working pretty hard, but I guess I could have worked harder. And if I did, my mother was telling me, there would be a reward at the end.

Then a Frisbee had hit me in the knee. It didn't really hurt, but I said, "OW!" and bent to pick it up. A boy—I'd thought he was a man, then—ran over to get it. "I'm so sorry," he said. "I'm a terrible shot with this thing."

"It's okay," I said, handing him the Frisbee back. I don't really remember what he looked like, just the overall impression that he'd been tall and gangly. He ran back to his friends, tossing the Frisbee in front of him, and everyone laughed, this gang of boys and girls, on their way to study French or chemistry or psychology. I'd never seen so many people who looked so happy in one place. And why shouldn't they be happy? Shining stars, every one of them, passing through on their way to a bigger, better life.

I opened the emails, one by one. And then, after I'd read them, I cleared my mother's browser history, shut the computer down, and went back to my own room, where I spent the next five hours staring at the ceiling.

Dear Miss Abramavicius,

We regret to inform you that we cannot offer you admission at this time. Our admissions process was very competitive this year, and we had to turn away many worthy candidates. We thank you for your interest and wish you the best of luck in your future endeavors.

Regards,
Georgetown University

Dear Miss Abramavicius,

It is with great regret that we must
tell you blah blah blah many qualified
applicants, etc.

Most sincerely,
Williams College

Dear Miss Abramavicius,

Too bad. So sad.

Best wishes for your future,
Virginia Polytechnic Institute
and State University

Dear Miss Abramavicius,

Nope.

Good luck, sucker,
The University of Virginia

CHAPTER THREE

THIS WAS NOT HAPPENING.

That's what I told myself: This was not happening. It could not be happening. I would not allow it to be happening.

I supposed this happened, occasionally, to other people. People who hadn't properly applied Ms. Pendleton's handy-dandy college admissions formula. People who misunderstood where they stood in the hierarchy of high school academia.

That was not me. Therefore, this could not be happening.

I felt . . . numb. Like I was watching a movie about someone else. I got up the next morning. I dissolved a packet of instant oatmeal in a bowl of hot water. And I went to school.

What I did not do was tell any of this to my mother. This wasn't the result of any conscious decision on my part: I just didn't open my mouth and make the words come out. It's so simple, really, not to tell people things. All you have to do is not say them.

This should not have seemed like a deep thought to me, because it wasn't.

At school I managed to avoid everyone, which is surprisingly easy to do when you don't have a phone. Somebody asked me if I was okay. It might have been Jim. It might have been Caroline. I told him/her/them I had a headache, which was not untrue. I felt a little like I was swimming through Jell-O.

That afternoon, I had to meet the rest of the senior student government officers at the Starbucks two blocks from campus. I caught a ride with Caroline, who is the secretary, and Mark Santos, who is the treasurer. I'm the vice president, a position I chose strategically because it involves less work than any of the other three main positions (I don't have to deal with money, keep the minutes, or delegate to other people), which frees me up for more activities than I could have managed otherwise. When we got there, Jim (our Fearless Leader) had already commandeered the long table under the window and was drinking a cup of coffee bigger than his head.

I sat down on Jim's left, and the smell of coffee was so strong I wasn't sure if it was coming from the cup or somehow emanating from his pores. "What is that?" I asked.

"Quad shot venti skim latte. No foam," he said.

"Foam is for sissies," Mark said sagely.

"Quad shot?" I asked.

"Four shots of delicious espresso," he confirmed.

"Sleep is also for sissies," Mark said.

Caroline snorted, pulling out her laptop. "Do I need to take minutes for this?" she asked.

"Probably not," Jim said. "I just wanted to talk about the formal away from the big group. Becca's asking for more money again." Becca O'Connell was the head of the Senior Formal Committee, which was in charge of doing all the work for the dance. Our job, basically, was to hold their purse for them. She'd already asked for extra money for better decorations, an extra photographer, and fancier snacks for the buffet.

"Again?" Caroline asked.

Jim shrugged. "She says they sold more tickets than they expected, so she had to get the Regent to move us to a bigger ballroom. She guesses there are either a lot of seniors taking underclassmen or people who don't go to Blanchard."

"Shouldn't the extra ticket money make up the difference?" I asked.

"She says they're still four hundred bucks short."

"That doesn't make any sense," Mark said. "And she should have cc'd me her numbers."

"I'll forward them to you," Jim said. "Oh, and they also want to hire the premium DJ instead of the regular DJ, and that's going to be three hundred extra, too."

"What does a premium DJ even do?" I asked. Admittedly, I had never been to a Blanchard senior formal, but putting on music for a high school dance didn't seem that hard. You mixed the fast songs and the slow songs together. You tried not to say anything too embarrassing or accidentally play polka music. I wasn't sure what a premium version of this would look like. The DJ agreed to wear matching socks?

"I don't know," Jim said, rubbing his eyes. "She sent me a brochure, but I didn't have time to read it."

"This is stupid," I said. "We don't need a premium DJ."

"I'll let you tell Becca that."

"Fine," I said. "I'll email her later. Next she'll want a petting zoo and a pony ride."

"Don't give her any ideas."

"Okay," Caroline said. "So Mark's going to check Becca's financials, and Mischa's going to lower the boom about the DJ. Anything else?"

I scooted my chair back from the table a little, because I was kind of hoping we were done, and I was also kind of wanting to go home. My phone was still in the box of rice, so I couldn't get any calls, but Nate had promised to give me a ride home at five, which was in ten minutes. I was supposed to meet him out front; he'd told me he was going to hang out at the bookstore next door.

But Jim said, "Actually, there was one more thing. Becca wants to have a banner printed up with a list of where everyone's going to college."

The Jell-O in which I was swimming seemed to get a little thicker. I felt something in my head that might have been an electric shock.

"A banner?" Mark said.

"What?" I said.

"Oh, that's nice," Caroline said.

I felt like the universe was contracting a little bit, like gravity was pulling in toward me and I was being compressed. My head went *throb, throb, throb.*

"But," I said. "Not everyone's decided yet. Not everyone's even found out where they've been accepted yet."

"The formal's not until the first week in May," Mark said. "We'll all have picked someplace by then. How much does she want for that?"

"Hundred twenty-five," Jim said. "The printer who did the tickets offered her a deal."

"Why would we have something like that up at the formal?" I asked. "That doesn't even make sense."

"She wants to put it up in the foyer outside of the ballroom, so people can have their pictures taken in front of their names."

"*Why?*"

"It's just another photo op. Jeez, Mischa, what's with you?"

"I'm fine," I said. "It's just another stupid waste of money."

"It's only a hundred bucks!" Mark said. "I think it sounds cool."

I was starting to twitch all over. I stirred the rest of the whipped cream into my Frappuccino and wished I'd gone with the decaf. Or maybe it was just too much sugar. I felt less numb and more . . . something else. Whatever I was feeling, it wasn't something I knew how to name. It was bad on so many different levels; it went beyond sad or angry or freaked out.

"All in favor?" Jim asked. Caroline and Mark both put up their hands. They stared at me.

"Whatever," I said.

"Good," he said. "She'll be happy we at least said yes to one thing she wanted."

I mashed the ice in my drink with my straw.

"So," Jim said to Mark while I stared at my cup. "I heard you were choosing between Penn and Rice. That's pretty sweet, man."

"Yeah," Mark said. "I'm leaning toward Penn, I think."

And then I'm pretty sure he kept talking, but Caroline had just closed her laptop, said, "What about you, You never texted me back last night."

"What?" I asked. Then, hoping maybe I could just sideways myself out of this conversation, I said, "No, thanks, Nate's picking me up."

"No, I meant which schools have you heard from."

"Oh," I said. "Oh. Well. You know, I'm still deciding."

"You're deciding who you heard from?"

"No, I mean, of course not, it's just, well, it's a lot to think about, you know? I need—I need to talk it over. With my mom."

She exchanged a glance with Jim and Mark. I could feel my face getting red. "I guess I'm not ready to talk about it just yet. It's all kind of . . ." I swallowed some Frappuccino. "New."

"Ooookay," she said. Her eyebrows were all knitted up like I had ceased to be a person she recognized. "So do you want to go dress shopping this weekend?"

Dress? What was a dress? Oy. She was talking about the formal again. "What? I—I—I don't even know if I'm going. To the formal."

"What are you talking about? Of course you're going!"

"It's, uh, I have this thing."

"No you don't," she said, rolling her eyes. "Look, my parents and I are going out to dinner on Saturday to celebrate Dartmouth and Columbia."

"You got into Columbia?"

"That's what I was texting you about last night! Didn't you get my message?"

"Um, no."

"So let's go shopping first, and then maybe you can come along to the dinner? My parents have been dying to know where you're going, too."

No way was I going to Caroline's Dartmouth/Columbia dinner. "Uh," I said.

"Mischa, come on."

"I'll go dress shopping with you," Mark offered.

"Shut up," she said. "Mischa," she wheedled. "It'll be so boring otherwise. My mom put up like twenty Facebook posts about it already. She's getting super annoying."

"Oh my God," Jim said. "My grandmother came up from Florida to take me shopping. Apparently my shoes are not Brown material."

"She made you buy new shoes?"

"Three pairs!" he said. "I don't even know."

"Mischa!" Caroline was saying again. "So Saturday?"

But I was starting to feel a little weird. Like everything in the room had suddenly gotten way too loud, and too bright, and too—too something. I grabbed Jim's phone off the table. "What time is it?" I said, glancing at the screen, and then I said, "Crap, I was supposed to meet Nate five minutes ago, I have to go, sorry." And then I bolted outside without looking at Caroline or anyone else again.

Nate wasn't out there, of course, because I was five minutes early, not five minutes late. I ran into the bookstore, hoping he would be there, but since I had no phone, I couldn't even text him. I checked the magazine section, but he wasn't there, and by then I was starting to feel really, really not good.

I don't know why it hadn't exactly hit me before, the magnitude of what was happening. I hadn't just been rejected by the best schools on my list. I'd been rejected from virtually *all* the schools on my list. There was nothing left.

Well, not nothing. I still hadn't heard from Paul Revere. My safety school.

Nate came around the corner. In his hand was a city guide to Atlanta.

"Hey!" he said brightly, then his expression went into concerned-Nate mode when he saw my face. "What's wrong?"

I didn't actually know how to answer that.

Wonderful. This was all wonderful. There was going to be a *banner*. My name was going to be *on it*. And I was going to have to pose with it, *in formal wear*. And meanwhile, Caroline was going to Dartmouth (or Columbia). And I would probably have to go to her stupid dinner, because otherwise I was going to look like a jerk. I was going to have to remember all the times we sat in trig together last year, getting back our tests and quizzes, and always, always comparing our scores. Mine were always higher. Always. She would pretend to slap me with her quiz, and I would pretend like I thought that was funny, and she would say, "I'll beat you next time!" and I would say, "Sure!" even though she never, ever did. But now she was going to Dartmouth (or Columbia), and her parents were taking her out for steak and a ten-dollar baked potato, and I was going to have to stand in front of a banner with my name next to Paul Revere University and act like I was happy about it.

It wasn't fair. It just wasn't fair.

I looked at Nate. He looked so happy, with his Atlanta book. I said, "I think I'm getting a migraine."

"Oh," he said. "Do you mean a migraine-migraine or a"— he made air quotes—"'migraine'?"

In answer, my knees kind of cut out from under me, and I sat down on the floor, hard. I hadn't fainted, and I was actually pretty happy about that. But I felt like I was either going to pass out, throw up, or have a heart attack.

My brain kept saying, *Oh no, oh no, oh no.*

I'd read once that nausea was a heart attack symptom in women. What else? Pain in the jaw? Did my jaw hurt? It kind of did. I was dying. *This is it,* I thought. *I am dying on the floor of the Barnes and Noble.* I looked up at the shelves above me. *In the manga section.*

"Whoa," he said. "You *are* sick." He pressed a hand to my forehead. Under different circumstances, I might have enjoyed it. "You're all hot."

Under different circumstances, I *really* would have enjoyed that.

He knelt down in front of me. "See, now you're supposed to say, *I know.* Or, like, if you're feeling especially generous, you could say that I, also, am all hot."

I just stared at him.

"Not up to banter?"

I shook my head. I wanted to tell him. I also didn't want to tell him. I said, "I'm kind of dizzy."

"Maybe it's an inner-ear thing."

"Yeah," I said. "Maybe."

"Okay, well, I'll take you home."

I actually didn't really want to go home. At least here there was Nate, who was not going to make me talk about stuff. At home, there was . . . my mother. "Can we just stay a little while?" I said. "I think I just need to rest a minute."

He pivoted to sit down next to me. "Okay," he said. "Do you want me to talk or shut up?"

"You can talk," I said, because if he was talking, it meant the voice in my head shrieking *OH MY GOD! OH MY GOD! OH MY GOD!* would have to be quiet. "But is it, like, okay if I don't talk back for a few minutes?"

"That's great," he said. "Because you know I really love the sound of my own voice, and I'm not too proud to admit it." He held up his Atlanta book. "How about I read you some of this excellent Atlanta travel guide? I can tell you all about the museums down there. You'll like that, right?"

I had to look away from him. "Not that one," I said.

He set the book down on his other side. "Okay, not that one," he said. He reached into the shelf behind him and pulled out a book, some paperback manga with two people on the cover, one with white hair and one with black. "Here we go: *Inuyasha,* volume one." He opened the cover. "This looks good. Everyone has great hair."

"You're reading it backward," I said. "Japanese books go the other way."

He smiled and flipped the book around. "See? I'm so glad you're here right now to tell me these things." He put his finger in the first dialogue bubble and started to read it out loud. It starts off by introducing Kagome, a schoolgirl who falls down a well and ends up in feudal Japan, like *Alice in Wonderland* but with time travel and blood and demons. And then there's a big battle where Inuyasha defeats some lady centipede monster who has way too many boobs.

"There are boobs in this book!" Nate exclaimed. "I did not see that coming!"

I sighed and leaned against him a little, and he either didn't notice—because there were six bare boobs in front of him—or didn't mind. He nudged me a little with his elbow. "I guess it's fun to be surprised, right?"

On another day I might have agreed with him.

CHAPTER FOUR

BY THE FOLLOWING TUESDAY I HAD GONE FROM NUMBNESS TO full-on panic. My phone had miraculously survived its trip inside the toilet, and every time it chirped, I jumped. I was like the collegiate version of Pavlov's dog. Or, actually, not the collegiate version. The no-college version. The "living at home in my mother's basement" version. The "Do you want fries with that?" version.

I'm not even sure why I was so jumpy. The only place I hadn't heard back from was Revere, a school so easy to get into that it was known occasionally as the high school on the hill. It existed, near as I could tell, to be a safety school. Nobody *actually* wanted to go there.

I went back through my old papers and pulled out my SAT scores, my old report cards, my essays, thinking maybe I'd missed something. Did I have some horrible grammatical mistake in my essay? Had I split an infinitive or used too many adverbs? I didn't think so, except I did use the word "thoroughly" three times, which was, in retrospect, a poor use of vocabulary. Had I unwittingly said something offensive? No, my discussion of how I wanted to be a pediatrician was totally benign (if not entirely honest; I have no idea what I want to do after college, but everybody loves pediatricians). My list of extracurriculars was decent but not so long that it made me look like I'd padded it too much. Everything was exactly the way I'd remembered it. I was a good candidate. I really was.

I wondered, briefly, if there was another Mischa Abramavicius applying to all the same schools as me, but the idea was pretty ridiculous. As far as I know, I'm the only one in the entire country.

While I ruminated about all this, Nate came to school in a revolving wardrobe of Emory sweatshirts. Caroline still couldn't decide between Dartmouth and Columbia, and Jim was dithering about Brown versus Stanford. Dr. Marlowe, our headmaster, who seemed to spend most of the day holed up in his office, was suddenly visible wandering the halls, shaking hands with chuffed-looking seniors. "Congratulations!" he would say. "Make sure you come back and visit!"

Meanwhile, I still had not heard from Revere.

It was a joke even to be worried about it. The average SATs there were 450 points lower than mine. I had a 3.98 GPA. My lowest grade was an A–, and I'd only ever had one of those, and it was in PE.

I grimaced, thinking of Ms. Erickson, my ninth-grade PE teacher, who had downgraded me for running the mile too slow because I'd had cramps that day. Ugh, I hated that woman.

But I was pretty sure an A– in ninth-grade gym didn't keep you from getting into college.

I walked into the bathroom before calculus that morning and stepped directly into the path of Meredith Dorsay, who was walking out. She stopped when she saw me, putting an arm out to block my path.

Meredith Dorsay was the scion of an old Virginia family that had owned several plantations before turning to railroads and then real estate development and then state politics. Meredith's father had been the black sheep of the family and had rebelled by marrying not the daughter of some other wealthy family, as had been expected, but the scientist who headed the ovarian cancer research division at NIH. Why this had been a scandal was puzzling to me; Nate had tried to explain that it had something to do with her lack of connections or her hair being too curly, but I'd never really understood. Rich people are just weird sometimes.

Anyway, Meredith had money, great gobs of it. If the universe was fair, she would have been stupid, or at least of middling intelligence, but instead Meredith had inherited her mind from her mother.

It's hard to survive this level of privilege while also maintaining a semblance of humility. Meredith had not done so. She was not humble. She was not kind. Actually, and rather unfortunately, she was something of a schmuck.

That's unfair. She was a schmuck of epic proportions. *The* schmuck. The schmuck's schmuck. All lesser schmucks trembled before her.

"Michelle," Meredith said. This was our own private joke. Well, it was *her* private joke. Our freshman PE teacher had steadfastly refused to call me by the right name all year, and while I'm pretty used to people bungling my last name, the first-name thing could not have been anything but deliberate. I'd been "Michelle" in her class until June, which everyone found hysterical. Nobody else seemed to remember it but Meredith, though.

"I thought you were in France," I said, ducking under her arm and stopping at the sink to fix my hair, because I didn't want to go into the stall and pee until she'd left the bathroom.

She snorted. "I went to L'Auberge Paris for lunch. Not France."

I got my brush out of my bag and started working on my hair. "Huh," I said.

"John Andrews got into UCLA," she said, crossing her arms.

"Did he?" I said, knowing perfectly well it was true, because I'd been in the room when he'd gotten the email.

"Marissa Singh is going to Oberlin."

When I didn't respond, she added, "Tara Goddard is going to Duke." She traced a finger along the edge of the sink next to me. "I haven't heard anything about where *you're* going, though."

I swallowed. "I'm a private person."

She chuckled. "Yeah, but that's the thing, isn't it? You aren't. I know every test score you've gotten in government this year. I know your SAT scores." She dropped her voice. "I even know you got an A− in gym freshman year." She made a *tsk* sound. "Didn't even know that was possible. But I don't know where you got into college." She leaned closer. "Why is that?"

I put my brush back in my backpack. I was going to have

40

to hold it until next period, because no way was I finishing this discussion. "Because it's none of your business? Why do you even care?"

"It's not that I care," she said. "I'm just curious."

"Those two things tend to be mutually dependent," I said, "and I'm late to class."

Her face lit. "You didn't get in."

I took a step toward the door, but she moved sideways to block me. "Who? Who rejected you? Harvard? Princeton?" Her eyes took on a greedy gleam. "Both?"

I checked her with my shoulder and moved past her, but she laughed and said, "It's okay, Michelle. We can't all be special snowflakes."

I spun around and glared at her.

She chuckled. "Someone has to dig the ditches."

I made it as far as my desk in calculus before I started dry-heaving.

"Mischa?" Mr. Bronstein said. "You okay?"

"Just—" I said as another spasm seized my stomach. "I'm not . . . no." An awful noise came up my throat, and everyone in the room made sounds of disgust, waiting for my breakfast to hit the floor. I bolted for the nurse's office, which was closer than the bathroom.

The nurse was running a thermometer over some freshman's forehead when I came in, and from the other room, I could hear the sounds of racking sobs. Wordlessly she handed me a wastebasket, which I heaved into for a minute. Nothing came up, though, and I sank down onto the nearest cot and put the trash can on the floor.

"Okay?" she asked.

I nodded, and she handed me a bottle of water from the

little refrigerator where she keeps antibiotics and stuff. "Try drinking little sips," she said soothingly. I did, and my stomach slowly unclenched.

I closed my eyes and breathed through my nose, because I was starting to feel like, now that I wasn't going to barf, I might just hyperventilate instead. Meredith knew. She didn't know what she knew, but she knew I hadn't gotten into anyplace really good, because if I had, I would have told everyone. She was probably telling people right now. But what did I expect? Everybody was going to figure it out at some point, unless I lied and said I'd gotten in someplace I hadn't. Everyone would know what a failure I was.

My mother would know. She would know, because I would have to tell her.

Damn.

I imagined her face. She would pretend to be okay with it. Her face would get that frozen look it gets sometimes, when something awful has happened—there's mold in the basement or the roof is leaking or whatever—and she would say, *We'll get through this.* Then she would go in the other room and, what? Cry? Rage? Wish I'd never been born, probably. My mother got pregnant with me while she was in law school, and my dad's not really in the picture. All I know about him is his name, and that I'm supposed to have his complexion, and he lives in Boston.

If Mom hadn't had me, maybe she'd have taken a different career track. She could have gone into some high-paying corporate-law position of the kind you can't really do if you're the single mother of a baby. Or maybe she could have even gotten married somewhere along the line. To someone who could have picked up the slack at home while she climbed the corporate ladder, or to someone rich who would have let her do the kind of pro bono work she likes to do when she has extra time. But no. She had me instead. And I was about to pull out her heart and stomp on it.

I'd already told Nate in a middle-of-the-night text confessional, and that had been bad enough. He'd said, *Are you sure?* and I'd said, *Yes, I'm sure,* and he'd said, *Not even VA Tech?* and I'd said, *Nope,* and he'd said, *Are you sure?* again, and then I'd had to turn my phone off because the whole scenario was so utterly unbearable.

I put the bottle of water down, because I didn't think I really deserved to feel better. Meredith was right. I wasn't special. I was just another peon, another salmon trying to make it upstream, and the current had been too much for me. The magnitude of my failure pulled me down, down, down, until I felt like I was at the bottom of the ocean, looking up at everyone around me through ten million gallons of water. I would never be able to make this up to Mom. Never.

I lay down for the rest of calculus and ended up running into Nate on my way to lunch. Today's Emory sweatshirt was navy blue with an embroidered crest, and I hated noticing that it made his eyes look even bluer than they really are. He walked with a bounce in his step, like a man who was on his way to his dream school, his dream life. I walked like a girl who had just spent the past ten minutes with her head in a trash can full of used Kleenex and dirty Band-Aids.

"Hey, gorgeous," he said, which annoyed me, because I knew I looked like hell. He fell into step alongside me and tucked a piece of hair behind my ear. "Any news?"

I shook my head. "Just the usual apocalypse."

"So no word from Revere?"

"Afraid not."

"Well, of course you'll get in there. It's like a joke to think you won't."

"Nate," I said. "It's already a joke. I just don't get it. Maybe . . . I don't know. I don't even know what went wrong."

"Did you see Ms. Pendleton yet?"

"What would I say to her?"

"I don't know. Maybe she could give you a pep talk or something."

"I don't need a pep talk. I need a school. UGGGHHHH! I can't believe I'm going to Revere."

"Okay, Snobby Snobberson," he said.

"Oh, like you'd be okay with going there!"

"It's a perfectly fine school."

"It's a perfectly fine school for people who didn't work that hard in high school!"

"Oh dear," he said. "Entitlement, thy name is Mischa."

"Shut up."

"Hey, none of this is my fault. Just try to have a little perspective."

"If you call this a First World problem," I said, "I will beat you to death right now."

He coughed.

"Look," I said. "If I end up at Revere, what was all this *for*? I might as well've just slept through the last four years. I just . . . I don't get it. I don't know what I did wrong!"

"Have you told your mom?"

"Oh my God. No. I don't even know what to tell her."

I didn't know how to explain to Nate the extent of what my mother had given up to send me to Blanchard. Even with my financial aid package, the part we were responsible for hurt pretty badly. I knew that money was coming out of my mother's retirement savings. She drove a fifteen-year-old car (which seemed to be having trouble keeping all the required parts attached). We hadn't taken a vacation in four years. That was all because of me. All so I could get into Revere. A school I could have gotten into, easily, from a public school for free, without spending every waking moment of the last four years studying or hunched over some stupid homework assignment that, as it turns out, was a total waste of time. We could have gone to the beach every summer. I could have had an after-school job. I could have dumped all my stupid extracurriculars and spent my weekends making money or hanging out with my friends, or maybe even taking road trips. I could have spent my last spring break in Florida instead of making posters for the freaking band booster club. Four wasted years. I could have done anything. I could have been *happy*.

"I just can't believe it," I said. "I can't believe I'm going to *Revere*."

Dear Ms. Abramavicius,

No. No no no no no. No. Also: NO.

Yours in sympathy (but not really),
Paul Revere University

CHAPTER FIVE

THE THING NO ONE TELLS YOU ABOUT HITTING BOTTOM IS
that you don't actually know when it happens. You have a moment where you think, *Ah! This is it. I am at the bottom. Nothing
can get worse.* You look around for the other things that live at
the Bottom, like those creepy fish with both eyes on one side of
their heads. You think, *Okay, here I am.* You take a breath and
wait to start bouncing back up.

And then things get worse, because what you thought was
the Bottom was just a ledge, just a momentary break before
you plunged down the rest of the way.

It's like being on a roller coaster: you free-fall eighty feet,
feeling the bottom drop out of your stomach, and then just as
you start to level out, down you go again. And by that point
you don't trust your vestibular sense anymore; you have no
idea what's coming next, and you think that there may in fact

be no bottom at all, and you'll just keep falling all the way through the earth until you pop out the other side and then go shooting off into space, where your eyes explode in the vacuum.

That was how I felt the moment I got the email from Revere, telling me that my epic failure was ten thousand times worse than I'd thought. I sat staring at my phone on my bed after school, waiting to fall through the earth, to shoot out of the atmosphere, for my blood vessels to pop. I wished, actually, that it had happened. I wouldn't have been remembered as the girl who failed. I would have been remembered as the girl who died. That seemed so, so much better. People would forget about me. Maybe Nate and Caroline would take longer. Maybe my mom would be sad for a while, but then I wouldn't have to tell her I'd screwed the pooch. She'd never have to know. People wouldn't sneer at her. They'd feel sorry for her. Maybe that would be better, in the long run.

But I kept breathing in and out. My heart kept beating. I had not actually been sucked into the center of the earth—I was still in my bedroom, with my broken Ikea dresser and my *Star Wars* poster over my bed. I looked at Rey, posed seriously with her eyebrows drawn down, her lightsaber at the ready, and thought, she never would have let this happen. She was special.

I'd thought I was special, too.

I took two Benadryls, because I knew I wouldn't sleep otherwise, deleted some text about this week's French club meetings, and went to bed. Then I had the wonderful experience of sleeping through my alarm the next morning.

• • •

I woke up in the middle of my mother's rant, which she was issuing from the end of my bed. It sounded suspiciously like she was shouting, "ALL SHALL LOVE ME AND DESPAIR!" but she probably wasn't. I tilted my head up and tried to focus on what she was saying.

"—meeting in an hour," she said. "You have ten minutes to be in the car, or I'm taking you in your pajamas."

I rubbed my eyes, regretting the second Benadryl. Everything always hits me a little harder than I think it will, which is why I don't drink. My mother says I have a sensitive system. My doctor says it has to do with my metabolism; I don't know. "I'm up," I said, even though I wasn't.

"You need to be upper than this," she said, yanking the blankets off my bed and leaving me shivering on the bare mattress.

I staggered into the bathroom and stared at my haggard face in the mirror, which is when I remembered about Revere, and then wondered how I'd forgotten about it for five minutes, and then remembered my mother's scary Galadriel impression in my bedroom.

"Ugh," I said.

"Mischa," my mother called. "Get going."

"I'm in the bathroom. I'm up," I called back, even though what I really wanted to say was that I wanted to go back to bed for the next hundred years and then wake up like Sleeping Beauty, after all of my problems had been solved by someone else.

I rubbed at the dark circle under my left eye, which, for some reason, was worse than the one on the opposite side, maybe because I'd slept on that part of my face. Did I look different? I thought maybe I did. This was the face of a person who has no future. All that lay ahead of me was the edge of a vast cliff. I wondered if other people would be able to tell just by the sight of me. Maybe they should be able to tell. Maybe I should warn them, in case I was somehow contagious.

I grabbed my mother's eyeliner pencil from the jar where she keeps such things, and across my forehead I wrote *FAILURE*.

Then I started to laugh, because I realized what I'd done. Not only had I leveled up to peak emo, the saddest creature living on this earth, I had written on my forehead while looking *in the mirror*. It wasn't enough that my forehead said *FAILURE*. My forehead said *FAILURE* backward. I laughed some more. This was really very funny. And not at all sad. Just funny.

So funny.

No, I told myself. No matter how bad things got, I would not be *this*. I would not be the girl who wrote *FAILURE* on her face. I got a wad of toilet paper and started to wipe it off.

It was stubborn, this eyeliner. I rubbed some more. My forehead was looking a little red. It was then that I realized I'd written *FAILURE* on my face not in my mother's blue eyeliner, but in my mother's blue *waterproof* eyeliner.

"Uh, Mom?" I called through the closed door. "You know that navy blue eyeliner?"

"You're putting on eyeliner? *Now?*"

"Hypothetically speaking," I replied. My rubbing grew desperate. The liner was not budging.

"That blue stuff is the devil, nothing takes it off."

By then I'd moved on to my mother's cold cream. It was not helping. "Nothing?" I asked, a little shrilly.

"Oh, you didn't," she said. "Let me see."

"No, no," I said, locking the door before she could open it. "It's fine. Just out of curiosity, why did you keep it?"

"I thought I threw it out! I never use it. Let me see how bad it is."

"It's fine!" I said. "Really!" I'd given up on the cold cream and was lathering my face with Dial. The liner was fading, but it was still completely visible. "What about peroxide?"

"On your *eyes*?"

"Right," I said. "Right. No. That would be bad." My forehead was getting massively red now. I took the bottle of peroxide and poured it on a wad of toilet paper and started to rub.

After a minute a lot of the eyeliner was off. But anyone standing within five feet of me would have been able to see it.

"Mischa, we have to leave in *five minutes*!"

Shoot shoot shoot.

I could not go to school with **FAILURE** written backward on my face, even if it was faded.

"How long does this stuff take to wear off?"

"Two or three days. I'm sure it's not as bad as you're thinking—let's go!"

I stared at myself in the mirror. It was definitely as bad as I was thinking. I could wear a hat, I thought. If Blanchard allowed hats in class, which they don't, and also that wouldn't get me out of the bathroom and past Mom, and if Mom saw this she would a) freak out and b) ask the reason why the word "failure" was inscribed on her daughter's face.

"Damn it," I muttered, and got the scissors out of the medicine cabinet. I brushed my hair over my forehead.

"Mischa!" Mom called. "I have my shoes on!"

I held the scissors parallel to my eyebrows. And I cut.

. . .

51

Nate found me in front of my locker fifteen minutes before first period, which was odd because he was never there that early.

"Hey," he said, his back pressed against the locker next to mine and looking, not at me, but out at the crowd of people milling around. "So I have this theory that it's the soy milk that's giving me heartburn, and I'm thinking about switching back to dairy." When I didn't answer, he turned and looked at me. "Whoa. Did you get bangs?" He leaned in to inspect my hastily chopped-off hair. "Did you do that yourself?" he asked. "Didn't we talk about cutting your own hair after the mom-bob incident of 2015?"

"Don't bring that up."

"It's like nineties grunge in the front, party in the back. Is that what you were going for? 'Cause frankly, it's kind of a mismatch."

"Nate," I said. "Please."

He snapped his mouth shut, put his fingers under my chin, and turned my head slowly left and right. "It's really not that bad," he said. "You just need someone with a steady hand to even it out. It looks like you did it with a Weedwacker."

"I was in kind of a hurry," I admitted.

"You can go get it fixed after school. I'll drive you, if you want."

I met his eyes. He stared at me for a long minute, and I wondered if he could see the word *FAILURE* written on my retinas. Or maybe it was the fact that I was just trying really, really hard not to cry. Anyway, whatever he saw made him say, "Okay. Let's go." And he grabbed me by the hand and pulled me down the hall, in the opposite direction from where we both had first period.

"Where are we going?"

"Art room," he said. "Mrs. Portland doesn't teach first period. Should be empty."

The art room *was* empty. "Up here," he said, patting the counter next to the sink and then opening and shutting cabinet doors until he found a plastic box full of scissors. "Here we go."

I hesitantly hoisted myself onto the counter, my feet dangling several inches over the floor.

"Nate," I said. "I'm not sure I can fix it. I'm the one who messed it up in the first place."

"Don't be silly," he said. "I'm going to fix it."

For a second, I really wanted to cry.

He approached with the scissors in one hand; then he flipped his backpack over his shoulder and pulled out a comb.

"Are you sure this is a good idea?" I asked.

"I'm very confident in my ability to cut in a straight line," he said. "Hold still."

He ran the comb through my bangs a few times to straighten them out and then set it down on the counter next to me. "Don't move," he said, his face about six inches from mine. "I'm going to try to even them out without making them any shorter."

"Okay," I said, because that sounded like a good plan. I had vivid, awful memories of my mother's attempts to cut my bangs when I was about eight. They kept being uneven, so she kept cutting them a little shorter until they were an inch and a half long. It had taken six months before they looked normal again. Also, I really, really didn't want anyone seeing my forehead today.

"Don't move your head," he said, holding my chin steady

with his left hand. I felt the edge of the scissors skimming my eyebrow from left to right as he took impossibly small snips. I focused on his face to keep from flinching as the cold metal blade skated over my forehead. His lower lip was anchored between his teeth, and his eyebrows were drawn down in concentration. I tried to focus on the little scar under his left eye, but it was hard when I could feel him breathing against my face and he was close enough to kiss. Finally Nate said, "There. I think it's better now."

I turned around to look at myself in the mirror behind me. My hedge-trimmer bangs were straight. They weren't even too short. It looked like something I'd done on purpose, with the aid of an actual hair-cutting professional. Best of all, the eyeliner was completely invisible.

"Thank you," I said. "Thank you so much. You are the best friend in the universe. God."

I turned around to look at him directly instead of in the mirror. "You're like a genie. How did you even do that?"

He held his hand out in front of him, palm down, and said, "Steady as a rock." Then he set both hands on my shoulders and stooped down to meet my eyes. "So do you want to tell me why it says 'failure' backward on your forehead?"

CHAPTER SIX

THAT NIGHT, I WAS LOOKING FORWARD TO TELLING MY MOTHER that I had been rejected from every last school I'd applied to. I puttered around the kitchen, setting the table and trying to decide the best way of describing my situation, short of just letting her have a look at my forehead.

I wondered if this kind of occasion called for the use of salad forks. Somehow I didn't think so.

I'd already had to tell her about the other schools. She'd heard about Admissions Day from some friends with high school kids, and she'd asked, so even though I'd really wanted to keep it to myself, I'd had to tell her.

Her face had sort of frozen up—like I'd known it would. She'd hugged me. And she'd told me Revere was lucky to be getting such a great student. But I'd known, even then, that she was disappointed. This, though . . . I didn't know how she was going to handle it.

So Mom and I sat down to Chili Night. The idea of filling my stomach with beans sounded particularly awful, and I stirred them around in my bowl.

"Something bothering you?" Mom asked.

I'd been waiting until after dinner to tell her, because I figured she'd take the news better on a full stomach.

"Not really," I said. "Um. How was work?"

"Oh," she said. "Same as usual."

"Fighting the good fight," I piped in.

"Well, I try. For all the good it does."

I set down my spoon, because this was a little more cynical than Mom usually got. "What do you mean?"

She put more cheese on top of her chili. "You know, Misch, we're not playing on a level field. Sometimes it's just depressing, that's all. You have no idea how lucky you are."

"Right," I said. "I mean, of course I do."

"Educated parent, middle-class upbringing. Best education you could get. I know it's rough, being on the lower side of the economic scale at school. But you're still starting about ten steps ahead of most people."

I had a sudden urge to fill my mouth with beans.

"I just mean, you've had a lot of great opportunities. Even if you end up at Revere next year, you'll have a real leg up."

"Mmph," I said, because my mouth was full.

"So try not to worry too much about it," she assured me.

"Grumph-umppph," I said, nodding vigorously.

"You didn't get your official letter from them yet, did you?"

I put my spoon back in my bowl and carried it into the

kitchen. "Not . . . no. I didn't get the acceptance yet," I said. I stuck the bowl in the sink and said, "Is that my phone?"

"I don't hear it."

"Oh, yeah! There it is! That must be Nate!"

"Can't you call him back?"

"I can't. He's having an. Um. A crisis."

"Nate's having a crisis."

"Yeah," I said. "It's bad. Bad crisis. Poor Nate."

"Mischa . . ."

"I have to go!" I called over my shoulder, scooping up my purse and my keys. "Nate needs me!"

"Nate needs a kick in the butt!"

"Good thing I'm wearing my shoes, then!" I said, and shut the door behind me.

I got to Nate's house half an hour later. His sister opened the door for me; she was thirteen and athletic and grumpy. "Oh, it's you," she said.

"Hey," I said. Rachel Miller neither liked nor disliked me; I existed outside the scope of her world, which consisted of school, other thirteen-year-olds, and softball. She played on some travel team that had practice or games almost every day, which seemed to have eaten Nate's parents' lives, but, on the bright side, it meant that Nate kind of got to do his own thing a lot, since he'd assured everyone that middle school softball was not a good use of his time. "Is Nate here?"

"He reads comic books now," she said.

"Oh," I said.

"Mom says he's regressing."

"Uh, I'm sure he's not regressing." She moved aside so I could come in. She was in her softball uniform, which probably meant she was on her way to practice, because she wasn't sweaty yet.

"I like your hair," she said.

"Thanks."

Nate was sitting in the living room reading while Robbie the robot vacuum zoomed around the room doing its nightly seven o'clock pass. On the coffee table was a fake skull; I patted it on the head as I sat down. "Hey, Maury," I said, addressing the molded plastic cranium. "Looking good." Memento Maury was a leftover Halloween decoration from years past; Nate found some kind of perverse pleasure in buying him new accessories whenever he thought of it. Currently he was wearing a beret and false eyelashes. I wondered if they were his mother's, or if he'd bought them specially. "Where are your parents?"

"Work. Then they're meeting Rachel at her game."

"Rachel has a game?"

"Yeah, she's there now."

"No, she's here. She just answered the door."

"Oh," he said. "Crap."

"Were you supposed to take her?"

He turned away from me and shouted, "RACHEL, WAS I SUPPOSED TO TAKE YOU TO SOFTBALL?"

"NO, FATIMA'S PICKING ME UP," she called back, and then a little more quietly, but not much, she added, "loser."

"I just love her," Nate said.

I sat down next to him on the modern, cream-colored couch that was just a tiny bit too firm to really be comfortable. Nate's whole house was like that—everything was very, very perfect in an interior-design kind of way. Sometimes I thought his mother had just opened a mid-century furniture catalog and ordered one of everything.

On the coffee table were volumes three and four of *Inuyasha*.

"You're still reading that?" I asked. "Are there more boobs?"

"In fact, there are!" he said. "But everyone just has the regular number. I feel kind of cheated."

I picked it up and flipped to a random page. "Wow," I said, pointing to a really hot girl with long hair and a sword. "How many does she have?"

He glared at me. "That's Lord Sesshomaru. He doesn't have any."

"Oh," I said, looking closer. "Yeah, you're right. He's super hot."

"You thought he was a girl!"

"Well, now I see he's not, and I think he's hot!"

"He's Inuyasha's evil brother," he said. "And he's *super* hot."

"Is everyone in this book super hot?"

"Pretty much. It's giving me some kind of an existential crisis, though."

"What? Why?"

He turned the page to show me another character. "Okay, here's the thing. See, Kagome is really the reincarnation of Kikyo. She's a priestess, right?"

"That's cool."

"Yeah, but even though she's her reincarnation, they aren't the same person. At all."

"Well, no, because Kikyo's dead."

"She actually comes back to life, but that's not what I mean. It's like, I always thought reincarnation meant the same person coming back to life over and over, but they're two totally different people."

"Oh. That's kind of what I thought it meant, too. The coming-back-to-life thing."

"I know! But it turns out that's Hindu reincarnation, and Buddhist reincarnation is different." He handed me another book from the bottom of the stack called *Zen Buddhism: A Primer.*

I flipped through the first few pages; it was riddled with Nate's handwriting, and he'd underlined a bunch of passages. Probably this is what he'd been working on instead of his *Heart of Darkness* paper, which was almost certainly not done yet. "So what did you figure out?"

He took the book back from me. "I'm only on page twenty, but I can tell you with a great degree of certainty that I have no understanding of Buddhism. Or any other Eastern religions, basically. It's kind of embarrassing."

"There's probably a class at Emory."

"There's probably a *department* at Emory. I just mean, I feel like I spent eleven and a half years in school, and maybe I should know what reincarnation is." He leaned back on the couch. "Or which way Japanese books go." He picked up a plastic tray from the coffee table, which held some kind of frozen chicken dinner. He took a bite and offered me some, which I declined.

"Chili Night," I said. "I'm kind of disappointed about the not-coming-back-to-life thing, though, because right now I think that might be my only shot."

"Don't say that."

I absentmindedly picked a carrot off the edge of the tray and ate it. It was mushy and tasted like it only dimly remembered having once been an actual vegetable.

"How did your mom take it?" he asked.

"I didn't actually tell her."

"What?" he asked, revealing a mouth full of half-chewed chicken. Then: "Pick up your feet."

I folded my legs under me on the couch as Robbie zipped past, like a motorized Frisbee on a mission. I had to raise my voice to be heard over the vacuum. "I couldn't. She was giving me the 'you are so privileged' speech, and I just couldn't tell her all my privileged prospects were circling the drain." I ate another carrot. "Actually, that's not right. They're not circling the drain. They have gone down the drain. My prospects have moved into the sewer."

"The sewer leads to the ocean, eventually," he offered helpfully.

"You're right," I said. "The sewer's too nice. I need an uglier metaphor." I slapped the couch. "A septic tank. My future resides in a septic tank. How am I supposed to tell my mother my future is in a septic tank? There's no way to sugarcoat 'septic tank.' The poop goes in, and it doesn't come back out again. That's what a septic tank is, Nate."

"You need to stop saying 'septic tank.'"

"Septic. Tank."

He rolled his eyes and stuck his tray down on the coffee table. "You can't just not tell her, though. I mean, you are telling her at some point, right?"

"Of course I'll tell her. Eventually."

"Like, before she tries to move you into a dorm at Revere?"

"Yes," I said, heaving a sigh. "Before that."

"You know," he said. "I read some article about a girl in Canada who lied to her parents and told them she'd graduated from high school and was going to some fancy college, and then she got up every morning and went someplace else. I think she kept it up for a couple of years."

I laughed. The idea was not entirely unappealing. "What tipped them off?"

"Uh, actually, she put a hit on them so they wouldn't find out."

"Jesus," I said.

"I'm just saying," he said quickly. "You might not want to let it get that far."

"I'm not going to murder my mother because I didn't get into college!"

"So wait," he said. "Does anyone know about this but me?"

"Um. No. Just you."

He scooted away from me on the couch.

"Oh, relax; I'm not going to kill you, either."

"I'm pretty sure that's what that Canadian girl said, too."

"Oh, shut up. By the way, if my mom asks, you're having a crisis."

"Me? Why am I having a crisis?"

"It was the only way I was getting out of the house."

"Throw me under the bus, why don't you."

"Consider yourself thrown." I pulled my knees up to my chest and hugged them. "Seriously, Nate. What am I going to do?"

He patted my back. "You'll figure something out. You can always go to community college and transfer in a year. It's not the disaster you're making it out to be."

"Right," I said. "Imagine telling my mother she's been

wearing the same pair of shoes for four years, but it's not a disaster that I'm going to community college next year."

"It'll be cheaper, at least," he said. "She might appreciate that."

"I guess."

"Really, though," he said. "I think you should see Ms. Pendleton tomorrow. Maybe she'll have a suggestion. Maybe there're some other schools with late deadlines you can apply to. Or someplace with rolling admissions."

"I guess," I said. "You're probably right."

"Of course I'm right." He put his arm around me, and I leaned into him. "Stop thinking about septic tanks."

"I'll try," I said, stifling a yawn. Robbie had finished his chores and plugged himself back into his docking station to charge, so it was suddenly very quiet. "Can we watch a movie?"

"Sure," he said, digging the remote out from between the couch cushions. "It's even your turn to pick. See?" He squeezed my shoulders. "Everything's getting better already."

I smiled weakly, mostly because I didn't want Nate to feel like he wasn't helping. But the truth was, my future had truly, legitimately been flushed.

CHAPTER SEVEN

I WOKE UP IN A SWEAT BECAUSE I'D HAD THE SHOWER DREAM again. It was not my favorite, and I had it so often on test nights that I'd actually started expecting it, except I didn't usually have it on normal nights. It goes like this: I'm in the shower, only somehow the drain stops working, and the whole thing starts filling up with water, faster and faster, until I'm treading water up by the ceiling, and then the water goes up over my head and I realize I'm drowning. The thing is, I don't have to drown; I could just open the shower door, but my entire calculus class is standing in my bathroom watching, and some of them are, like, taking notes? So if I open it, I will wash out of the shower and wind up naked on my bathroom floor in front of everyone.

I never open the door. I always drown.

• • •

At school, I made a beeline for Ms. Pendleton's office. A good night's sleep (nightmare notwithstanding) had taken the edge off my feeling sorry for myself, and I had a new thought: I was being screwed over. I hadn't gotten into that septic tank by myself. I'd done everything right. I could accept not getting into Harvard, Princeton, and maybe a few of the others. But Revere? No. That didn't make any sense.

Someone had made a mistake. It *had* to have been a mistake.

There was a sign on Ms. Pendleton's door saying she was out for the day. I smacked my forehead against the wood, then I did it again.

Bebe Tandoh, who was getting a drink from the water fountain across the hall, said, "She was out yesterday, too. You okay?"

Looking at Bebe made me feel even more like something the cat dragged in; her aunt's a Ghanaian fashion designer, and every summer Bebe goes to stay with her relatives in Accra and comes back with a closetful of the most amazing clothes you've ever seen. She was wearing these lime-green gladiator sandals that made her look like a cross between Lupita Nyong'o and Xena: Warrior Princess. I was wearing my two-year-old sneakers with the beginnings of a hole in the toe. I wondered where Bebe was going to college.

"Yeah," I said. "I'm okay."

Then I turned around and walked out of the building.

I'd driven my mother to work that morning because I had a French club meeting after school, so I went and sat in my car. I turned on the radio. I turned off the radio.

I googled the admissions office of Revere on my phone. I recognized the name of the assistant admissions dean, Nicole

Smythe, from my rejection letter. I wondered if she'd been the one to sign it, or if it had been some stupid intern.

An intern. Did they have interns in admissions offices? Or maybe not interns. Maybe just entry-level people who did the preliminary sorting into "yes" and "no" piles based on test scores and GPAs. Maybe my file had landed in the wrong pile somehow. That was the only explanation I could think of. There was a mistake somewhere in the process. I turned the key in the ignition and left the parking lot.

Revere is only twenty minutes from my house, which is one of the reasons it was my safety school; if my financial aid situation got really bad, I could live at home and commute, which would save the room and board money. It was supposed to have been my worst-case scenario. Ha.

I had to park a block away from the admissions office, in front of some academic building called Matlin Hall, which had people coming and going from it in droves. I wondered what they taught there for a second before I remembered that I didn't care.

I had to step over a couple of kids who were studying in the middle of a walkway in front of the building. One of them reached out as I passed and tugged my shoelace loose. I scowled at him.

"Are you a freshman?" he asked, his voice a teasing mockery that set my teeth on edge.

"No," I said coldly, bending down to retie my shoe. "I don't go here."

"Ooh," his friend said. "Fresh meat. One if by land, two if by sea, girl." Which managed to be both the grossest and most ridiculous pickup line I'd ever heard.

"Does that line often work for you?" I asked.

"Every night, baby."

Good lord. I looked them over—white boys with backward baseball caps, one thin, one fat, both with bad skin. The one who had hit on me wore a slightly dead-behind-the-eyes expression.

This. This, here, was the school that had rejected me. This guy, who couldn't even come up with a pickup line that made sense, had gotten in here. They'd taken *him*.

"What were your SAT scores?" I asked. He replied with a scandalously low number, smirking, as if it were something to be proud of. "If you come by my room later, I can help you study."

"Study what? I just said I don't go here."

They both laughed. "It's okay," he said. "I like stupid girls."

"Oh, ew," I said. Then I picked up the notebook they were studying from and stuffed it into the nearest trash can.

I took the steps to the admissions building two at a time, wishing I'd worn a dress that day instead of the yoga pants I'd slept in the night before. Inside, I found a secretary sitting in the giant lobby. She was young and blond and smiling a little too wide. "May I help you?" she asked.

"Yes," I said confidently. "I'm here to see Dean Smythe."

"And you are . . ."

"Mischa Abramavicius," I said.

She frowned. "Do you have an appointment."

"Yes." I glanced at the clock. "For ten-fifteen."

"Hmm. I don't have you down."

"I've come a long way," I said. "I really do need to see her."

She drew her mouth up to one side. I wondered how many

other college rejects had shown up demanding to meet with Dean Smythe. Maybe I should have called ahead and made an appointment. Except that I doubt she would have seen me.

"I'm afraid Dean Smythe is in meetings all day," she said.

"I only need ten minutes," I said.

"She's just not available. Is there someone else who can help you? Perhaps someone in the financial aid office?"

"It's—It's not exactly a financial aid issue," I said.

"Can I ask what this is regarding?"

I scowled. "It's a private matter."

"Honey," she said quietly. "If this is because of an admissions decision—"

"It's not," I said quickly. *Stupid yoga pants.*

"Okay, if it is . . ."

I scrambled for some legitimate reason to be talking to Smythe. Why did anyone come to see her, except to talk about why they didn't get in? If they had gotten in, they wouldn't need to talk to her. Her usefulness to the students has a pretty limited shelf life. "It's for an interview!" I said quickly. "I'm interviewing her for my school paper. I'm doing an article about demystifying the admissions process."

She looked at me doubtfully. "And you're not in school today because . . ."

"I go to a private school," I said. "It's an in-service day for the teachers."

"Hmm," she said.

"Please," I added.

She gestured to the waiting area, which was filled with several overstuffed chairs and a couch. Nobody else was there, because the decisions had already been mailed out. Probably the whole admissions staff was at a bar somewhere getting roaring drunk and laughing at all the pathetic people they'd rejected. "If you want to wait," she said, "she'll be on a lunch break at twelve. She might be able to talk to you while she's eating."

"Thank you," I said gratefully, and then remembered that I didn't have anything with me that looked plausibly school newspapery, like a camera or a recorder or, you know, a notebook or a pencil. "I left my stuff in my car," I said. "I'll be right back."

She waved me off, and I went out to get my government notebook, which I turned to a blank page, and a pen.

It occurred to me that I should have stayed for homeroom, because any minute now my mother would be getting a call to tell her I hadn't shown up for school. Which meant that about ten seconds after that, my phone was going to start blowing up with my mom freaking out because she thought I was dead in a ditch somewhere. I decided to stave off disaster and sent her a text.

Stomachache on my way into school this morning. I went home but I don't think Mr. Bronstein checked me in first, so don't be surprised if you get a call.

Are you OK? Did you throw up?

I decided to cut things short. *Other kind of stomachache.*

Oh dear. Do you need me to come home?

I'm fine. Don't come home.

Please don't come home, I thought. *Please don't come home and discover that I am not there.*

Are you sure?

No no. I'm OK.

OK. I'll pick up some probiotics on my way home. Eat yogurt.

Will do.

And wash your hands.

Seriously??

That taken care of, I stashed my phone in my backpack and settled in to wait. I pulled out my government book and opened to page 524 to start the reading I'd need to have done for tomorrow. I looked down at my book. Then I started laughing hysterically because I realized that I could do nothing, *literally* nothing, for the rest of the year—I could skip all my classes, never read a page, draw cartoon characters on my exams, whatever I wanted—and it would make absolutely no difference. None. None! Well, I suppose if I really jacked things up badly enough, they could refuse to give me my diploma. That would be worse. Slightly.

I put my book away and spent the next hour and a half googling pictures of cats.

There are a lot of pictures of cats on the Internet. Fat cats. Fluffy cats. Cats sitting in flowerpots. Cats with bunnies. Cats with goats. Cats with other cats. I don't know why looking at pictures of other people's cats is such a pleasant way to pass the time. Sometimes there are videos. Cats climbing into fishbowls. Cats running away from zucchinis. Why are cats so scared of zucchini? I don't know. I thought, *College is for suckers. I can just look at cat pictures every day for the rest of my life and then die. That's not so bad.*

I looked up because the secretary at the desk was waving her arms and pointing toward a woman walking into the building. *Dean Smythe,* she mouthed once she had my attention. I jumped up and hauled over to her as soon as she was through the door.

"Dean Smythe!" I said. "It's Mischa Abramavicius. From Blanchard?"

She looked at me blankly, and I had to jog to keep up with her. "It's nice to meet you, Mischa. Is there something I can do for you?"

"Ah," I said. "Yeah, the secretary said it got left off your calendar, but we were supposed to do an interview today, for my school paper. The secretary said you might be able to work me in during lunch?"

She looked darkly at the secretary as we walked by. "Did she," she said. The secretary quailed and pretended to read an email.

"Yes, so is that okay? I only need a few minutes."

"Fine, Mischa."

I followed her into her office and sat down on the other side of the desk while she pulled out a lunch bag and unwrapped a sandwich. "I'll have to eat while we talk," she said. "I have another meeting in half an hour."

"That's fine," I said. "I just have a few questions."

"Well, let's get started," she said.

"Okay. Um, first, what percentage of applicants did you accept this year?"

"It was about 70%," she said, licking mayonnaise off her upper lip. "This was a particularly competitive year."

I wrote the number down because it's what I was supposed to be doing. *Seventy percent?* I thought. I was in the bottom 30% of applicants? That had to be a mistake. Had to be.

"So do you have any safeguards in place for the admissions office? To make sure nothing throws a wrench into the process?"

She took a big bite of sandwich and answered me with her mouth full. "What do you mean?"

"I mean in case someone makes a mistake someplace along the way. Like, if someone puts a student in the wrong pile, like, someone sneezes and accidentally puts the valedictorian in the 'no' pile. Is someone double-checking that?"

"We have multiple people reviewing the applications, if that's what you mean."

"Okay," I said. "But, like, if someone, someone who was very qualified, got put in the 'no' pile by mistake, like, because they were confused with somebody else or they just hit the wrong button or something, does anybody ever go back and double-check that?"

She put her sandwich down on the desk. "Let's be honest here, Mischa. This isn't for a school project."

I was writing down the word "safeguard," but I paused. "Um," I said.

"If I look you up in my computer right now," she said, "I will find that you applied here and did not get in, correct?"

I set my pen down. "You would probably find that."

"And you think that was a mistake on our part." She shook her head. "Mischa, we had a very highly qualified applicant pool this year. We had to turn down a lot of good students."

"But," I said. "But no, you don't understand. I have a 3.98 GPA! I had a 1580 on the SATs!"

But she was already pulling up my file.

"I'm sorry, Mischa," she said. "Your test scores were good, but some of your grades were very poor."

"Poor?" I said. "No. I mean, I know I got that one A– in gym, but . . ."

"Honey," she said. "It's okay not to get into your first-choice college," she said. "There's a college out there for everyone, even people who struggled in high school."

"I did not struggle. At all."

"Mischa," she said soothingly, which made me want to punch her. "Honey. It's okay. I'm not very good at math, either."

"Not good at . . . *what*??"

She turned the monitor around to face me. She'd pulled up a digital copy of my transcript, and I got up to look at it. My GPA was in the upper right corner. It was not a 3.98.

"No, no, that's just wrong. That's not me."

"Born January 5, 2000?" she asked.

"Yeah, but that's not me."

"Are there other Mischa Abramaviciuses at Blanchard?"

"No," I said. "Just me. But maybe they put my name on someone else's transcript. That isn't me!" I was scanning down the list of courses . . . the classes were all right. And most of the grades were fine. But, randomly, it was showing a D in geometry, a D in Algebra II, and a D+ in my sophomore world history class.

Dean Smythe had gotten up from her desk and was steering me out of the office by the shoulders. "You can always transfer in for the spring semester," she said. "Or next year, if you do well at your next-choice school."

"But I didn't have a next-choice school! Your piece-of-crap school was my safety!"

"Susan," she was saying to the secretary. "Call campus security."

"Don't bother," I said. "I'm leaving." And I stormed out to my car.

Sitting in the driver's seat with the engine idling, I pulled out my phone. My finger hovered over my mother's picture in my contacts list. I played out the conversation we would have in my head. It went like this:

Me: Mom! Something terrible has happened!

Mom: Oh, no, dearest offspring, do you have to go to the hospital? Seeing as you told me you left school early today because you were sick.

Me: Uh, no, I am not actually sick.

Mom: You lied about being sick? You *skipped school*?

Me: Yes, but only because I had to strong-arm myself into a meeting with the admissions dean at Revere.

Mom: Oh! To talk about their honors program?

Me: Not exactly.

Mom: To discuss your financial aid package?

Me: No . . .

Mom: Well, what was it? They must be so excited you're going there.

Me: Yeah, heh, funny story . . . so I was kind of rejected from every school I applied to, which I kind of forgot to mention before? And I know this sounds super bad, but listen! I think something went wrong with my transcript, not that I have any physical evidence of that, but I did see it on Dean Smythe's computer screen for like two whole seconds and then she said I was bad at math and threatened to call security on me.

Mom: You're not going to college?

Me: Did you hear what I said about the transcript?

Mom: YOU'RE NOT GOING TO COLLEGE?

I did not call my mother.

Instead, I sent a text to Nate.

Someone is messing with me.

• • •

The next morning, I tried to see Pendleton again, but she was still out, and now the sign on her door said she'd be out the rest of the week. So I went into the main office to see Mrs. Hadley, the registrar. Mrs. Hadley shares the front office with Ms. Richmond, the receptionist, and Ms. Thompson, the assistant to Dr. Marlowe. The three of them are all over sixty, and every year at Halloween, they dress up as the three witches from *Macbeth*, which is actually kind of great, except for that one year Ms. Richmond tripped over a cauldron and broke her toe.

For the hundredth time, I smacked my knee into the giant cardboard box that blocked the way to her desk, which has been there since midway through junior year and was a testament to Ms. Richmond's office-keeping ability. The official story was that she'd accidentally ordered five hundred reams of paper instead of fifty, and since no one could lift the box to return it to Office Depot, it was stuck there until all the paper was used up. The unofficial story was that it contained a dead body. Whose body depended on whom you asked; the prevailing theory these days was that it was Mr. Pelletier's mother, whom he'd murdered in some Norman Bates–esque fit of oedipal pique.

Nate and I had decided that Oedipal Pique would be an excellent name for a racehorse.

"Hi, Mrs. Hadley," I said. She was seventy at least and kind of hard of hearing, so I had to raise my voice.

"Do you need a late pass?" she asked.

"Um, no," I said. "It's just, there seems to be a problem with my transcript? I wanted to talk to Ms. Pendleton about it, but she's not here, and I was wondering if you could print me out a copy?"

"Sure. What was your name again?"

"Mischa. Abramavicius."

She pulled up the file and printed it out. "Here you go," she said, handing it to me. "Does it seem to check out?"

I scanned down the page: 3.98 GPA. And As everywhere, except that one stinking gym class. It was fine. It matched all of my report cards at home perfectly.

"Yeah," I said quietly. "It does. Can I keep this?"

"Well, sure," she said. "It's your transcript."

I walked out of the office with my transcript and flipped through it again.

If the woman at Revere hadn't shown me the version she had, I'd never have known there was a problem. It would have been one of those inexplicable things. I just didn't get into college. It dawned on me that this could be happening to people every day. How would anyone know? We're trusting the process because we don't have a choice.

Someone had sent out a faulty transcript. But it wasn't the one Blanchard had in the computer. Which seemed to imply one thing: someone had done it on purpose and then covered their tracks.

It occurred to me that I might be getting a little paranoid. But maybe some paranoia was in order.

Before ninth grade I was always just the smart kid at my regular public school. But then some rather unfortunate things went down at the high school I should have attended, and my mother decided she was not sending her only offspring to take her chances someplace that had recently dealt with a fairly epic scandal, in which it came out that the varsity cheer squad was pimping out the football team in exchange for drugs.

It was a bad year for Chinn Ridge High. And the principal's

speech to the middle school PTA that these were anomalies and the school did not have a problem with drugs, prostitution, or evil cheerleaders did nothing to reassure my mother. By January she'd assembled information packets from four different private schools; by February I'd bought a secondhand navy blue interview suit and had the "What famous dead person would you have dinner with?" conversation four times, and by April I had my admissions letter from Blanchard.

Mom was thrilled. I was filled with this fizzy optimism I'd never felt before, because I had a chance to be great, to go to school with the best and the brightest and blow them all away. I was going to be somebody. Somebody amazing.

I was going to show Mom that it'd all been worth it.

I found Nate in front of his locker after school the next day, since he had something he wanted to tell me in person before I went home. My phone was blowing up because I'd missed Monday's French club meeting plus one for Students for Sober Driving yesterday, but I didn't really know what to say to people, so I turned it off.

"Nate," I said, "someone has royally screwed me over."

"I know," he said. "That's what I wanted to talk to you about. I might know some people who can help."

"People who can help," I said. "Who are these people? Like, one of those college coaches?"

"Okay," he said. "Don't freak out."

"I've been freaking out for a week," I said. "I'm already at an eleven on the freaking-out scale. It doesn't go up any higher."

"You know Emily Sreenivasan?"

I blinked at him. He and Emily had gone out for a whopping three weeks last fall, before she dumped him via text in the middle of a chemistry quiz.

"I didn't realize you guys still hung out. What was it that she called you?"

"That was a long time ago."

"Oh, right. She called you a neurotic troglodyte."

"Let's move on," he said.

"During a *test*."

"Could you let this go?"

"Which you proceeded to *flunk*."

"The point is," he said through his teeth, "this problem falls under Emily's area of expertise."

"Screwed-up transcripts?"

"Nothing that specific," he said. "But I'll let them explain."

"Them? Emily and who else?"

"Just . . . just wait. You'll see."

I followed Nate down to the basement, which was mostly devoid of people at this time of the afternoon, and toward the computer lab at the end of the hall, where the computer science classes meet.

Emily Sreenivasan.

They'd been kind of a mismatch, I'd thought at the time, but then I thought everyone was kind of a mismatch with Nate.

I realize this is kind of unfair of me.

To my credit, I actually had tried to tell Nate how I felt about him. Just to clear the air, I guess. But my timing was off. It was freshman year. The conversation went something like this:

Me: Hey, so there's this guy I like—

Nate: Is it Jim? You should ask him out.

Me: No—

Nate: You should! And then you guys could go out with me and Colin.

Me: Colin Braverman?

Nate: Yeah, didn't I tell you? He asked me out after French yesterday.

And there was really no way to come back from that, you know? Except the next year I'd gotten up the guts to try again. And it had gone the exact same way, except this time he'd been going out with some girl from Sidwell he met at the Barnes and Noble.

I figured two hints were probably as much as I could stand to drop, since both times I went home and felt horrible for like three days, because, as it turns out, I do not take rejection all that well.

I wish I'd known that the implied no from Nate was just the universe's way of gearing me up for the big NNNNOOOOO I would be hearing from colleges later. Maybe I would have found a better way to deal with it.

I was about to open the door when I got a text from Leo Michaels saying, *Why aren't you in French club?*

"Oh crap," I said. I texted, *I thought that was Monday.*

Right. You missed the Monday meeting, too.

Nate, who was reading over my shoulder, said, "He can't argue if you don't answer him."

"I can't just ghost on Leo."

"Then tell him you're sick."

"Fine," I said. I texted, *Super bad headache, on my way home, sorry.*

He texted back, *YOU SUCK.*

"See?" Nate said. "That's why I told you not to answer him."

I sighed, because I knew I'd have to deal with French club drama later, and put my phone away.

The door to the computer lab was locked.

"No one's here," I said. "They probably lock it at the end of the day so nobody steals the computers or whatever."

"They're here," he said. He knocked three times.

"Cute Nate?" said a voice from the other side of the door, which might or might not have been Emily's.

"Cute?" I whispered to Nate, but he just shook his head and smiled, like this was an old joke that he pretended to be annoyed by.

"Yeah," he said.

"Did you bring food?"

"What? No. Of course not."

"Not even chips?"

"Could you just open the door?"

The door swung open. The person speaking, as it turned out, wasn't Emily, who was sitting at the long table in front of the room, typing away on what was definitely not a school-issued laptop, but Shira Gastman. Which was very strange because I couldn't think of a single thing she and Emily had in common, and also because Shira looked soberer than I'd ever seen her before.

"What are you doing here?" I asked.

"Not eating chips, I guess," she said. She went and sat down across from Emily, who did not look up from what she was doing. "Emily," she said. Then, louder: *"Emily."*

"Hello, Mischa. Cute Nate," Emily said, her eyes still locked on the screen.

"Her ladyship will be with you shortly," Shira said, rolling her eyes to the ceiling.

"It's not my fault," Emily said, "that you have no focus."

"I focus plenty," Shira said. "You're just showing off."

Nate cleared his throat into his fist, but I saw him stifle a smile. If Emily was showing off her mad focus skills, I guessed it was probably for his benefit, not mine.

"Shira," said a warning voice from down on the floor, where there was a third person I hadn't seen. Bebe Tandoh sat surrounded by computer parts like a little kid in the middle of an A+ Lego session, in her ubiquitous fabulous shoes. She had a tiny screwdriver behind her ear and was holding a circuit board an inch from her eye. She didn't look up when we came in, and I stopped to watch her put the circuit board down and pick up some kind of computer chip. "I'm almost done here," she said. "Just a sec."

I looked at Nate. "What is this?" I asked.

"Officially," said Shira, "we're the girls' STEM club."

I was pretty familiar with Blanchard's extracurricular offerings. "We don't have a girls' STEM club," I said.

Emily broke eye contact with her laptop and shut the screen, leaning back and stretching her arms over her head. "Technically we do," she said. "We just don't recruit."

"Also," said Shira, "our sponsor is dead."

"She's not dead," Bebe said from the floor. "She's in Boca."

"Same difference," Shira said.

Emily shook her head. "Here's the rundown: We had a girls' STEM club freshman year. Our sponsor was Ms. Silverman. She retired and moved to Boca. But when Ms. Ishikawa took over, she didn't want to run two clubs, so she tried to roll us into the coed STEM club."

"So we went rogue," Shira said.

"We made a deal with Ms. Ishikawa," Bebe said. "We keep

our club status, she doesn't have to come to meetings, and once a month one of us hands in a sheet with a list of whatever we did."

"Some of it's even accurate," Shira said.

"And in return, we get a key to the computer lab and a share of the Blanchard Community Cash."

Ah. The Blanchard Community Cash was a fund set up by the school for extracurriculars—every school-sponsored club was entitled to two hundred bucks a year for expenses. Most of the clubs used it for snacks and stuff that we ate during meetings, or supplies for posters or flyers or whatever, but it didn't seem like Emily and company were using it that way. I wondered what they *were* using it for.

"So that's the official story," Bebe said. "If anyone asks."

"Is there an unofficial story?" I asked.

Emily waved an elegant hand at Nate. "Cute Nate, you can go now."

"What? I . . ."

"Girl talk," Shira said. "You know."

"Right," he said. "You guys are going to paint your nails and talk about boys."

"Of course," Bebe said. "What else do girls talk about?"

"Bras," said Shira. "Pantyhose. Hot guys named Ryan."

"Oooh," said Bebe. "And Chris. Don't forget Chris."

"Our periods," Shira added. "Cramps. Tampons. Trips to the gyno."

"Fine," Nate said. "I'll go."

"But you're my ride!" I protested.

"We'll make sure Mischa gets home," Emily said. "Don't worry your pretty little head about it."

I grabbed Nate's wrist. "Don't leave," I said.

"What we have to discuss," Bebe said, "is not for Cute Nate's ears."

"You'll be fine," he said. "Call me later."

"Bye, Cute Nate," Shira called to his retreating back. Nate shook his head and kept walking.

"So, Mischa," Emily said. "Have a seat."

I sat down in the third chair, which I guessed was normally Bebe's when she wasn't disemboweling computers. The whiteboard at the front of the room had a bunch of lines of computer code scribbled on it, interspersed with a lot of profanity.

"Cute Nate tells us you have a problem that might be in our wheelhouse."

I looked over at Bebe again. She'd pulled the keyboard out of the laptop she was working on—like, I didn't even know that was possible—and was sticking something into a slot inside. Without looking up, I said, "I'm not exactly sure what your wheelhouse is."

Shira said, "Let's just say that our little syndicate has some experience with the problems of hacking."

I looked up from Bebe, who was screwing her patient back together. For all of her reputation, Shira seemed almost alarmingly sober. She grinned at me. It was unnerving.

"Syndicate," I repeated.

Emily spun a business card at me from across the table. On it was printed THE OPHELIA SYNDICATE, and then there was an email address: OpheliaOne@Ophelia.com.

I wondered who they normally handed these out to. It seemed . . . rather not secret to have business cards. Also: rather pretentious. They were embossed. There was a little picture in the corner, some kind of flower.

"You have a logo," I said. I read the card a second time. "The Ophelia Syndicate?"

"This is very off the record, Mischa," Emily said.

"Right," I said. "So you're, like, gamers?"

"We are not gamers!" Emily said indignantly.

"Really," Bebe said. "Don't call us that. We don't play games."

"We're hackers," Emily said.

"What do you hack?"

"Oh. A little of this. A little of that. Just believe that we're in a position to uncover what happened to you. There are two possibilities: either this was an accident, or someone did this to you on purpose. Did you try getting an updated copy of your transcript?"

"Yeah," I said. "I did. The one they gave me in the office had the grades right."

Emily and Shira exchanged a glance. "It wasn't an accident, then," Emily said. "Someone would have had to change the transcript and then change it back again after it was sent out to your colleges."

"There's no way that was an accident," Bebe agreed. "So apparently someone doesn't like you very much."

Emily leaned back in her chair with her arms crossed behind her head. "Well, well," she said. "Always-in-the-front-row Mischa has an enemy. And here I always thought you were boring."

CHAPTER EIGHT

BEBE DUMPED HER COMPUTER PARTS INTO A BOX AND CAME TO sit next to Emily, who was drumming her chrome-painted fingernails on the table. Shira was standing at the whiteboard with a dry-erase marker in her hand.

"So," she said. "Who hates you? Besides the obvious."

"What do you mean, 'besides the obvious'?"

"Honey," she said. "Meredith Dorsay's been gunning for you since we were freshmen. Why is that, by the way?"

"I'm not really sure," I said. "She kind of hates anyone she thinks might be getting better grades than her, doesn't she?"

"To a point," Emily said. "But you seem to be a special case."

"You haven't heard what she's been saying," Shira added.

I winced. "What has she been saying?"

"That the reason you aren't telling people where you're

going is that you didn't get in anywhere," Shira replied. "Oh, and that you lied about your SAT scores."

"God." I closed my eyes. "And I'm sure everyone believes her, too."

"Well, technically, she's half-right," said Shira. "Anyway, I think we can agree that she hates you. Did you pee in her cornflakes freshman year or something?"

"Honestly," I said. "I didn't do anything."

Freshman year, Meredith and I had been in the same classes for English, Algebra II, and PE, which seems like a lot, but for a small school like Blanchard, it really isn't. She'd pretty much ignored me until the end of the third week, when we'd gotten our essays about *Wuthering Heights* back. I'd gotten an A. She'd gotten a B+.

The next week, we'd had a problem set due in math. I'd gotten a 98. She'd gotten a 94.

Apparently, she'd been considered the smartest kid in her grade back in middle school, and here I was, a nobody from some third-rate public school with a home haircut and shoes from Target, and I was showing her up. The next time we got a math quiz back, my grade had been five points higher, and I could see that she was stewing. I didn't realize it was about me, not really. I thought it was the grade. I didn't have any friends yet; I hadn't started hanging out with Nate or Caroline, so I went up to her after class and said, "Hey, we could study together sometime. If you want."

This had been the wrong thing to say.

She'd sneered at me and said, "I don't need help from *you*."

I'd been too stunned to say anything back. Caroline, who had been in that class, too, had brushed by me and said, "Here's some free advice: don't let her see your grades."

"What?"

"Trust me. Just don't let her see them."

And I'd tried. I'd flipped my papers over as soon as they were handed back, and I could see her neck always craning to check out my work. But after a while I was sick of it. I was getting 98s and 100s and hiding them, and what was the point of doing the work and then acting like I was ashamed of it? What was she going to do, throw me in a dumpster?

So I stopped hiding them. And that's when it began, whatever stupid competition we had going. If I made a point in class, she one-upped it. If I did a trig problem in four steps, she'd let the teacher know that it could be done in three. If my sonnet had a syllable with the wrong inflection, she'd make sure to point it out to the rest of the class. I couldn't put a toe out of line without her being all over it. It was exhausting. On the upside, it meant my work was always letter perfect. It had to be.

"I think maybe she's just super competitive," I said.

"And you applied to a lot of the same schools," Emily pointed out.

"Yeah," I said. "I guess so."

"Schools that, historically, don't take more than one or two people from Blanchard every year."

"I don't know," I said. "This seems pretty low, even for Meredith." But truthfully, I was starting to wonder.

They exchanged a glance. "Do you have someone else in mind?"

"No," I said. "I don't."

Emily wrinkled her nose at me. "Well," she said, "either this was revenge, or someone had something to gain by shredding your transcript. Someone else who was applying to the same schools as you, maybe? Any other possibilities you can think of?"

Shira wiped off a space on the whiteboard and made two columns. "A" was revenge. "B" was personal gain. Five minutes later we sat back and looked at the board.

Category A was Meredith. I honestly couldn't think of anyone else. ("Because you're so boring," Emily told me.)

Category B consisted of all the other students I knew who'd applied to Harvard and Princeton. Which included Meredith again, plus about fifteen other people, and probably left out a bunch of others who were being quiet about having applied.

Shira leaned back and tapped her lip. "Why are we limiting ourselves to students?"

"You think it could be a teacher?" Emily asked.

She shrugged. "Maybe. Maybe one of them's got it in for you?"

I closed my eyes for a minute. "Well, there's Mr. Bender, maybe."

Everyone perked up. "Really?" Emily said. "Why him?"

Mr. Bender had only been teaching at Blanchard for a few years; he was around twenty-five and looked like a senior, unless he remembered to shave, and then he looked like a sophomore. He was cute, I guess, one of those men who was probably a huge nerd but had recently shelled out for a gym membership. There were girls flirting with him constantly, and I thought he was, frankly, pretty gross, though I seemed to be alone in that assessment. Well, actually Meredith Dorsay despised him, too, but that was kind of her default setting.

"I caught him with Beth Reinhardt between classes last year."

Emily cocked her head to one side. "Define 'caught him.'"

"They were alone in his room with the door locked," I said.

"Locked," Emily said. "Not shut."

"Locked," I confirmed. "And the blinds were down."

"Holy crap," Bebe said. "Beth Reinhardt. She's as dumb as a rock."

It was, unfortunately, true. Beth's father was famous for having been the senator from New Hampshire. Beth's mother was famous for having been an extra on *Baywatch*. Beth, at Blanchard, was famous for having accused Ms. Templeton, the biology teacher, of sexual harassment for using the word "cleavage" while discussing cell division.

"I'm not sure if Mr. Bender knows I know. But Beth definitely does. I ran into her in the hall afterward, and she was all sweaty and red in the face."

Bebe said, "Ew."

"Add Beth to the list," Emily said. "Mr. Bender, too."

"Um," Shira said. "Full disclosure: I caught Mr. Bender with someone else last fall."

"Who?"

"Willa Jenkins. I saw her get out of his car at Starbucks."

"Willa," said Bebe. "Wait, aren't she and Beth pretty good friends?"

"Yeah," I said. "They are."

Bebe said, "Ew."

"So we suspect Bender was getting it on with at least two different students," Emily said.

"At least?" I asked.

"Two is a pattern."

"Yeah, but why go after me, even if he did know that I knew?"

"Where did Beth and Willa apply? Do you know?"

"Beth's a legacy at Princeton, I'm pretty sure. And I heard Willa got into Williams."

"Well, that's interesting," Emily said. "Maybe he's getting the competition out of the way for his lady friends?" She dropped her voice. "Or in exchange for—ahem—favors?"

Shira said, "Ew."

"Or it could be a coincidence. It's not like there aren't a ton of us applying to the same schools."

"It's an avenue worth pursuing," Emily said, fiddling with the ends of her hair. "But one other thing occurs to me. A couple of Ds shouldn't have kept you out of Revere, especially with good SAT scores—it doesn't make any sense. It's possible they got into other parts of your packet."

"Like my test scores?"

"No way," Bebe said. "ETS is pretty much unhackable. People have been trying for years. It's too hard."

"Well, the only other piece that came from the school and not from me was my letters of recommendation—oh no, no, no. My letters." I sat back from the table and made eye contact with Emily. Shira let out a low whistle.

"That actually has the potential to be worse than the grades," Emily said. "A lot worse."

The admissions equation flashed along the backs of my eyelids.

The R factor—which accounted for the quality of the letters of recommendation—rarely meant anything, unless the letters were bizarrely good. Or bizarrely bad. If my letters had been hacked, if someone had put something really bad in there, called me a felon, said I bit the head off a live chicken during class . . . my admissions number could have been decimated. "Oh my God," I said. "Oh my God."

"Deep breaths, Mischa," Emily said.

"Okay," I said. "Okay. Okay." I breathed a few more times.

"But how could we even find out what's in those letters? They're anonymous. I can't get my own copies."

"Couple of possibilities," Emily said. "We could pose as a college and ask Blanchard to send a copy to a fake address. Or we could hack the system ourselves."

I said, "Can you do that?"

"Somebody already did."

I left with my OpheliaOne card tucked into my pocket, sitting in the passenger seat of Emily's car as she drove me home on her way to whatever she was doing next. She drove a five-year-old BMW, bright red and way too clean to belong to an eighteen-year-old.

"What do I do now?" I asked.

"You wait," she said. "When we get a plan in place, I'll call you."

I rubbed the skin between my eyes. This was my entire future, and I was leaving it in someone else's hands. I was trusting Emily and Company because I had no choice. The school wouldn't have believed me; the transcript they had on file for me was the right one, and the only evidence I had was what I'd seen with my own eyeballs.

I suppose I could have told my mother.

My mother.

I couldn't tell my mother.

"This is a nightmare," I muttered.

"It is," Emily agreed.

I sifted through the contents of the cup holder next to me: two bottles of nail polish and a keychain of the starship *Enterprise*. "It's like . . . it's like I was just walking along, minding my own business, and someone randomly shoved me off a cliff," I said. My eyes started to ache, and I turned my face away from Emily and coughed into my hand.

She turned onto my street and pulled up in front of my house. Before I could get out, she reached across and took hold of my hand, which reminded me, for some reason, that she used to go out with Nate, which made my insides feel strange. I looked over to see what she wanted, and she gave me an intense stare. I looked at her. She looked back. She had, I thought, the longest eyelashes in the world. "You need to separate yourself from this," she said. "Don't confuse College Applicant Mischa with the real person."

I looked down at her hand. She was wearing a ring with a blue stone in the middle and flowers on either side, the same flowers that were on the Ophelia card. I wondered again what they were. "What do you mean?" I asked.

"Think about it this way. At any point in your life, you are two people. There's the Mischa you think you are, and then there's the Mischa everyone else sees. The second one is the one who gets you into college, or not. That's the one who applies for jobs, and mortgages, and gets written about in the paper. Call her the Mischa-bot, if you will. Your brand. Your avatar. You've worked for the last twelve years programming her with all the bits you want her to have. The right classes. The right extra-curriculars. All that garbage you do as a means to an end."

"And now someone's reprogrammed my avatar."

"Exactly."

"Can we fix it?"

She let go of my hand and put hers back on the gearshift, which I recognized as a dismissal. "I guess we'll find out," she said. "But, Mischa, remember. That avatar is not you."

CHAPTER NINE

WHEN I GOT HOME THAT AFTERNOON, MY MOM WAS ALREADY there, buzzing around the kitchen making some kind of left-over casserole that she called "glop," which both of us would drown in mango chutney to try to mask the taste of three-day-old chicken and cream of Choose Your Own Adventure soup.

"Hey," she said, while I came in and got myself some water. "So the guys at work heard about how you're going to Revere next year."

I tried not to choke on my water. "Mm-hm."

"And they got together and got you something." She picked an envelope off the counter and handed it to me.

"They didn't have to—" I started.

"It's like the circle of life," she said. "We all put money in for baby showers, weddings, housewarmings. It all cycles around. Now it's your turn."

"But I don't even work there."

"Just open it."

I opened the envelope. In it was a card that said *CONGRAT-ULATIONS!* in big bubble letters, while a bunch of Dalmatian puppies wearing mortarboards pranced around looking winsome. The inside said, "We know you'll be SPOTTED doing great things!" and then there was a hundred-dollar gift card to Macy's.

"Wow," I said, tearing my eyes away from the faces of the mocking dogs. "That was really nice of everyone."

"I thought we could go after dinner," she said. "Pick out some stuff for your dorm room. They're having a sale."

"I don't know," I hedged. "Isn't it kind of early for that? Don't people usually do that at the end of the summer?"

"Yes, and everything will be all picked over," she said, taking the card back from me. "Come on. I know you're bummed about Revere. This'll help you get over it."

I wasn't sure which was worse, that she thought, somehow, that a new bedspread and shower caddy would be enough for me to forget that I'd be going to my safety school, or that, in fact, nothing so good as that was going to happen. I needed to tell her.

"You know," I said. "I was thinking of applying to a couple of other schools. Places with rolling admissions or late deadlines. Just so I have some more, uh, choices."

"Oh. Really?"

"It just seems like a good idea."

"Hmm. You're probably right. Still, though," she said, tapping my arm with the envelope. "We can go pick stuff out. Wherever you go, you'll have a room."

"Can't I just take my stuff from home?"

"You're not going to want to haul your sheets and towels back and forth every time you come home, Mischa."

I sighed. "I guess you're right."

"Great! We'll go after dinner."

"Okay," I said, and then, because my mother was looking at me expectantly, I added, "Yay!"

After dinner we made our way up to the Tysons mall, where Macy's was having a white sale and the aisles were filled with people elbowing each other over bargains. My mother went to look at towels while I stood, despondent, in front of a selection of extra-long twin comforters.

I didn't much want to think about matching dust ruffles and shams right then. This was a waste of time and money, and I was considering telling my mom so when someone to the left of me pulled the package of bedding out of my hands.

Of course it was Meredith Dorsay. Why she was shopping at Macy's was another issue. I'm pretty sure her mother imports her linens directly from France.

"What are you doing here?" I asked.

"God, you're rude," she said. "I'm here with Amy Gregston. She's going to Cambridge this summer so she has to buy everything early."

I spied Amy down the aisle, frowning at a package of sheets and muttering about thread count. I didn't ask if she meant Massachusetts or England, because I couldn't stomach caring.

"So where are you going, anyway?" she asked. "You never did say."

I was about to tell her I hadn't decided yet (which was technically true) when over my shoulder I heard, "Revere."

The answer came from my mother, who had come to stand on my other side. "Mischa's going to Revere."

Meredith's smile ate her face. "Really? Revere? Oh. That's a really great school for you."

I let the slap pass over me. My mother, however, had gone rather stiff. "They have a great internship program," she said defensively.

"Oh, really? I hadn't thought too much about internship programs." Meredith pushed the package of bedding back into my hands. "You should get this one," she said. "It suits you." Then she turned around and went off to find Amy, who had a blue towel in one hand and a beige one in the other, weighing them like Lady Justice.

I looked down at the bedding I was holding, and only then realized it was SpongeBob.

"Charming girl," my mother said flatly.

"Oh yes," I said, putting the comforter back on the shelf. "She's a peach."

"Did you pick one?" she asked, gesturing toward the packages of bedding. "I assume you didn't actually want the SpongeBob."

Good lord, I could not have cared less about bedding or towels or matching throw pillows. She held something up in front of my face; it was some kind of a bucket with lots of compartments. "It's to take your shampoo and stuff," she said excitedly. "To the showers. See? There's even a spot for your razor."

"Hey," I said. "Look at that."

"They have blue and orange," she said. "Which do you think?"

"Um. I don't know. Orange, I guess."

"That's a good choice," she said. "Everyone else will pick blue."

I grabbed the nearest bedding set off the shelf—something paisley. "This one," I said.

"Perfect. Here." She thrust the shower caddy at me, and I grabbed it with my fingertips, then she piled a couple of bath towels on top of everything, pulled out her phone, and said, "Smile!"

"What?"

"For the folks at work. So they can see what you bought. Everyone's so proud of you, Mischa."

"Mom—"

"They just want to be supportive." She snapped a picture of me, then frowned at her phone. "Let's get another one. You're not smiling." Then she put her phone down and said, "Mischa," probably because my eyes were filling with tears, and my only consolation was that Meredith Dorsay was not there to see.

"Don't," I said. "Just don't, okay?"

CHAPTER TEN

On Monday I got up, I went to school, I did not cry in public, and I went home.

After dinner Caroline messaged me three selfies where she was modeling different dresses in front of a three-way mirror.

Can't decide, she said.

I rubbed my eyes. I was so tired.

The blue one, I said. *The red one won't stay up while you're dancing.*

What about the pink one?

The pink one was too tight, but of course I couldn't get away with that much honesty so I said, *The blue one makes you look more collegiate.*

She said, *YEAH IT DOES!*

I was about to turn my phone off because I was not really in the mood for this when I got a text from Emily. She'd put this app on my phone the other day called TalkOff, which deletes all your texts two minutes after they're seen and is supposedly 100% anonymous, and it makes a little *bloop* sound when a message comes through.

The message said, *Meet me at my house at 11:30. Wear something dark.*

Eleven-thirty? I wondered how she thought I was going to get out of the house that late on a school night. My mother was usually asleep by then, but I felt a little weird disappearing with the car in the middle of the night. Even if she didn't notice, there was a good chance one of the neighbors would.

That might be a problem, I texted back.

The phone rang. I picked up, and Emily said, "This is tiresome, Mischa."

"Sorry, what?"

"We are attempting to render our services unto you, for which you are not paying us, by the way. The least you could do is actually show up when we call you."

"You know," I said. "Not everyone has their own Beemer."

"Your boyfriend," she said, "has a car."

"He's not my—"

"Shush. Borrow your mother's car. Borrow Cute Nate's car. Borrow the Queen of England's car; I do not care. But be at my house by eleven-thirty. We have things to do."

"Fine," I said.

"I'm glad we understand each other," she said, and hung up.

I weighed the possibility of making off with my mother's car—which was prone to dropping key parts at inopportune moments—and asking Nate for help yet again. I called Nate.

"I have a summons," I explained. "From Emily."

"I see," he said. "If I give you a ride, can I come along?"

"Not up to me," I said.

"No," he agreed. "It's probably not. I'll pick you up and drive you over there, if you want."

"Thanks, Nate," I said.

"Don't mention it. Well, it's okay if you want to mention it sometime. Mentioning it is probably fine."

"Nate."

"Mischa."

"I'll see you at eleven."

Nate and I arrived at 11:28 at Emily's house, which is about a mile away from Blanchard. It's one of those big square houses with all-glass walls that you see on design shows. Emily and Shira were in the basement, her parents presumably asleep, both girls wearing black leggings and T-shirts with their hair tied back.

"Uh," I said. "Are we breaking in someplace?"

"In fact, we are!" Shira said jovially. "Isn't it wonderful?"

"What?" I said. "Where are we breaking in?"

"Hello? Blanchard?" Shira said. "Where else would we go?"

"To look at the transcripts? I thought you were going to hack into those remotely."

"Well, yes, that was the idea," said Emily. "But that didn't happen quite the way I'd hoped."

"Didn't happen?"

"I was hoping those files would be stored on Blanchard's cloud. But they aren't backed up there. I couldn't find them."

"Isn't that strange?"

"It is strange," Emily said. "But they must be on Mrs. Hadley's hard drive, so we're going to access them the old-fashioned way."

"And how are we getting into the building?"

"Also the old-fashioned way." Emily glanced at Nate. "Are you coming? You're not really dressed for it."

"Sorry," he said. "I didn't realize this was a costume event."

"You can wait in the car," she said, and we followed her out the front door.

"Isn't this an awful lot of people to break into the school with?" I asked. "We're kind of conspicuous."

Emily got in the car, with Shira riding next to her. Nate and I squashed ourselves into the backseat. "We're not all going inside," she said. "We need contingencies. And contingencies for the contingencies."

Emily alternated driving with tying her hair up in a bun and shoving it into a beanie. A few minutes later we pulled into Blanchard's driveway, where the guard who manned the entry booth had long since gone home. The gate across the entrance lane was up, and after we'd driven by it, Emily shut off the headlights. Then she picked up her phone and dialed. "Bebe," she said. "Darling."

"Where's Bebe?" I asked.

"Hopefully in the vicinity of an exterior door." She cocked her head toward the phone. "Auditorium, she says." She put the phone down and pulled the car into a spot behind a dumpster.

"We're kind of far from the building, aren't we?" asked Nate.

"You can see the booth from here. You"—she indicated

Nate—"are going to stay here and keep watch. If you see headlights coming down that road, you call us. Whatever happens, don't let anyone see you."

"She's really getting into this," Shira said.

"Look, we are all aware that what we are doing could get us arrested and expelled, right? Like, that's a real thing that could happen if we aren't careful?" Emily reached back to switch off the dome light so it wouldn't turn on when we opened the doors, and the three of us got out, leaving Nate to wait.

"How long do you think this'll take?" he asked.

"If we can't get what we want in half an hour, we're leaving. It's just too risky otherwise." She leveled a finger at him. "Don't do anything that turns on any light."

"What?"

"It'll draw attention to the car! Honestly, people."

"So I'm just going to be sitting here. In the dark. By myself. Doing nothing."

"Not doing nothing," Emily said in a tone of strained forbearance. "You're going to be watching for other cars."

"Yay," he said. "How fun that will be."

Emily shut the car door, and the three of us made our way quietly toward the side of the school, where there was a locked fire door leading out of the auditorium. When we got there, Shira knocked two times on the door, and it opened. On the other side, Bebe was holding the door open with one hand and a box of take-out lo mein noodles with the other, a pair of chopsticks sticking out of the top.

"Took you long enough," she said. "It's massively boring in here. Like, you'd think there'd be more to do, but Mrs. White's emails really aren't that interesting."

"You were reading her emails?" I asked.

"I was joking."

"You know she's having an affair with Mr. Bender, right?" I asked.

They turned toward me and stared for a few seconds. "Her, too? Now how did you figure that one out?"

"They both go out for lunch twice a week. Separately. And then they come back and eat a sandwich during third period."

Emily looked impressed. "Nate put that one together, actually," I admitted.

"Why didn't you mention this before?"

"I—I don't know. I guess I didn't think it was important."

"From now on," Emily said, "everything is important." She checked the time on her phone and nodded at Bebe. "Did you check the building?"

"Nobody home," she said. "I did a round at seven and another one half an hour ago. Ms. Erickson was the last one here."

"Where were you hiding?"

"Boys' locker room." She shuddered. "I was going to do the girls', but the lacrosse team was here until six."

"So where'd you get the takeout?" I asked, pointing at the lo mein.

"Faculty fridge," she said, turning the box so I could see the other side, where *Lisa White* was written in black marker. She teaches AP English, but not my section.

"You took her lunch?"

She gave me a dark look. "She docked me ten points on a quiz for writing in purple ink." She slurped the noodles into her mouth. "Time to pay the piper."

We made our way to the front office, which was closed for the night. Before she tried the door, Emily opened the bag slung over her arm, saying, "This is the part where we put gloves on."

"Is that really necessary?"

"No," said Shira. "It's stupid."

"It's a precaution. We're about to get intimate with Mrs. Hadley's keyboard." When nobody moved, she said, "Just put on your damn gloves."

We did. Emily put her hand on the door.

It was locked.

"Hmm," she said. She glanced at Bebe. "You didn't happen to find a stash of keys somewhere, did you?" Bebe shook her head.

"Ah well," Emily said, pulling her wallet out of her purse and extracting her Starbucks card. "The old-fashioned way, right?" She slid the credit card into the crack in the door, then gave it an extra push when she met the locking mechanism. The door popped open.

"You've got such great life skills, Emily," said Shira.

"Thank you, love."

"Can we turn on the lights?" Bebe asked.

"No," said Emily.

"There's no one here!"

"Not worth it," said Emily. "Let's go." Guided by the beams of Emily's and Bebe's flashlights, we made our way to Mrs. Hadley's desk. Emily sat down in her chair. Bebe, who was behind me, smacked into the giant box next to the desk and swore loudly.

"Would you be quiet?" Emily hissed.

"It's fine," Bebe said, limping around to the other side of the desk. "I didn't really need all ten of those toes anyway."

Emily turned on Mrs. Hadley's computer, and we watched the screen flicker to life. "Mischa, check in with Nate while this starts up, would you?"

"Fine," I said. I texted Nate, *We found a dead body.*

Really?

No. Everything OK there?

Fine, but I am SO BORED.

I put my phone away. "Nate's fine."

By then the computer was on, and Emily was typing a password from a piece of paper Shira had extracted from her pocket. "How do you have Mrs. Hadley's password?"

"I emailed her a keylogger yesterday attached to a Word file," Shira said.

"A keylogger?"

"It's like a virus," she explained as Emily typed. "You put it on someone's system, and it records everything they type and then sends it to you."

"What if they find it?"

"I spoofed the admissions office at George Mason. It'll look like it came from there."

"Should I be scared of you guys?"

"Probably. We're in," Emily said. "Okay." She pulled up Windows Explorer and started scrolling. "This looks promising." She clicked on something called "IGradeBook."

A message popped up on the screen. "Oh, *come on,*" she said.

"What is that?" I said. "They want a second password?"

"They're using two-factor authentication on this," she said.

"Can you—I don't know—override it?"

"Not easily."

"So what does that mean?"

"It means," she said, "that we can't get the transcript files. Not tonight, anyway."

Bebe said, "What do we have access to?"

Emily backed out of the IGradeBook screen and went back to the list of folders.

"Memos. Lots of memos." She clicked some more. "Databases of college addresses. Databases of alumni donors."

"Why would Mrs. Hadley be looking at those?"

"They're shared files," Emily said. "She's probably not." She kept scanning. But then my phone rang in my pocket.

"It's Nate," I said, answering it.

"There's a car coming," he whispered. "It just came through the gate—wait, now it's going toward the building."

"Cops?" I asked.

"Don't think so."

I looked up at the girls. "Someone's coming."

"Wait—here are the letters of recommendation," Emily said, still reading from the list of files.

"We have to leave!"

"Wait," she said again. "Now, where are yours?"

"Emily," Shira said.

"Which side of the building?" I asked Nate as Shira pressed her face against mine to hear both sides of the conversation.

"Front entrance," he said. "I still can't see who, but if they're going in the front door, they're probably heading for the main office."

"Shoot," Shira said. "Hang on, ladies." And then she slipped out the door.

"Where is she going?"

"She's going to make some noise somewhere else in the building. Emily," Bebe said. "We have to go."

"They're listed by student ID number," Emily said.

"I don't know my ID number," I said.

"Well, then, I'm going to have to go through all of them."

"There's no time!"

Just then I heard the front door of the building open and close with a bang. Bebe and I crouched behind the desk. "Emily," Bebe hissed.

"If the numbers were assigned alphabetically, she'd be toward the top of the list."

"Emily," I said.

"That's it!" she whispered. "I'm printing them out." She clicked something and then closed the files.

I heard the sound of shoes in the hallway outside just as the printer started to whir.

The footsteps stopped. Bebe killed her flashlight, and we huddled under the desk, but I realized with a sinking horror that the monitor was still glowing. I lunged toward the outlet and unplugged the computer's power strip right as the door opened.

The three of us were piled on top of each other under the desk; Emily had my letters balled up in her hand, having already grabbed them off the printer. Bebe's knee was mashed into my nose, and my body was sandwiched between Emily's legs, her chin digging into my boob. We held our collective breath.

Then we heard the sound of a car alarm going off.

Whoever was in the room—a man, I realized—swore. And then went back out, shutting the door behind him.

I climbed off Emily. "Let's go," she said. "Let's go now."

We peeked through the doorway, long enough to see the front door fly open as whoever it was went out to attend to his car, and we slipped out the other way, back toward the auditorium.

I called Nate as we ran down the hallway. "Things just got less boring," I said.

"I gathered that."

"Meet us at the auditorium door," I said. "We're almost there."

"I've got Shira," he said. "And—oh *crap*. That's Pelletier."

As the assistant head of the school, Mr. Pelletier was in charge of maintaining order and doling out punishments while Dr. Marlowe shook hands and kissed babies (metaphorically speaking). If you got caught smoking by the dumpster, you saw Mr. Pelletier. If you got caught cheating, you saw Mr. Pelletier. Except nobody really called him Mr. Pelletier except to his face. To each other, we mostly just called him Bad Cop.

"How can you see that far?" I asked.

"Because he's driving this way, and he's the only one on campus who drives a silver Lexus convertible. Crap. Crap. He's doing a circle around the building—don't come out yet."

"We're already at the door!"

"If you come out," Nate said, "he'll see you."

"If we don't come out, he'll see *you*!"

"Oops," he said. "I think he just saw us."

Through the phone I heard Shira saying, "Why are you taking your shirt off?" and then the line died.

"What just happened?" Emily asked.

"It's Pelletier," I said. "And he's seen them."

"Great," Bebe said. "We're all screwed."

A text came through from Shira. Emily flashed it at me. It said, *Come out now, but go toward the guard booth.*

We exchanged glances before carefully opening the door and making our way out. About 150 feet away, Nate and Shira were being pulled out of the backseat of the car. I could see the dim light of the streetlamps reflecting off their bare skin. They were both shirtless, muttering things to Pelletier I couldn't hear while Shira put her shirt back on and Nate made some joke that made her put her head in her hands in a way that was both shameful and rather un-Shira-like. Emily had to grab my arm and pull me away from the scene.

We ran past the guard booth and waited, crouching on the ground on the other side.

"Do you think he'll call the police?" I asked.

"For Nate and Shira? Probably not. They weren't in the building. I don't think they'd bother with the cops for two people making out in their car."

Five minutes later Emily's car rolled by, and we jumped in. Nate was still shirtless.

"Any reason that's still off?" I asked.

"I was in the moment," he said. Shira, who was in the front seat, laughed. "You were right," she said, nudging Emily's knee with her fist. "He does know how to kiss."

Nate, throwing me a nervous look, said, "Please. Your saliva's all over the car. Were you *trying* to eat my face?"

I chewed on my lip.

"What did he say to you?" Emily asked.

"Threw us off campus. Gave us a warning. Lectured us about condoms."

Emily turned on the dome light and uncrumpled the papers in her hands.

"Did you get them?" I asked.

"Most of them," she said. "Some of it got cut off when you unplugged everything." She handed the pages to me.

I read out loud:

"'To Whom It May Concern: It is only with grave reservations that I write this letter. On the one hand, Mischa is a very bright student, as her test scores attest. She has strong natural abilities in reading and writing, which can be seen when she applies herself.'" I swallowed. "'However . . .'"

"However?"

"'However, she has demonstrated an alarming tendency toward academic dishonesty. Many of her papers are liberally cribbed from Internet sources, and, after some interrogating, she admitted that her term paper had been purchased online—' What the *hell*?"

Everyone in the car was silent while I finished reading the rest of the letter inside my head. "It doesn't get better," I said.

"Wow," Nate said. "Ms. Augerman loved you."

"Yeah," I said. "She did."

"What about the other one?" Emily said. "There were two."

I glanced at the letter from Mr. Jensen, which I only had half of because the printer had been cut off in the middle. "More of the same," I said. "I cheat on my papers and knock over liquor stores in my spare time."

"Well," Emily said. "I guess we know why you didn't get into Revere."

"What do you think happened to the real letters?" Nate asked. "Are they still in there somewhere?"

"I didn't see anything else," Emily said. "But then I didn't really have a ton of time to poke around. However," she went on, "we could replace these with our own. Just write some ourselves."

"Doesn't help a whole lot without also fixing the transcript," I said.

"That," she said, "is going to be a bigger challenge."

Nate dropped me off in front of my house an hour later. His shirt was back on, alas. I said, "So. You and Shira."

"Are you criticizing me for making out with Shira Gastman for fifteen seconds? I think prison would have been worse."

"Yeah. Of course it would."

He grinned at me in the dark. "You aren't jealous, are you?"

"No," I said. "Shira's not my type."

"Mischa," he said.

"Thanks for the ride," I said.

"Mischa."

"I have to go to bed." I held up the printouts of my letters. I wasn't sure what to do with them, because I didn't especially want my mother to find them. "Or I have to go rob a 7-Eleven. I haven't decided."

I hid the letters under my mattress.

CHAPTER ELEVEN

WHEN I WAS A LITTLE KID, MY MOTHER AND I HAD A SUNDAY-morning routine. First we would make a real breakfast—eggs or waffles or blintzes or something like that—then we would clean the house for an hour, and then, when we were done, we'd walk three blocks to the local park, which had a pond behind it, and feed peas to the ducks.

We'd have the longest conversations. I'd tell her about my friends. She'd tell me about stuff at work. And in between, we'd just sit and stare at the pond. I don't know why staring at water is so relaxing, but I guess it is for everyone, or it wouldn't be so expensive to live by the beach or a lake or whatever. I remember one time we found a robin's nest in the tree next to the pond, and there were eggs in it—tiny and blue and perfect. It amazed me that something so complicated as a bird could come out of something barely bigger than a jelly bean.

One of the things we used to talk about was my grandmother.

She died when I was pretty young; apparently, she had that bad gene that makes you get ovarian cancer. Mom and Grandma had kind of a weird relationship, which I didn't witness a lot of, but I got the sense that they weren't exactly spending much time together at the duck pond.

Grandma had been a refugee, and she and her own mother had arrived in Chicago with nothing but the goodwill of Third Cousin Moishe—who I'm named for—who put them up in his tiny apartment. Two weeks after they arrived, the cousin enrolled her in kindergarten, where on the first day the boys in her class called my tiny, malnourished grandmother a communist and stole her milk money.

They hadn't realized, of course, that to a small child used to fearing the Soviet secret police, a few brats with fists were not particularly scary.

"I showed them who's a communist," she later told me. "The next day, I made a knife out of the handle of a broken teacup and took it to school in my pocket." She always cackled when she told that story. "Boy, those little turds ran fast!"

When she wasn't attempting to shiv her classmates on the playground, Grandma learned English, grew up, worked at a shoe store to put herself through college, and had my mother, telling her bedtime stories about princesses and clever third sons, but also about Vilnius and the Soviet deportations, because she didn't want my mother to forget the extent of the opportunities she'd been given. She'd wanted my mother to be a doctor but had been reasonably content with her choice to go to law school, until Mom got pregnant in her last year by a man she'd met in a bar on three-dollar-mojito night.

I got up the nerve to ask my mother about that down at the duck pond when I was about twelve, because we'd just learned about abortion at school, and before that I hadn't realized that my mom actually had a choice in whether to have me or not.

"What did Grandma say?" I asked, once I'd gotten up the guts. I'm still not exactly sure why I wanted to know so badly—I just did. I guess it was some kind of perverse curiosity.

Mom threw some peas to the ducks. She was frowning and not looking at me, like this was not a conversation she really wanted to have. "Oh, well. You know."

"That's what she said?"

"Why are you asking me this?"

"I don't know." I pulled a handful of grass out of the ground and threw it a few feet. "I was just wondering."

She exhaled. "Well, I told her I wasn't leaving school, and I was still going to graduate and get a job, and everything would be fine. And everything was fine." She poked me in the shoulder. "See? I'm always right."

She still hadn't told me what Grandma said. "But . . . ," I said. "But . . ."

"Honey," she said. "You know, Grandma got out of Vilnius, but a lot of other people didn't."

Of course I knew this already; there's a reason my mother has no cousins or aunts or uncles. If the Nazis hadn't gotten you before 1945, there was a good chance the Soviets either killed you or deported you (which usually amounted to the same thing). "But she didn't feel guilty about that, did she? None of that was her fault."

"Well, I don't think she felt guilty, exactly. It was more that she felt like since she'd made it, she needed to do something with the life she'd been given."

"Like she wanted to show she survived for a reason?"

"No. She knew it was just luck. But she felt like she owed it to everyone else to do all the things they couldn't. She wanted to do what they couldn't, and then she wanted me to do what *she* couldn't. She always used to say, 'Opportunity is responsibility!'" My mom laughed, but only a little bit.

I hadn't asked any more after that, because I knew beating around the bush when I heard it. And I also knew whatever disappointment Grandma had felt in finding out about my existence, she'd eventually gotten over it. But I felt kind of weird, too. Like I also owed something to all those people who hadn't made it. I had opportunities that they didn't.

At some point we started skipping our Sunday breakfasts. I was too tired to get up for them, and no one really wanted to clean the house first thing in the morning, either, and then I had too much homework and I was too old for the park anyway. So four times a month became two, and then, sometime in middle school, they dropped out altogether. It's not like I miss them, exactly. It was a little-kid thing, getting up early to eat waffles and feed ducks. I honestly can't remember the last time I did either.

I wonder what Grandma would say, if she'd lived long enough to know I wasn't going to college.

The next day, I remembered as I was driving to school with my mother, it was teacher appreciation day, which meant that the SGA bought buckets of flowers at the local Safeway and

handed them out to the staff. Caroline and Mark had volunteered to pick up the flowers, and then the rest of the SGA was
supposed to deliver them during our respective lunch periods,
along with five-dollar Starbucks cards. The juniors had the brilliant idea of making us wear silly hats while we did this; they'd
also wanted us to sing, but, thankfully, Jim had killed that idea.

Caroline pulled up to Blanchard's front entrance in her
little blue Toyota at lunchtime, the backseat filled with buckets
of roses, and popped her trunk open. The juniors, who were
bizarrely energetic that morning, said, "Woo!" and started
unloading the buckets and sticking the roses into bud vases,
which were recycled from the year before. Mark got out of the
passenger seat and leaned against the car.

"Are you okay?" I asked, because he was kind of listing to
one side.

"He's been like this all morning," Caroline said. "He fell
asleep when I was putting the buckets in the car."

"I said I was sorry," he told Caroline.

"You drooled on my upholstery!"

To me, he said, "I was up until four doing a linear algebra
packet."

"Ugh," I said.

"Just buck up or something, okay? This is important.
OKAY," said Caroline, addressing the group. "We've divided
the teachers by class. Come get your lists and let's get it done."

She passed out lists to everyone, and we picked up our
shoe boxes full of bud vases from the juniors. "I thought we
could double up," she told me. "That way we can talk while we
do it. I haven't seen you in forever."

"Sounds good," I said, even though it kind of didn't. I
wished I was home in my bed. Or anywhere but Blanchard,

really. I pulled on my sparkly purple top hat and went off with Caroline to make my rounds.

"So," she said. "I was going to go shopping for shoes to go with my formal dress this weekend, if you want to come. We could look for dresses for you at the same time, if you want."

"Oh," I said, because some part of my brain was still under my mattress with those horrible letters. "Let me check my schedule, okay?"

"I was thinking maybe Saturday," she said. "So did you decide yet?"

"Decide?"

"Which school you're going to. I know you didn't want to talk about it before."

"Um, no. Still thinking. And I, uh, haven't heard from everyone yet."

She turned to look at me. "Seriously?"

"Yeah, you know." I was blessedly saved because we were outside Ms. Kim's room, and she was on our list.

Ms. Kim teaches US history, and the class was full of juniors getting ready for the AP. "Blanchard loves its teachers!" we said in unison, and then plunked her flower down on the desk with her card.

"Thank you," she said. "Now shoo! They're taking a quiz."

"Oh," Caroline said. "Sorry."

We quickly backed out of the room. "Maybe we should try a different approach?" she said. "We sound like cheerleaders on Valium."

"Maybe just one of us should say it?" I asked.

"Yeah, I think that would be better. So I just can't decide what to do," she said. "It's such a big decision. What if I'm wrong?"

I pulled out the next flower in anticipation of Ms. Kelley's room. "What are you talking about?"

"Hello? Dartmouth or Columbia. I just don't know what to do, and it's *killing* me."

I blinked a few times, because I didn't really know what to say. Legitimately, her biggest problem was choosing between Dartmouth and Columbia.

"I mean, Dartmouth was my first choice. Mindy Kaling went there. Did you know that?"

"Yeah, I heard that somewhere."

"I love her."

"She's funny," I agreed.

I opened the door to Ms. Kelley's room. "Blanchard loves its teachers," I said, and then sort of flung the flower onto the desk and walked back out.

"But," she continued. "If I go to Columbia, I get to be in New York, and that's worth something, too. There are a lot of opportunities in the city. That's huge. Right?"

"There's a lot of stuff in New York."

"Yeah! There's so many jobs, and internships, plus all the fun stuff to do like restaurants and pubs and those cool bodegas with the cats—"

"Wait. What?"

"The little grocery stores. They're called bodegas. And they all have cats."

"Why?"

"To keep the rats out, I guess. And they have their own social media and everything."

"The cats do?"

"So there's all that, and Dartmouth's cool, but it's kind of in . . ."

"New Hampshire."

"Right."

"Which probably also has cats."

"Yeah, I'm sure they do, but—"

I opened the door to Mr. Robles's room. "Blanchard looooves its teachers," I said, and gave him his flower. He was eating a sandwich at his desk. "Uh, thanks," he said.

"Yeah, fine," I said.

"So what would you do?" Caroline asked as we walked out of the room.

Jeez, what a question.

"Mischa?"

"What?"

"What would you do? It's like, this is my whole life resting on this decision. I can't even sleep at night. I just lie there and lie there and—"

I walked into Ms. Bromley's room. "BLANCHARD LOVES ITS TEACHERS," I said, and then slammed the flower down on her desk.

"Are you hungry?" Caroline asked out in the hallway. "You sound hungry."

"I'm fine. Was that the last one?"

"There's just Ms. Ramirez, but she's my next class anyway."

"Okay," I said.

"Okay," she said. "Look, call me about Saturday, okay? I *need* to hear your thoughts on DOC."

"DOC?"

"Dartmouth or Columbia." She frowned. "I guess I could have called it COD, but I don't think that sounds right."

"I have a quiz next period," I said. "I should proba-bly study."

"Yeah, okay," she said. "So I'll see you on Saturday, and we'll talk then."

I hadn't actually agreed to Saturday, and I definitely did not want to talk about DOC (or COD), but I said, "Sure."

"Do some research!" she called to me as she walked down to Ms. Ramirez's room.

I went back toward the cafeteria to get a cookie before next period and ran into Jim in the hallway. "Success?" he asked.

"Yeah," I said. "I'm just hungry. I wanted a cookie."

"A cookie sounds excellent," he said. "Maybe even two cookies."

Then we stopped because there was singing. In the theater room some of the juniors were singing the Blanchard alma mater to Ms. Drury and her class of sophomore drama students. At the end they did a kick line. "Woo!" they shouted.

"Were we ever that young?" Jim asked.

"No," I said. "We weren't."

CHAPTER TWELVE

I GOT TO SCHOOL IN TIME FOR BREAKFAST A FEW DAYS LATER, which meant hot chocolate and cold cereal. I was almost never there that early, but it was a nice perk for the kids who live closer, because they could come in before school for study groups and whatnot on test days. A crew of sophomores was at the table under the window, working on a problem set for precalc, and a pair of freshmen were doing a Latin translation at the table behind me.

I was there early because I'd gotten a note the night before from Emily, telling me it was time to start talking about our next move.

Jim was sitting at a table by himself, reading, and I went and sat next to him, glancing down at the magazine he had propped under his tray—the *Lancet*, it looked like, or some other medical journal. "What are you reading about?"

"The gut biome," he said, showing me the article before dropping it back on the table. He marked the end of the section he'd read by scoring the end of the paragraph with his thumbnail, leaving a little dent in the paper.

"The . . ."

"It's the range of bacteria that live in your digestive tract," he explained.

"There's an appetite killer."

"Nah." He showed me a table with figures that meant little to me. "See, they did these studies on mice that showed that what was living in their guts changed their brains somehow. They could make them more or less anxious depending on what was living down there."

"Really?"

"Yeah. So, like, eating yogurt can change your behavior."

"Yogurt."

"Well, technically it's the bacteria in the yogurt. There's a theory that someday they'll have bacteria that you can take instead of antidepressants. And others you can take instead of antibiotics and stuff. Like, you'll have good bacteria that eat your strep or whatever."

"Or your mono."

"Or your mono. Did you know," he went on, "that most of the cells in your body are not you? You're, like, 45% you and 55% bugs that live on you. In you."

"Holy . . . *seriously?*"

"Seriously."

"I'm—I'm not sure how I feel about that." I took a bite of my cereal. "Like I need a shower, maybe."

"Well, if you didn't have all those bugs, you'd die."

"Yeah, I get that, but still." I shuddered. "I'm squicked."

I took a sip of my watery hot chocolate and got a mouthful of undissolved chocolate powder, which made me gag.

"So dramatic," he said, thumping me on the back.

I was going to explain to him that I'd swallowed a bunch of Swiss Miss, but then I saw that Shira had come in. She was sitting at a table by the door, her eyes unfocused, staring at a spot on the wall that meant nothing to anybody. "Hey," I said. "I'm going to go, but I'll see you later, right?"

"You're going to sit with Shira Gastman?" he asked, which was fair, because it was kind of an odd thing for me to do.

"Yeah," I said. "We have . . . stuff."

"Should I be worried about you? Like, we're not going to find you high in the bathroom later, right?"

"I'll see you in physics," I said.

I headed over to the table where Shira was sitting.

"Hey," I said.

I watched the glassiness drain from her eyes. It was kind of a terrifying thing to see.

"Why do you do that?" I asked. "It's . . . I mean honestly, it's kind of creepy."

Shira's eyes crinkled at the corners. "There's an art to manipulating people's perceptions of you, so that you can get them off your back," Shira said. "It's like those butterflies. What are they called? Viceroys. They look like monarchs, which are poisonous, so that no one will eat them. But they aren't poisonous at all. It's just a really clever piece of genetic engineering."

"Isn't it boring, though? Staring out the window all day?"

"There are worse things," she said, "than being bored." She reached into her backpack and pulled out a stack of paper several inches thick.

"What is this?" I asked.

Emily had just wandered in, looking half-asleep, her braid of thick hair tied up in a knot at the back of her head. She plunked a Starbucks cup with two teabags floating in it down next to me and then sank into her chair. "Bebe's not coming," she said.

"Sick?" Shira asked.

"Unconscious," she replied. "She was up until four writing a government paper." She gestured at the pile of paper Shira had dumped in front of us. "Tell Mischa what you made, you industrious little creature."

Shira gave her a tight little smile. "This," she said, "is a spreadsheet I compiled from online. A list of the colleges people from Blanchard got into."

"You checked everyone's Twitter and Instagram?"

"And Tumblr and Facebook," she said. She pointed toward a pink line of highlighter. "I marked everyone who got into one of the schools you applied to. Pink for Harvard. Yellow for Princeton. Blue for Williams, et cetera."

"What about Revere?" I said, because it didn't seem to have a corresponding color in the chart she'd made on the first page.

She laughed drily. "Nobody hacked you to get a spot at Revere, honey."

I looked down at the list. There was a lot of highlighter there. "According to this, we can reasonably suspect everyone."

"Actually," she said, "we can't. Blanchard's system uses two-factor authentication, right? So it wasn't enough to have a motive. Whoever did this also had to have access."

I frowned. "What does access look like?"

"A faculty cell phone, most likely. Unless it was a faculty member using his own cell phone."

"You're still thinking of Mr. Bender."

"Look at the list," Emily said. "Willa applied to four of the same schools as you. Beth applied to three. And here's what we know about Mr. Bender: One, he's married. Two, he was having an affair with Mrs. White. Three, he was caught in a compromising situation with two different students. It's a solid lead. We already know he's a slime."

This all seemed to be true. Particularly the slime part.

"What we need to do," Emily went on, "is determine if Beth and Willa had grades changed. Unfortunately, we have to do that without the use of the transcript files."

"Because you still can't get into those," Shira added.

"Shut up," Emily replied. "But I do have a plan." She leaned forward so that her elbows were on her knees and grinned. "The Teacher of the Year nominations are due in two weeks."

I coughed. Every year Blanchard put up a candidate for the Independent School Teacher of the Year award; generally, this was the kind of award that went to someone who was helping underprivileged youth get into the Ivies or taking classes of kids to build schools in Central America. It did not go to chemistry teachers whose two most notable achievements were a) flirting with students and b) having well-defined deltoids. "The ISTY? We're nominating *Bender*?"

"We're going to say we are. And we're going to interview some of his best students for quotes. Starting with Beth Reinhardt."

"Only I can't do that," I said. "Beth knows I saw her with Mr. Bender."

"It can't be you," Shira agreed. "And it needs to be someone she'll spill to. Someone she likes. Someone hot. Someone who kisses like the devil and makes you want to smack your mama."

"Shira," Emily said. "Stop trolling Mischa."

"Fine," she said. "So. Nate?"

CHAPTER THIRTEEN

AFTER THE END OF SEVENTH PERIOD, THE OPHELIAS AND I SAT huddled in the empty art room, hunched over Emily's phone, which was set to speaker.

"I can't believe I'm the honey trap," Nate lamented through the phone. "Look what you've reduced me to."

"You're not the honey trap," Bebe said. "A honey trap is someone who tricks their mark into cheating. You're just asking some questions."

"This shouldn't be too hard," Shira said. "Beth's as dumb as a rock."

"Then why did you tell me to undo the top two buttons of my shirt?"

"We need to work all our advantages," Bebe said. "Plus your hair's on point today, so that's good."

"My hair?"

"You're supposed to be finding Beth," Emily reminded him.

"Doesn't my hair always look like this?"

"Nate," I said. "Focus."

"Fine," he said. "I'm putting my phone in my shirt pocket. You might want to mute it on your end so she can't hear you discussing my hair."

Emily clicked the mute button on the phone. I said, "Seriously, do you think he's up for this? You know Beth wants in his pants big-time."

"He's been through worse," Emily said. "We may never deflate his ego, though."

"Are you recording?" Shira asked. Emily nodded.

"Is that, you know, legal?" I whispered.

"Virginia's a one-party recording state," she said. "As long as Nate knows, it's totally legal."

"Wow," I said. "So I could record my conversations with anyone?"

"Legally, yes you could."

"Huh," I said.

By now Nate had found Beth. "Hey, Beth," he said. "Do you have a minute?"

"For you? Absolutely," she said.

There was some chitchat while Nate explained about the ISTY award and led her into some more private location that he didn't identify over the phone. When there was a squeak, Bebe said, "They're in the dining hall. That's the noise the chairs make on the floor."

"So," Nate said. "The committee and I wanted to talk to a few of Mr. Bender's best students before we submit the packet. Get a better idea what he's like. Maybe some quotations we can use?"

"Hmm," she said. "Is that really all you wanted to talk about?"

There was a rustling noise. Papers, I thought. Maybe Nate was taking notes. "Weeeell," he said, drawing the word out over three beats. "For the most part," he said.

"Is he flirting?" I asked. "Why is he flirting?"

"Because that's why we sent him. Shush!"

"For the most part?" Beth said. "Huh."

Pause. Pause. Pause. More shuffling papers.

"He's really dragging this out," Emily said.

"I think he's nervous," I said.

"Is it the boobs?" Shira asked. "'Cause she is kind of stacked."

"I bet it's the boobs," Bebe agreed. "I bet he's staring at them right now."

"Would you stop?" I said.

Beth said, "So what are you doing this weekend?"

"Oh," he said. "Finishing up this nomination packet. After that, who knows?"

"Who knows," Beth repeated. "Who indeed."

"Ew. What does that even mean?" I asked.

"Mischa," Emily said. "Shut up."

"So," he prodded. "Mr. Bender. Thoughts?"

"He's okay," she said. Her tone was off. I wished we could have seen her face.

"Okay? Someone said you did really well in his class."

"Really. Who told you that?"

"Um," Nate said. I could imagine the wheels turning inside his brain. *Don't say me,* I thought. *Don't say me.*

"Don't say it," Shira murmured. "Don't say Willa Jenkins."

"I think it was Willa."

Emily said, "Ugh."

"Willa said that?"

"It might have been someone else," he said hastily.

"He is *really* bad at this," Bebe said incredulously.

"What else did Willa say?"

"Uh, just that she had a really good time in his class. She learned a lot about, uh, polyatomic ions. And, uh, bonds. Bonds are so, you know. Bondy. Don't you think? I always thought covalent bonds were a little dirty. Sharing ions and all that."

"We need to get him out of there," Emily said. "He's a complete train wreck."

"Do you want to go someplace?" Beth asked.

"What?"

"Someplace more private." She dropped her voice. "We can talk about bonds all you want."

"This is private," he said. "Here's private. Here's good."

"You're such a freak!"

"What? Wait. No. That's not what I meant."

"It's not?"

"I think I may have given you the wrong idea."

"WHO WANTS TO GO GET NATE?" Shira shouted, laughing.

"It's not that I don't like you. It's just that I. Uh."

"You, uh, what?"

"I'm celibate. Right now. I gave up, you know. Sex. Not sex! I mean, yes, sex, but also dating. Uh. For Lent."

"Wait, aren't you Jewish?"

"Hey," he said in a strangled voice, "look at you! All knowing my religious background. Whoever said you were du— hey! There's Colin! Did you know he has a tattoo now?"

"Who said I was what?" Beth said irritably.

"Nothing! Ha! Ha! Uh. So. Mr. Bender? He's great, right?"

"Bebe," Emily said. "Go get Nate."

Bebe was halfway to the door when Beth said, "You know what? I changed my mind. I don't think I have a minute to talk about this."

"But—"

"I gotta go." There was the sound of her getting up from her chair, and then she added, "Your shirt's unbuttoned, by the way."

"Well," I said after we'd hung up the phone. "I'm not sure what that told us, except that Nate has no future in espionage."

"It told us that whatever was going on, Beth and Willa both knew about each other," Emily said, glancing at Shira. "Do we know where they're going to school yet?"

"Beth's going to Brown. I just found it on Instagram this morning."

"Brown!" Bebe exclaimed. "How the heck did she get into Brown?"

"What about Willa?" Emily asked.

"Georgetown."

Emily glanced over to me. "That sound right to you?"

"I guess it's possible. But Beth at Brown? No. No way."

A minute later Nate burst into the room. "Don't ever make me do that again."

We all stared at him without speaking.

"How could we?" Emily asked. "You gave up having a brain. You know. For Lent."

"Right," he said. "Never mind."

"We're not going to get anything out of them without

subterfuge," Emily said. "And we need proof before we can do anything."

"Well, how would we get proof?"

"Emails," Shira said. "If there's anything between Bender and Beth or Willa, that'd be all the proof we need."

"And how are we going to get a look at their emails?" I asked.

"Leave that," Emily said, "to me."

CHAPTER FOURTEEN

My mother came home the next day with a sticker on the bumper of her car that read MY DAUGHTER AND MY MONEY GO TO PAUL REVERE. And underneath was the school motto: UNA SI PER TERRAM, SI PER MARE DUAE.

"Look!" she said, feigning pride. "I ordered it in the mail, and it came today."

"Hey," I said weakly, "you got a bumper sticker."

"They also had a weather vane. I was going to put it in the yard, but I don't think the HOA would let me."

"A weather vane?"

"Sure. It's a replica of the one on their library. Paul Revere on his horse. I thought, since I can't put it in the yard, I might hang it on the wall."

"You're going to hang a weather vane on the wall?"

"As an objet d'art," she explained.

"Mom," I said. "I think that's overkill."

I knew all this was born of the fact that my mother didn't want me to feel bad. Her intentions were kind, at least. And I felt like a giant pile of manure because I was not, and never would be, going to Paul Revere. If the Ophelias and I managed to fix things, I'd be going someplace better. If we didn't, I wouldn't be going anyplace at all.

I couldn't tell her any of this, though. So I said, "I think we should go on vacation."

"What?"

"Vacation. This summer. Like, you know how you're always saying you want to go to California? See the Getty and the Santa Monica Pier? Let's just go."

"I don't think we really can," she said. "With those tuition payments coming."

"We haven't been anywhere in four years," I said.

"I know," she said, and what she telegraphed with her eyes was *because of you.* "But until we find out about your financial aid package, I'm not sure we should make any firm plans. Do you know when they're likely to send that out?"

My eyes cut away. "No," I said. "I'll have to check."

"Well, go ahead and check," she said. "And let me know."

"Sure. I'll let you know."

The following day I was at my locker when Bebe breezed by. Her hair was in this sort of puff-braid queue (it went braid section, puff section, braid section, puff section) that swung when she walked. She grinned at me and stopped, her heels coming to a clicking halt. "We have emails," she said.

"Emails?"

"Keep up, Mischa. The Bender emails. We're meeting at Nate's after school."

"Why Nate's?"

"Emily's parents are getting ready for a party, and he lives closer than the rest of us."

"All right," I said. "So what was in the emails?"

"We'll talk about it then."

"Can't you just tell me now?"

"No." She pulled her wallet out of her backpack, opened it, and handed me a business card not unlike the one Emily had given me. "In case you need me," she said. "That's my private email."

I looked down at Bebe's card, which listed as her email address OpheliaTwo@ophelia.com. The flower in the corner was different from Emily's; Emily's was tiny and blue, Bebe's yellow with a purple center.

"Bebe," I asked. "Where are you going next year?"

"What? You mean college?"

"Yeah. I was just wondering. You guys never talk about it. Not with me, anyway."

"Oh. I haven't actually decided yet. I'm taking a gap year first, though."

"A gap year," I said. "Your parents don't mind?"

"No," she said. "I want to spend some time with my grandparents in Accra, and my aunt says I can work for her for part of the year. Plus I want to travel some."

That sounded sort of like standing at the edge of a huge pit and not knowing what was at the bottom. "But," I said. "How will you even know what to do?"

"What do you mean?"

"I don't know. It just sounds kind of scary."

"It's not scary. If I go to college, I'm not really sure what I want to study yet."

"You don't want to do computer science?"

"Maybe, I guess, but it's not the only thing I'm interested in. I might do a business IT track, or maybe international relations. I just don't know."

"I don't know, either," I said. "I kind of thought I'd figure it out when I got there."

"That works, too," she said. "I just don't want to do it that way." The bell rang, and she said, "I've gotta go. I'll see you later, okay?"

"Yeah," I said. "Bye." I was looking down at her Ophelia-Two card again, at the little flower in the corner. It was a pansy, I realized. Like from the speech Ophelia gives in *Hamlet* about the flowers. Pansies are for thoughts.

Mr. Pelletier was coming down the hall toward me. "You have about thirty seconds to get to class." He clapped his hands at me like I was a dog and said, "Chop, chop!"

"I'm going," I said, still staring at the card. "Sorry. I was just thinking."

Nate and I got to his house ten minutes after seventh period. "Why are we doing this at my house, again?" he asked as he dropped his backpack by the front door. Rachel, who was already home, had pounced on him the second we'd walked in and kept trying to take his wallet out of his back pocket while he spun in a circle and tried to avoid her grabby little hands.

"Would you *quit*?" he said, finally getting fed up and batting her away.

"I just need twenty bucks," she whined.

"I don't have twenty bucks."

"Liar. You got all that money from Grandma."

"Go mow a lawn," he said. I followed him into his room, and he shut the door in Rachel's face.

"I'm telling," she said through the door.

"Good for you!" He sighed. "Did we really have to meet *here*?"

"We're doing it here because you live closest," I said. "At least that's what Bebe said."

He twisted his mouth sideways.

"Why are you being weird? Is this because of Emily? Because you guys used to . . . ," I hedged, then said, "go out?" Which is not actually how I had been intending to finish the sentence.

"It's not that," he said.

"Is it 'cause you made out with Shira?"

"I didn't make out with Shira. I pretended to make out with Shira."

"Right. I forgot. You were *pretending* to know how to kiss." He could barely contain his smile. "Are you jealous?"

"No! Why would I be?"

"I don't know. Maybe you want to make out with Shira?"

"I already told you. I don't have a thing for Shira."

"I wouldn't blame you," he said. "She has that dimple."

"What dimple?" I said.

"In her left cheek. When she laughs."

"I hadn't noticed her dimple."

"Well, in that case, maybe—" he started, but then there was a banging at the front door, which turned out to be Emily and Bebe, so I never found out what he'd been planning to say.

Rachel, who had changed into her softball uniform, got to the door before we did. "Oh," she said to Emily. "It's *you*."

Emily said, a little darkly, "Hello, *Rachel*."

To Bebe, Rachel said, "You're, like, really tall."

"Rachel," said Nate. "Go somewhere else."

"What? It's good to be tall. I wish I was taller." Turning back to Bebe, she went on, "There's this surgery where they break your legs and stretch them out so you grow more, but my mom totally said no."

"They don't do that to people who are five-four!" Nate said.

"They do if you pay them enough!"

"I'll break your legs," said Emily, which was enough to convince Rachel to flounce back to her room. "I hope you have food. Does your mother still keep those macaroons around?"

"No," he said.

"Bebe's hungry," she said.

"I'm fine," Bebe said.

"No, you're not."

"It's okay," Nate said. "We'll get something. For Bebe."

Nate found a plate of leftover hors d'oeuvres from a dinner party his parents had thrown a few nights before and grabbed it—little tart shells with unidentifiable fillings, and some mushroom caps stuffed with either old French cheese or, possibly, old French toothpaste. He brought the plate into his bedroom, where Emily was already firing up her laptop on his desk, having swept Nate's books and laptop into a pile on the floor.

"Cute Nate," Emily said. "I'm thinking you may not want to be in the room for this."

"You're showing up at my house and then kicking me out?" he said incredulously.

"Cute Nate stays," I insisted. "If it wasn't for him, we'd all have gotten arrested the other night."

"Mischa," Emily said. "The less he knows, the better for him. What we're doing today isn't exactly legal. If he's here, he loses his deniability."

I glanced over my shoulder at Nate. "Maybe you should go," I said.

"No. I'll stay." He sat down on the edge of the bed. "Mischa'll just tell me everything later anyway. This way, maybe I can talk you out of doing something really stupid."

"Not likely," Bebe said.

Shira came stomping down the hall and flung the door open. She was wearing a T-shirt that said PROPERTY OF MORLOCK ATHLETIC DEPARTMENT (EST. 802701). "Your sister just insulted my haircut," she told Nate.

"Yeah," he said. "Sorry about that."

Seeing the lack of seating, she went over to Bebe, bumping her hip out of the way so they could share Nate's recliner. Next to her, on the windowsill, was Memento Maury, who had lost the beret (but kept the eyelashes) and was wearing a pair of Groucho Marx glasses, which were half falling off because Maury, being a skull, had no ears. She picked him up and turned him around to face her, and Emily grabbed him out of her hands.

"Alas, poor Yorick!" she cried. Then, frowning: "What have they done to you?"

"That's Maury," I said.

She scowled at the skull, then pulled his glasses down slightly as if she might make eye contact. "Oh," she said. "Very clever." Handing Maury back to Shira, she said, "So I hear you have emails."

Shira handed them over, and as Emily scanned them, she said, "I have several, actually. I couldn't get into Bender's, so all the ones I have are from Beth. It looks like whatever was going on, they usually discussed it in person. The emails are pretty vague."

Emily reached for a mushroom cap off the tray, which Nate had set down on the end of the bed, and ate it with a frown. "These are terrible," Emily muttered.

Shira held up Maury and said, in a very high-pitched New York accent, "And such small portions!"

Nate and I groaned, and she said, "What? He's a man of infinite jest!"

Bebe snorted. Emily rolled her eyes. Shira showed off the dimple in her left cheek.

"What can you pick out?" I asked Emily, trying to ignore Shira and Maury.

"He was giving them something. But I can't tell if it was a better grade or what."

Shira pulled one of the emails out of the stack—it was marked with yellow highlighter—and handed it to me. "Read the marked section, if you would."

I scanned it. The pertinent section said, *Your class performance needs to be better if you want to avoid suspicion. Meet me at the Starbucks on Ridgemont at eleven tomorrow. Do NOT mention to anyone. That you brought Willa in is bad enough.*

The reply from Beth said, *Are you bringing them with you?*
Answer: *Yes.*

Nate, who was reading over my shoulder, said, "That's weird."

"Weird, how?"

"Well, if he was doing it with Beth and Willa, he's being

kind of cold about it. He doesn't sound very happy for a man who's sleeping with four people at the same time."

"Four?" I asked.

"Including his wife," he said. "And Mrs. White."

"Maybe he got tired," Shira said. "He's not exactly a spring chicken."

"I think it's weird that Beth and Willa even knew about each other," Bebe said. "And what was that part about Beth bringing Willa in on it? That's just nasty."

Emily tapped her pen against her lip. "Have we considered that we might be wrong about this? Maybe he wasn't fooling around with Beth and Willa."

"Well, he was doing *something* with them."

"What are you thinking?" Bebe asked.

"I'm not sure," Emily said. "But I think Nate's right. I don't think he was sleeping with them. Did you check the messages between Beth and Willa?"

"I tried. There aren't any."

"They probably just text each other," I said.

"That's what I figured," she said. "Only texts are a lot harder to get into, even if you weren't looking for something that's a year old, which we are."

I had a thought. "You said you spoofed an email to Mrs. Hadley and made it look like it came from the admissions office at GMU."

"Yes," Emily said. "I did do that."

"Could you spoof Willa? Send an email to Beth, pretending to be her? Ask some questions that way?"

Emily smiled slowly. "What would you ask?"

As it turned out, spoofing someone's email is not all that hard. All you have to do is create a new email address that looks like the old email address, and then make it so that it has the name you want in the "from" field. Willa's real email is WJENX@gmail.com. Our spoofed email came from WJENX@mail.com. When it popped up on Beth's phone, it would look like it came from Willa, provided she didn't bother to double-check the email address. And since Willa and Beth never emailed each other, she might not notice the difference even if she did.

I made a mental note never to discuss anything really private except in person.

"Okay," Emily said. "What shall I ask Miss Reinhardt?"

"Not you," I said. "She'll know you aren't Willa."

"I wasn't planning on doing a video chat," she said.

"You use too many ten-cent words," I said.

"You don't exactly sound like a third-grader, either."

"I can sound more like Willa than you can."

"Fine," she said. "By all means, you do it."

I sat down and stretched my fingers over the keys. Willa. Willa played lacrosse. Willa liked those sugary coffee drinks with flavored syrup and sprinkles. Willa wore glitter eye shadow at eight in the morning and boots with sundresses. I tried to channel my inner pumpkin spice latte.

Hey, I wrote.

"Add an emoji," Bebe said, poking me in the arm. "She'd totally open with an emoji."

Hey 🐱! What's up?

Two minutes later: *Why are you emailing me?*

I wrote back: *My phone's out of power. I've just been thinking about some stuff. Did you talk to Nate?*

About Bender? Yeah 😒. He was practically drooling all over me, but he wouldn't seal the deal. I think he might be 100% gay.

Over my shoulder I heard Nate snort. I typed back, *His hair tho* 🖤 🖤 🖤

I know, right? I just want to bite his face.

"Ugh," said Nate.

"Bet you're sorry you checked out her boobs now," Bebe said.

"How could you—oh never mind."

But, I wrote, *do you think we handled the situation with Bender the right way? I guess I've been thinking about it again.*

Beth: *You're not feeling guilty now.*

Me: *Maybe.*

Beth: *Why?*

I turned to Nate. "What do I say now?"

Nate: "I have no idea. Say something or she's going to get suspicious."

Me: "What? What?"

Beth: *So did you see what Bebe Tandoh was wearing today?*

Bebe: "Excuse me?"

Nate: "Back on track. Get her back on track."

Me: *I'm just worried. Do you think we'll get caught?*

Beth: *By WHO? The only one who knows is Bender, unless he told Mrs. White, and she's sure not telling anyone.*

"Mrs. White," I said. "They knew about that. They knew they were having an affair."

Nate said, "Whoa. Whoa. Wait. Beth and Willa weren't sleeping with him." He ran his finger under the words "she's sure not telling anyone." "They were *blackmailing* him."

"You're just guessing," Emily said.

"Yeah, but that's how it reads. They got dirt on him, and they were using it. That explains why he was so nasty with Beth. Because she was threatening him."

Beth: *Are you still there?*

Me: *Yeah. Sorry. Just thinking. Do you think it was worth it?*

Beth: *Well, obviously it wasn't.*

Me: *Why not?*

Beth: *Are you losing it? You need to forget about this.*

"End it," Emily said. "You aren't getting anything else."

Me: *You know, I think you're right. I think we should just pretend this conversation never happened.*

Beth: 🐻

"Well," I said, pushing back from the computer. "That was interesting. Why do you suppose she said it wasn't worth it?"

"Maybe she thinks she would have gotten into Brown even with the bad chem grade?"

"That seems like a stretch."

Nate said, "Check the emails between Bender and Mrs. White. Whatever was going on, I bet she knew about it."

"I'll have to get her email address, then," Emily said. "I need a directory."

Nate pulled his out of his desk drawer and handed it over, and she turned to the faculty section.

"How long will that take?" I asked.

"Depends on her," she said.

We sat there watching Emily type. After a minute she said, "Is this really the best use of your time? Watching me?"

I shrugged. Without turning around, she said, "Somebody make me a sandwich."

"Right," Nate said. "Why did we break up again?"

"Because I dumped you. Oh, and don't use that low-fat cheese," she said. "I'll know."

•••

Nate and I went off to make a full-fat grilled cheese sandwich. While we were standing in the kitchen, my phone pinged with a text from Caroline.

It said, *Shopping this weekend: we need to talk about DOC!*

I deleted it and put my phone away. "What do you think?" I said.

"I'm reserving judgment. Did you want a sandwich?"

"Pass. I'm full-up on those mushroom things."

"You know, if we're right about this, and it was Bender and we can prove it, that really changes things."

"I know," I said. "I'm trying not to get my hopes up."

"Hope is good," he said. "I recommend it. This is done." He flipped the sandwich onto a plate.

"Do you think she wants a pickle?" I asked.

"Oh dear God. I'm not getting her a pickle."

He carried the plate down the hall and set it in front of Emily.

"You didn't make *me* a sandwich?" Shira teased.

"You didn't ask," I said.

"I left the cheese on the counter," Nate said. "Help yourself."

Emily said, "No pickle?"

I said, "See, I told you."

Bebe said, "I love everyone here, but I do have other things to do with my life."

"Okay," Emily said, taking a bite of her sandwich. "So I got into Mrs. White's emails. There's only one problem. She deletes everything in her inbox more than three months old. So I don't have anything from him to her. However," she said, holding up a finger. "She didn't bother to delete the sent messages. I have all the ones from her to him. And those are rather interesting."

She pulled up a series of screenshots she'd taken. Unfortunately, his emails weren't quoted in her outgoing messages, and hers were pretty terse. But they were also telling.

The first one said: *What are you going to do?*

The second: *You can't. If you get caught, you'll never work again.*

The third: *Use the answers to last year's exam. It buys you some time. Then tell your wife they're lying because they did badly on the test.*

The fourth: *Don't worry about Marlowe. They won't go to him.*

The fifth: *I love you.*

"Wow," I said. "Mrs. White is kind of a psycho."

"So," Bebe said. "They were blackmailing him for the answers to the final. But he screwed them over and gave them the ones from the year before."

"Nothing to do with the transcripts," Shira added.

"That doesn't mean it wasn't him," I insisted. "What if there was something else later, something there's no email record for?"

"I don't think it was him," Emily said. "He was already scared of losing his job because of the thing with Mrs. White. I don't think he would have taken the risk."

"You don't know that, though."

Emily turned away from the computer and leaned back, so that her elbows were hooked over the back of the chair. "You're familiar with the theorem of Occam's razor?"

I nodded. "The simplest explanation is usually the correct one."

"Right. We have a very well defined explanation here. He was having an affair. Beth Reinhardt caught him, decided to blackmail him for the exam answers, and brought her best friend in on it because they both suck at chem. He double-crossed them."

"Did they tell his wife?" Bebe wondered.

"I don't know," Emily said. "From our perspective, it doesn't matter. But we do know that there's no record of any further emails between him and Beth. It wasn't Bender who changed your transcript. I'm sure it wasn't."

"So where does that leave us?" I asked.

She gestured around Nate's room. "It leaves us here," she said, getting up and handing Nate back her empty plate. "Thanks for the sandwich."

I was climbing into my bed that night, exhausted and frustrated, when I got a text from Emily.

Wakey, wakey, it said.

I'm still awake, I said, *barely.*

Good, she said. *I found one other thing in Mrs. White's sent emails.*

Why are you still reading her emails?

I was just looking to see if there was anything unusual. It's not like I enjoy snooping.

She totally enjoyed it. *What did you find?* I asked, because I did actually want to know.

So it turns out Mrs. White is Amy Gregston's adviser, and Amy asked her to help her get an unofficial copy of her transcript. She was applying to some class at the Corcoran over winter break, and she needed to show her art grades, so Mrs. Hadley forwarded it to Mrs. White and then she forwarded it to the Corcoran with a letter of recommendation.

And?

And the transcript shows her getting an A in junior year English. Only I was in that class with Amy, and she didn't get an A.

Are you sure?

She got a B+ and she was really, really mad about it. So yeah, I'm sure.

Maybe she did some extra credit?

After the final?

I settled myself in my bed, because I really was tired. I tucked my comforter up under my armpits. *But Amy only applied to schools on the west coast.*

That's right. Her dad's out there and she wanted to be closer to him. She's going to Stanford.

We didn't apply to any of the same schools.

No. You didn't. And I checked her transcript and she didn't have Bender for chem, so there's no connection there, either, in case you were wondering.

So what does that mean?

I don't know. There's some connection we aren't seeing.

CHAPTER FIFTEEN

MY MOTHER SPENT ALL DAY SATURDAY AT THE OFFICE, CATCHING up on work, which she does about two Saturdays a month. I got a call from her around five, telling me she wouldn't be home for dinner.

"I'm sorry," she said. "I was supposed to be done at four, but my computer crashed, and I had to start a case file over from scratch."

"It's okay," I said.

"I think there's leftovers," she said.

Leftover glop, she meant. "Sure," I said. "That sounds great."

I pulled the glop out of the refrigerator. I pulled the tinfoil off the bowl. I pulled out my phone and took a picture, then texted it to Nate.

Save me, my text said.

What IS that?

Dinner, unless you help me. Please help me.

What's in it?

It's leftovers of leftovers. I'm not really sure.

Maybe you should learn to cook.

I'll get right on that.

I'll give you dinner, he said, *if you read my government paper for me.*

That was due yesterday!

Look, do you want real food or not?

I'll do it. Please hurry. I think it just moved.

Nate picked me up half an hour later, and we dug around in his kitchen for leftovers because his parents were at some kind of benefit dinner. Nate's sister was sleeping over at a friend's house, and Nate had been left to feed himself. Fortunately, he was pretty good at that.

"I can't believe I came all the way to your house to eat your leftovers instead of my leftovers."

"I can take you back," he said. "You can still have the gloop."

"Glop." I took out a bowl. "What's this one?"

"Baked ziti, I think."

"How old?" I asked, peeling back the edge of the saran wrap.

"Two days."

"Oh. Good. That's safe." I handed him the bowl, and he stuck it in the microwave. Just as it beeped, the front door opened, and in walked Nate's parents, his mother in a woman-of-a-certain-age burgundy dress with a matching jacket, and his father in the black suit he wore when a tux was too formal but a regular suit was too casual. His dad was on the phone and disappeared into the other room, giving us a friendly smile and a wave.

"Your grandmother called," Nate's mother said, kissing him on the cheek. "Hello, Mischa."

"Hi, Ms. Miller."

"How is Grandma?" Nate asked.

"Old," she said. "She's had him on the phone for forty minutes. I think she's moved on from talking about disinheriting your uncle to complaining about her health."

"Is she sick?" Nate asked.

"No," she said flatly.

"How was your dinner?" I asked.

Ms. Miller rolled her eyes. "Oh, Mischa. I don't even know why we go to these banquets; it's like they're all being catered by cooking-school dropouts. If it's not covered with a balsamic reduction, it's a raspberry glaze, because no one can eat dinner anymore unless it's coated with sugar. Is this filet mignon or a piece of pie? Honestly, it's all just so jejune." She put her doggie bag down on the counter, because I guess jejune leftovers are better than no leftovers.

Jejune, Nate mouthed at me. I smothered a grin in my hand. "Have you considered," Nate said to his mother, "that it isn't an apple confit you're eating, but a jar of Gerber? Maybe next time you should wear a bib."

"Don't be absurd," she said, ruffling his hair.

Absurd, he mouthed, but his mother had already left the kitchen, either to change out of her dress or to try to save her husband from the never-ending phone call.

"Five months," Nate said. "I will be in Atlanta in five months."

"Don't worry," I said. "I'm sure they'll visit."

"Yes. I'm sure they will." He laughed. "There is not enough medication in the whole world to get me through Parents' Weekend."

"Now you're being absurd," I said. Then: "Medication?"

He gave me a look.

"You're not taking medication," I said, followed by, "are you?" Probably this is the kind of thing I should have known after four years of friendship. But it's not like I make a habit of raiding people's medicine cabinets. That would be rude. And jejune.

"Well, I was," he said. "Quite a bit of it."

I hesitated, because sometimes I can't tell when Nate is joking and when he's being serious. "Really?"

"Yeah. I was. You know, antidepressants. For about two years."

"Oh," I said. "I didn't know that." I knew he was in therapy, but I didn't know he'd been taking antidepressants. And I didn't realize you could start taking antidepressants and then stop. . . . I kind of figured once you were on them, you had to stay on them forever.

There wasn't a whole lot I knew about Nate from the period before we'd met. I knew he'd been a crazy-successful student, which was how he'd gotten into Blanchard in the first place. I knew he used to play soccer. I knew he quit both of those things because he'd had some kind of a burnout that he never, ever talked about, but that other people had talked about in hushed tones freshman year.

"Mischa," he said. "It's not like you never heard this story."

I shrugged. "I heard some rumors, but I tried not to pay too much attention to them."

"Why? Weren't you curious?"

"I guess. But satisfying my curiosity by listening to a bunch of gossip seems pretty cheap."

He slung an arm over my shoulder. "This is why you're my favorite," he said. "But you're wondering now, right?"

"I—I guess."

He smoothed his hair out of his face. "Okay. I had a breakdown when I was fourteen." He laughed. "It was awesome."

This was kind of in line with what I'd already heard. "That doesn't sound particularly funny."

"It wasn't, at the time. Well, maybe it kind of was. Who has a breakdown when they're fourteen?"

"What happened?"

"Combination of things, I guess. School. Soccer. Parents." He picked up a napkin from the tray on the counter and started tearing it into tiny little pieces.

"You sometimes like boys," I added.

"You know," he said thoughtfully, his hands going still, "you'd think that would have contributed, but oddly enough, no one ever cared about that."

"Nobody?"

"Well, Grandma thought it was a phase. She still thinks it's a phase. If I marry a man, she'll show up at the wedding, stand up to make a toast, and say, 'Joseph is a lovely man, and I'm so very happy for my delightful grandson, who is both a prince and the apple of my eye. This is, however, a phase.'"

"And if you marry a woman?"

"Well, she'll just take that as proof she was right."

"How much does that bother you?"

"On a scale of one to ten? Like a two. Midway between a sigh and an eye roll."

"That's not so bad, I guess."

"Yeah, that really wasn't the problem. It was just, I went from school to soccer practice, to homework, to sleep. Day after day after day. I got really tired. I had a stomachache all the time. I stopped eating."

"That must have freaked out your parents."

"They didn't really notice."

"They didn't notice? You eat like a linebacker."

"So anyway, that spring my travel team was in the regional finals. And we lost by one point."

"Oh."

"Yeah," he said. "And I started crying. Like, little-kid crying. The loud, ugly kind."

"I mean, that sounds normal."

"Crying for fifteen minutes would have been normal. But I couldn't stop. It was like once I started, I couldn't find the off switch." He looked away sharply, and I was really sorry I'd asked. This was something that had hurt him. That still hurt him.

"I get it," I said. "You don't have to say any more."

"I didn't even tell you the good part yet."

It didn't sound like this story had a good part, but I said, "Okay. So you cried."

"I cried for *four hours*. My parents started yelling at me for 'attention seeking.' And then I started hyperventilating. And then I passed out." He flung the wadded-up napkin onto the table. "About an eighth-grade soccer game. I cried until I passed out about an eighth-grade soccer game. I didn't cry that much when my *grandfather* died."

"It wasn't about the soccer game."

He shrugged. "It wasn't. And it was. I don't know." He

rubbed his eyes. "They took me to this place called Meadow House. It's like, inpatient psych care for teenagers. I stayed there a month."

"A month?"

"Yeah. I was on a whole cocktail of drugs. Antidepressants, antianxiety stuff. Something to make me sleep at night. Lots of therapy." He smiled a little wanly. "They didn't want to put me in with the kids there for drugs, so my therapy group was me and four kids with eating disorders."

I tried to imagine a younger Nate, without his easy smile, all alone in a place full of kids too sick to be at home. I wondered if any of his friends had come to visit. I wondered if he'd even wanted them to. Maybe once you hit a place that low, you just want to be alone so you don't have to pretend anymore. I grabbed his pinky finger into my fist and squeezed it, which made him smile, just barely, without looking at me. His eyes were on our hands.

"But you got better," I said.

"I did. Mostly I realized that if I didn't start setting boundaries with people, my life was going to be hell." He turned to look at me and ran a finger over my forehead, smoothing the wrinkles there. "You're frowning."

"I'm sorry. I'm sorry that happened to you."

I wondered at what point in the process the Millers had started funneling Nate's sister into travel softball and extra tutoring and twice-weekly clarinet lessons, if it had been before Nate's breakdown or after. I wondered if he'd burned out, and his parents had taken all that energy and moved it to her, just like that. Like they had a very specific amount of mental and physical energy to apply to child-rearing, and they weren't going to waste it on the kid who wasn't going anywhere. The situation put me in mind of locusts, devouring a field and then, once everything was gone, moving on to the next. They'd used Nate all the way up.

Or maybe he was just letting them think they had.

"Also," I said, "I'm just thinking that I was an odd friend for you to pick."

"You are a little odd, it's true."

I elbowed him in the gut. "I mean, if you were looking to break from your overachieving past."

"Not really. You're kind of wonky with the studying and stuff, but that's you. You don't care about what I do. I could flunk all my classes, and I don't think you'd even notice."

"Of course I'd notice!" I protested.

"I didn't mean it in a bad way. It's just like, if I ask for help, you help. And if I don't ask for help, you don't help."

"You say that like that's not what everyone does."

He laughed at me. "Mischa, that isn't what everyone does, trust me." He reached over and picked up the bag of his parents' leftovers. "Did you still want the ziti, or did you want to try the jejune steak?"

"Oh," I said. "The ziti, I think," but he'd already grabbed a fork and was eating out of the white paper box.

"Wow," he said. "I can't believe it. My mother was right."

"It's bad?"

He held out the fork, and I took a bite. "Ergh," I said. I stuck my face into the sink and drank some water out of the tap while he laughed. "What is that? Candied meat?"

Nate's mother had come back into the kitchen and said, "I told you. You laughed, but I told you."

"Yes, Mom," Nate said, giving her a one-armed hug and a kiss on the cheek. "You told us."

CHAPTER SIXTEEN

ON MONDAY MORNING I HAD TO GO TO THE DENTIST.

I lay back in the chair for forty minutes while the hygienist yelled at me for inadequate flossing and I stared at a poster of a beach on the ceiling.

"Open wider," she said, and I obliged as she attempted to extract either a chunk of tartar or my eternal soul from between my molars. Whatever it was, it wasn't coming out.

"You need to take better care of your teeth," she said.

"I rush wice a ray," I mumbled around the metal implement of death.

"You should try an electric brush," she said. "We sell them here. Forty bucks and they come with an extra brush head." She leaned into my gums, and something gave way. "There we go."

"Ow," I said.

"You're fine."

"I'n *reeding*."

"You're fine."

Two pints of blood later, I got to school just as lunch was starting. I walked into the cafeteria, where Jim was sitting at the table under the window with Caroline, Mark, and Molly St. Andrews. I thought about taking my tray out into the hallway, when Jim beckoned me over.

As I approached, their conversation stalled. I found myself staring, not at their faces, but at their shirts.

I realized, belatedly, that this was College Sweatshirt Day. I'd gotten an email reminder about it last week and deleted it. Every senior in the dining hall had their selected school emblazoned on their chest like Superman's family crest—the thing everyone thinks is an *S* but isn't an *S* because . . . I don't know. It's just not an *S*. Anyway, every person had some kind of trademarked logo on their torso, except me.

The good people of table three stared at my blank chest. Jim cleared his throat. "You want to sit, Vicious?" he asked.

"Don't call her that," Caroline hissed.

"What?" he asked.

"Get a clue," she whispered.

I blinked at both of them, because this made no sense. So I didn't have a sweatshirt on. So what?

"It's okay," I said. Jim had, in fact, never, to my face, used my real name, not since we were in class together freshman year and our English teacher butchered my last name taking the roll. But he always said it with this tiny little smile, like it was our private joke, that made it charming instead of mean.

Jim pushed out the chair in front of me with his foot. "Grab a seat, Mischa," he said.

I closed my eyes. I sat down, because people were already starting to stare at me.

Last year Dina Myer's father had a heart attack. He was in the ICU for days before he finally pulled through. He's fine now, so far as I know, except that he spends all his free time at some yoga studio, presumably assuming the corpse pose and trying really hard not to overidentify. Anyway, everyone in our class walked on eggshells around her for weeks, because her dad was (hypothetically) dying, and no one knew what might make her burst into tears. That's how everyone was looking at me. Like someone was *dying*.

Jim and Caroline were holding hands. Were they together? I wondered when that had happened and how I hadn't known. Admittedly, I had been pretty distracted lately.

Or maybe they'd been together six months, and I hadn't even noticed. Was that possible?

"Hey," I said. "You guys are . . ."

They glanced at each other, at me, with eyes full of . . . what? Pity?

"The meatloaf looks great today!" I said way too loudly.

"It's shepherd's pie," Mark said quietly.

"Oh," I said. "Right. The potatoes."

"To be fair," Jim said, "meatloaf is usually served with potatoes, too. I kind of thought it was meatloaf at first."

"Yeah," Caroline agreed. "It does have that kind of look, doesn't it? It's very, you know. Meaty."

"It's okay," I said. "It's not meatloaf."

"So," Caroline said. "Mischa, you know, my step-cousin went to Revere. He really liked it."

I stalled with my shepherd's pie an inch from my mouth. "Revere?" I asked.

"Yeah," she said. "They have a really good internship program."

Had I mentioned Revere to anyone? Besides Nate. And the Ophelias. And my mother. My mother. My mother had run into Meredith at the mall. My mother had told Meredith I was going to Revere.

Meredith effing Dorsay.

I considered telling them I wasn't going to Revere, but what was I going to say? I was going no place? Wasn't that worse? At least this way my mother wasn't going to hear I had no acceptances at all from someone else. I suddenly understood the way everyone was looking at me. It wasn't just pity; it was also fear. And it's not like I didn't understand why I was scary. I was a reminder of how precarious everything was for all of us. Our lives were like a very neatly ordered stack of dominos, precisely lined up. But you pull one out, and the whole system goes haywire. There's no margin for error. None at all.

Inside my pocket my phone buzzed, and I pulled it out.

It was a text from Emily. It said: *This is your rescue call.*

I looked around but didn't see her. *Where are you?* I texted back.

Hallway, she replied, and I craned my neck to look out. Emily was leaning against the door frame, her keys dangling from one hand. She raised her eyebrows at me before typing something else into her phone.

Are you coming?

I got up and grabbed my tray. "I just remembered: I'm meeting Ms. Wentworth in ten minutes," I said. "I should get over there."

No one said a word. They just watched me leave the table.

As I crossed in front of where Meredith Dorsay was sitting, someone—I'm not sure who—very loudly went *cough-cough-cough* "SAFETY SCHOOL," and the entire table erupted in laughter.

"Oh, grow up!" Caroline shouted from the other side of the cafeteria. But I just hunched my shoulders and kept walking.

Emily fell in next to me as I passed her. "That looked fairly painful," she said.

"It wasn't the best five minutes of my life, no. Thanks, by the way." It was then that I realized Emily wasn't wearing a college shirt. She was wearing a tank top with that same flower, the one from her ring and the Ophelia card, printed on it.

"Where's your sweatshirt?" I asked.

"It's eighty degrees out," she said. "These people are sheep."

From behind us, I heard "Baaa."

Followed by another "Baaa."

I turned and saw Shira and Bebe, followed by Nate, who said, "Moo," and then, "Sorry, I'm an iconoclast."

None of them, I realized, were wearing their shirts.

"Don't start," I said to Nate. "I know you own like ten of them."

"Don't pick on Cute Nate," Shira said. "He's a very nice cow. Bull. Do bulls moo?"

Bebe pulled out her phone and said, "I'll look it up."

"I didn't realize you guys had B lunch," I said.

"Bulls moo," Bebe told Shira. "That's a thing."

"Oh, we don't," Emily replied, ignoring the conversation about the verbal tics of cattle. "But the lunch buffet over at the

Hyderabad Café is always totally picked over by twelve-thirty, and they have free lassis on Mondays."

"So you guys are just skipping?"

"Skipping," Emily said. "Or taking a lunch meeting. Whatever you want to call it."

"Will we be back in time for next period?" I asked, a little reflexively.

Shira laughed. "Not if we're doing it right."

"Honestly, Mischa," Emily said. "What is it that you think they can do to you now?"

I stopped walking long enough that Shira bumped into me. "Nothing," I said. "They can't do anything."

My plate was filled with samosas and nothing else. Emily, who was eating about twelve different things, looked at my lunch and said, "Gack."

"I like fried food," I explained.

"Apparently. Hey, as long as you and your gallbladder have some kind of understanding, who am I to intrude?"

She picked up an idli and ate it. "So," she said. "Bebe may have figured out how Beth got into Brown."

I looked to Bebe, who had just put half a tandoori chicken wing in her mouth and was making the sign for either *I am chewing* or *I am choking*.

"Beatrice, do you need the Heimlich?" Shira asked.

Bebe shook her head vigorously. "Chew-ing," she said with her mouth full. "Choking is this." She put her hands around her own neck.

"You were pointing to your esophagus."

She swallowed. "I was pointing to my jaw!" She put down the bony remnants of the wing. "Anyway, yeah. I got bored last night and googled Beth's dad. He's been a busy beaver."

"What did he do?"

She typed into her phone and set it in the middle of the table. Nate and I squished our heads together to read the screen. Emily and Shira, who had presumably already seen it, kept eating.

"They named a *building* after him?" Nate said incredulously.

"It's not a building," I said. "It's a wing. Of the biology building. Which he endowed."

"I wonder how much it costs to endow a wing," Nate said, scrolling down on the phone.

"In this case, one point two million," Bebe said. The straw of Shira's lassi popped out of her mouth, and she whistled.

"Wow," I said. "That's. Wow."

"So what does this tell us?" Nate asked. "Maybe nobody changed Beth's grades at all. Maybe it was just the money."

"Perhaps," Emily agreed. "That's a distinct possibility."

"Which means we have no leads," I said.

"Except Amy," Emily said. "And that weird English grade."

"But you don't even know for sure that she had the B+!" I said. "You might be wrong about that. In which case, we're right back where we started."

"We have other leads," Bebe said. "Remember the list we made up."

I made a mental tally of what we'd done so far: we'd put a virus on Mrs. Hadley's computer, broken into the school, stolen Mrs. White's email address, read her private email, and pretended to be Willa Jenkins to talk to Beth Reinhardt.

It was starting to seem like we were involved in a lot of criminal activity with no actual results. I wondered what the penalty was for all this, if we got caught. Skipping school was one thing; there was literally nothing worse that could happen to me on that front. But getting in trouble with the police . . . that was something else.

"No," I said. "We really don't have leads. We have suspicions. Which are not leads. A lead requires just the tiniest amount of tangible evidence, and we have nothing." I smashed a samosa with my fork. "This whole thing has been a complete waste. We've committed *felonies*. And for nothing."

Emily leaned back from the table. "What are you saying?"

"I'm saying I want to stop," I said. "There's no point. I don't want to risk getting in even more trouble. This has turned into a wild-goose chase. One of us is going to end up arrested."

Emily said, "We know what we're doing. We're not getting arrested."

"I can't take that chance! Do you even understand? I have nothing right now. Nothing. If I end up with a record, I won't even be able to get a job. Do you get it? Do you get what's at stake for me? No. You don't. If you guys get caught, so what? Your parents will hire a lawyer. Maybe you'll get a few months of probation, and then your record gets wiped at the end. I don't have that option. I'll just get screwed."

"I was under the impression," said Emily blandly, "that your mother *is* a lawyer."

"She's not a *criminal* lawyer." I pushed my chair back to get up. "Look. It's not like I don't appreciate all the time you've put into this and everything else, because I do. I really do. It's just—I can't take these kinds of risks. I'm sorry."

Bebe and Shira exchanged an unreadable glance, but

Emily's eyes were only for me. "Are you sure about this?" she said. "If we stop now, there's no chance of changing your transcript back. Or your letters."

"I'm sure," I said.

Nate said, "I'll drive you back to school, I guess."

In the car Nate said, "What are you going to do now?"

"I don't know," I said. "I need to think. I just can't let things get any worse. I can't get arrested. Do you understand?"

"Not wanting things to get worse? Of course I understand."

"So you don't think I'm making a mistake?"

"I think what you decide to do is none of my business. I'm not going to tell you what to do."

"Thank you," I said.

He put his arm around me. "Come here," he said.

"What?"

"Just come here." He pulled me next to him, and then I did what I'd been wanting to do from the beginning: I broke down and sobbed.

As I was crying noisily into his shoulder, his hand rubbing up and down my arm, I realized I'd been kidding myself for the last four years. I didn't like Nate. I didn't have a crush on Nate. I didn't have a thing for Nate.

I was in love with Nate.

CHAPTER SEVENTEEN

I DIDN'T PARTICULARLY WANT TO GO BACK TO SCHOOL AFTER that, but I did, because I had a student government meeting and I didn't want to leave everyone in the lurch.

The SGA meetings were generally held in Ms. Wentworth's room, since she's our faculty adviser, despite the fact that she rarely shows up. We pushed four desks together to make a long table at the front of the room, and I sat between Jim and Caroline, while Mark, who had been up too late doing his math again, strained to keep his eyes open on Jim's other side. The eight class reps sat in the front row, along with Meredith Dorsay, who was our representative on Blanchard's board of directors. She sat with her arms crossed in smug satisfaction while Caroline typed up the minutes, Jim called on the reps to report, and I stewed in my own fury.

"Meredith," Jim said, which jolted me out of my fantasy of

ruining Meredith's sixty-dollar blowout by shoving her head in a toilet. "You have a report from the board?"

"Yes," she said, standing up, which was super unnecessary, since it's not like we wouldn't have been able to hear her otherwise. "The board is donating eleven hundred dollars toward the senior class all-night grad party this year. I should have their check by the end of the week."

"Make sure Mark gets that," Jim said, but Mark had momentarily nodded off, and Jim had to elbow him back into action. "Narcolepsy boy. Stay with us."

Mark jolted upright, saying, "Yes! The check. I will take the check."

"For eleven hundred dollars," Jim prompted.

"Right," Mark said, making a note. "Eleven . . . hundred . . . check . . . to . . . bank."

"That's less than they donated last year," I blurted out.

"Excuse me?" Meredith said.

"According to the records, the board gave the seniors thirteen hundred dollars for last year's party."

Meredith smoothed an invisible wrinkle in her sleeve. "Because last year's class was bigger."

"By four people," I said.

"Right. It was bigger by four people. Which is bigger."

"Do you mean to tell me that those extra four people were worth fifty dollars each?" I asked.

"I suppose fifty dollars would seem like a lot to some people," she said.

"I suppose asking for *parity* would have seemed like too much work for *some people*," I said.

Caroline said quietly, "Mischa, what are you doing? It's two hundred dollars. We can make up the difference."

Loudly, Meredith said, "Are you getting all this in the minutes, Caroline?"

Caroline gruffly said, "That's my job."

"Ladies," Jim said. "Should we move on?"

"No," I said.

"No," Meredith said. "Maybe Michelle would like to go talk to the board? You can ask them for more money, and then tell them what great use you've made of the scholarship they already gave you."

I stood up fast enough to knock my chair over. Caroline's mouth popped open, but I noticed she didn't actually say anything. One of the junior class reps said, "Oh no she didn't." Jim's hand shot out and grabbed my arm. "Vicious," he said. "Sit down."

"Let go of me," I hissed.

"I don't think so," he said. "Meredith, that was uncalled for."

"I'm just saying, if she thinks she can do my job better, she should go ahead and try."

"I'm adjourning this meeting," Jim said.

"We haven't heard from the freshmen yet," Caroline pointed out.

Jim turned to the two freshmen reps, who were watching this whole exchange with bug-eyed terror. "Do you guys have anything that can't keep?"

They shook their heads vigorously.

"Great. I move to adjourn the meeting," he said.

"Second," Caroline said, slamming her laptop shut.

Look at me, I willed. *Look at me right now.* But she didn't.

"And we're done," Jim said. "Mischa, come with me. Meredith," he shot over his shoulder, since he was already dragging me from the room. "Put a muzzle on it."

Out in the hallway he turned to me and said, "You want to tell me what that even was?"

"She's incompetent," I said.

"She's awful, but she's not incompetent. You know she has no control over how much money the board gives us for that party."

"She could have asked for more."

"How do you know she didn't?"

"She—"

"Look, it doesn't even matter! We have a budget surplus, and if we don't use it, it's just going to go to the juniors for next year anyway."

"Then the juniors should have it."

"Hey," he said, resting a hand on my shoulder, which I shrugged off. "It's not like I'm not sympathetic here. Meredith's a snake. But if you're going to be gunning for her in every meeting for the rest of the year, it's going to be a long three months."

"You're right," I said.

"Of course I am," he said. "Do you want to get a coffee or something? I have another hour before I have to be at tennis."

"No," I said. "Thanks. I should go home. Or something. I don't know."

"Okay," he said. Then, frowning: "You're not going to . . ."

"To what?"

He let out a long exhalation. "To jump off a bridge. Or whatever."

"No," I said, then felt worse, because that seemed to be the logical next step for me—not necessarily to jump off a bridge, but to *want* to jump off a bridge. "I'm not jumping off anything."

"Okay. Good. I mean, you would tell me, right?"

"Yeah, I'd tell you. But I'm not. I promise."

He turned to go, but then stopped to say, "Caroline said you guys were supposed to go shopping last weekend."

"I—I guess I forgot."

"Maybe you should call her," he said.

"Yeah," I said. "I know."

I was walking out of the building when I got a text from Penny Ford, the president of Students for Sober Driving. It said, *Meeting tomorrow at six. Please bring work supplies!*

I thought really hard about spiking my phone into the ground.

CHAPTER EIGHTEEN

CAROLINE WAS SUPPOSED TO BE MY RIDE HOME AFTER THE SGA meeting, but I just couldn't deal with listening to half an hour of conversation about DOC (or COD), so I bolted out the door without looking back. I got out my phone to text Nate, but then I remembered that he has therapy on Thursdays. Tucked into the little pocket of my purse was Emily's Ophelia Syndicate card, with the little flower in the corner. I ran my fingers over the embossing. Then I texted Emily.

I told myself it was because she lives like a mile from the school and picking me up wouldn't have been a big deal for her. *Are you busy?* I texted.

Yes, she texted back after a few seconds. I had to roll my eyes.

Was that your only question? she asked.

If I ask you to pick me up, can you not ask why?

What a strange request. Would I care why?

No, I said, *you wouldn't.*

Then please don't tell me.

Thanks.

I put my phone in my pocket and sank onto a bench that was slightly damp from last night's rain. A few minutes later my phone buzzed again.

It might help, Emily said, *if you told me where you were.*

Oh. I'm still at school. I'm outside the side door.

<SIGH>, she typed. *If you want me to drop everything to pick you up someplace with no questions asked, you might as well be someplace INTERESTING.*

Sorry, I said.

You should be.

I put the phone away again. She was right, though. I was boring. My main interests were school and, oh yeah, more school. I didn't play in a band. I didn't speak three languages or know how to disembowel a computer or collect first-edition romance novels. I'd never been anywhere or done anything, because I'd kind of thought those were things you did after high school. Like being interesting was some kind of a payoff. I wondered what Emily had been up to when I called. Probably hacking into a bank or something.

Emily pulled up in her BMW two minutes later.

"You were still at school," I said. "You could have mentioned that."

"I was in the computer lab finishing a CS project with Bebe. Did you want to wait longer? I can circle the block a few times."

"No," I said. "I'll get in."

I went around the front of the car and got in next to her,

and she pulled away without asking me where I wanted to go. She turned right at the light like she was heading for the Beltway, so I said, "Where are we going?"

"I was taking you home," she said. "Was that not what you wanted?"

"No, home is fine," I said. Then: "If I hadn't called, what were you going to do?"

She turned and looked at me over the tops of her sunglasses. "I was going to go home and read a book."

"Really?"

She didn't answer. A second later I asked, "What book?"

She turned into the next shopping center and pulled on the parking brake. "Mischa," she said. "What's up?"

"Nothing," I said. "Well, not nothing. It's just . . . I had SGA today."

"Okay."

"I do a lot of clubs, actually." I remembered the increasingly angry texts from Leo Michaels about my poor French club attendance. "Or at least I'm supposed to, and, you know, I go to school, and I study and write papers and stuff. And that's kind of . . . it."

"Oh. You're bored."

"I guess."

"There must be something you like to do."

I shrugged. I guess I like binge-watching shows on Netflix, but that doesn't seem like a nonboring way to be spending my free time. "I don't even know," I said honestly. "Is that weird?"

"Depends," she said. "How badly have you always wanted to be an android?"

"What is wrong with me?"

"You mean, why are you so boring?"

"Yeah."

"Well, you chose it."

"So what do I do?"

"Unchoose it? I don't know. What are you asking me for?"
I shrugged again.

"All right," she said, drumming her fingers on the steering wheel. "What did you like to do for fun before you came to Blanchard?"

I had to think back. Middle school seemed like it was a really long time ago; I could barely remember being the same age as Rachel Miller, which was probably a good thing. What did I like back then? I liked that *Young Justice* cartoon about all the teenage superheroes. I liked *Star Wars*. I liked books about dogs where the dog doesn't die at the end. I liked babysitting my neighbor's cat when she went on vacation; she was a Persian, so I would have to sit on the couch with her, brushing her over and over while she purred and nibbled on my forearm.

I said, "On Sundays, my mom and I used to get up early to feed the ducks. We used to thaw out frozen peas and take them down to this pond by our house."

"Peas?"

"They're better for them than bread," I explained.

She looked at me skeptically. She said, "Ducks."

"Ducks."

"Hang on," she said, and then she got out of the car.

"Are you coming back?" I called after her, but she'd left me alone. I went to turn the radio on, but she'd taken the keys with her. "Oookay," I said to no one. "I guess I'm just going to sit here."

I absentmindedly played with the bottles of nail polish in her cup holder—the chrome color she usually wore and a dark red called Evening Sherry. I opened the chrome and swiped a stripe down my left thumbnail. It was pretty, like a silver-scaled fish.

Emily reappeared a moment later with a paper sack in her hand. "What is that?" I asked.

"Peas," she said, pulling out a box of Farmer Jackson's Finest and nodding toward the convenience store on the other side of the parking lot. "There's a pond behind Blanchard. Shira used to skip there freshman year."

"You want to feed the ducks?"

"No," she said. "*You* want to feed the ducks." She drove out of the parking lot and back around the far side of Blanchard, where there was nothing but a neighborhood of nice houses and—yes—a pond. There were several little duck families, mallards with shiny-headed fathers and demure-colored mothers and fuzzy yellow babies.

"Babies!" I said. "There are baby ducks!"

"Hope there aren't any turtles in there," she said. "They eat the babies."

"No they don't."

"They do."

"Why did you tell me that? Ugh." I threw a handful of peas at her, and she laughed.

"They'll be fine," she said. "Duck parents are very protective."

"Right. Good on the duck parents."

We took turns tossing peas to the ducks. I don't know why I like them so much—the ducks, I mean, not the peas. Maybe it's the quacking. It's a nice noise for an animal to make, quacking. Quack. Quack. It's a good sound.

"Did you just quack?" Emily asked.

"What? No."

"You did. You said quack."

"I did not. Shut up."

"Quack," she said. "Quack, quack."

"You have food in your teeth."

"Oh. Really?"

"No. Just stop quacking."

She stared out at the pond. After a while she said, "You're right, though. It is kind of meditative."

I nodded. It was such an odd thing, just to exist with no real purpose. The sun was hot on the top of my head, the air smelled like wet grass (which was soaking through my jeans), and I was kind of happy. There was nothing at all besides the pond and the ducks and the sky and the peas. And Emily, I guess.

"Did you watch *Young Justice* when you were a kid?" I asked.

"Oh. Sure," she said. Then, smiling, she added, "I had a huge crush on Nightwing when I was twelve."

"Right," I said. "Because he's a—"

"A hacker, yeah."

"I had a little bit of a thing for Kid Flash," I said. "Also, maybe for Aqualad."

"'Cause he's broody."

"'Cause he's broody. Superboy, though . . ."

"Oh, no. Hard pass."

"Yeah, definitely not." Two of the ducklings were chasing each other while their mother looked on. It was sort of amazing to watch them; no matter where the mom went, the babies followed as if they were tied to her by an invisible string. I wished I could have picked one up and touched its fuzzy yellow dandelion feathers, but I was pretty sure Mama Duck would not have appreciated it. I tossed a few peas to the tiny siblings to break up the fight. Behind them was a bed of pansies, which reminded me of Bebe's Ophelia card. "So I was wondering," I said.

"The Blue Beetle," she said, pointing at me. "I would definitely go out with the Blue Beetle."

"No," I said. "I mean, yes, the Blue Beetle's awesome, but I was wondering about the whole 'syndicate' thing. Why Ophelia? We are talking about the Ophelia that's in *Hamlet*, right? The one who commits suicide?"

"Does she?" she said, raising an eyebrow. "Are you sure?"

"I'm pretty sure she does," I said. "We read it in English last fall."

"Ahhhh," Emily said. "But remember, *Hamlet* came out in 1603. Six years after *Romeo and Juliet*, which features another girl who"—she made air quotes with her fingers—"'dies' under mysterious circumstances."

I tossed a few peas to Big Mama, who had to eat fast before her babies got there. "So your theory," I said, passing the box back to Emily, "is that Ophelia's suicide was a redo of the fake death plot in *Romeo and Juliet*?"

"And not just that. Gertrude was in on it."

"Wait. What?"

"Think about it," Emily said. "Gertrude tells her unstable, homicidal son that his girlfriend is dead, after he's already killed three other people, including two of his own friends."

"You think she lied. To protect Ophelia from Hamlet."

"Exactly," she said. "She was playing in a rigged game. Hamlet and Claudius had all the power. So she hacked the narrative."

"Um. Then shouldn't you be the Gertrude Syndicate?"

"No," Emily said. "The Gertrude Syndicate sounds awful." She tossed the last handful of peas to the crowd of babies. "Sometimes you have to wink at accuracy for the sake of aesthetics." She stretched her arms over her head, then balled up the empty box and stuffed it back in the bag. "We're out of peas," she said.

We both got up and walked back toward the car. I wanted to ask Emily if she'd done all this because she felt sorry for me, but I already knew that she had. Still, though. A pity duck-feeding was better than nothing. She drove me home, and we listened to the radio. Halfway through the second song, I realized she was humming. So I hummed, too.

After she dropped me off, I pulled out my phone and started a memo. I titled it Mischa Abramavicius Bucket List.

Number One: Feed ducks.

I put an *X* next to it.

Number Two: I looked down at my silver-striped thumbnail. *Find signature nail polish.*

I stream-of-consciousnessed the next few things on the list.

Go ice skating at Rockefeller Center.

Swim with the moon jellies in Palau.

See the terra-cotta soldiers in Beijing.

Tell Nate I love him.

I looked at that last one for a long time. And then, like a little coward, I deleted it.

CHAPTER NINETEEN

THE NEXT DAY WAS AN IN-SERVICE DAY. NORMALLY, I WOULD have used it to study. I was behind in every subject, and my teachers were starting to notice; I was getting lots of notes on quizzes that said things like *Let's talk* or *Come see me*. I didn't want to talk. I didn't want to go see them. What would I say? "I thought your class was relevant to my future, but as it turns out, I was wrong!" So after I spent the morning adding things to the Mischa Abramavicius Bucket List and watching *Star Wars* (plus two episodes of *Young Justice*), I was on my way to do the most unpleasant task of my life: I was going to tell my mother about Revere.

I could have waited for her to get home, but I thought it might make more sense to tell her in a neutral, semipublic location, where she'd be less likely to melt down. Or, at least if she stopped breathing, it would be easier to find the paramedics.

I was going to tell her. I was going to tell her today. Today would be the day.

Yep, today.

I took the bus to the Metro, and the Metro into Arlington, never mind that it cost me almost eight dollars one way. I swear, DC must have the only public transit system in the world built exclusively for rich people. After I got off the train, I left the station and turned my toes in the direction of my mother's office, which was five blocks away.

My steps started out confident. Measured. Even.

I was going to come clean. I wouldn't have to lie anymore. But.

Here's the thing that kept ringing inside my brain, every third step. *This isn't my fault.*

It isn't my fault.

It isn't my fault.

On the third block, there was a street preacher.

Arlington isn't exactly the kind of place where one normally finds street preachers. Unless maybe they're ironic street preachers. Maybe that's what this was. An ironic mission. I braced myself to hear about Jesus's ambivalence.

"You have to be accountable!" he said to me as I approached, because I was too lazy to cross the street like everyone else. "Accountability is the cornerstone of a civil society!"

This was a little odd, coming from a street preacher. He had a short beard and was wearing a light blue button-down shirt. He was a little better dressed than you might expect.

"People need to take responsibility for their actions!" he cried.

I stopped just past him and turned around. "Accountability?"

He glanced at me and frowned.

"Accountability means owning your screw-ups," I said. "Accountability's good."

He looked a little uncomfortable. "Right."

"So what about when you have to own up to something you didn't do?"

"Hang on," he said, touching the side of his face. "To be clear, what are we talking about here?"

"That doesn't matter. Just, is it right or wrong to take the consequences for someone else?"

"Well, wrong. Usually."

"Usually?"

"Nothing's absolute."

"Ugh," I said. "That's not even an answer."

He sighed and looked down at his shoes. He looked kind of familiar. Or maybe it was the voice. I'm usually better at remembering voices than faces. I'm not really sure why that is.

He was looking at me, too. He said, "Have we met somewhere before?"

I was pretty sure we hadn't, because I don't usually talk to street preachers. "I don't think so?"

He snapped his fingers and pointed at me. "Debra Miller's seder. You were there two years in a row. You're Nate's friend."

The truth is I go to the Millers' seder every year; Mom's agnostic and doesn't really go in for that kind of thing, so if I want my parsley-and-salt-water fix, I have to get it elsewhere. I scanned his face: dark brown hair, blue eyes, dark brown beard. Wait. The beard. *"Rabbi Perez?"*

"Actually, it's just Doug now," he said, which was when I remembered why he'd stopped coming to Debra Miller's seders: he'd quit. Or retired, I guess. His contract came up for renewal, and he just walked away.

"You preach on the street now?" I said incredulously. "I mean, no offense."

He laughed, hard. "What?"

"You were preaching! On the street! About accountability!"

He laughed some more. Then he took a Bluetooth earpiece out of his ear. "I run the bakery across the street," he said. "One of the managers forgot to order coffee and tried to blame somebody else."

I put my hand over my eyes.

"Listen," he said. "Do you want a donut? You seem like you could use a donut."

I wasn't especially hungry, but I also wasn't quite ready to meet my maker yet (by that I meant my mother). So I said, "Sure, I'll eat a donut."

I followed Rabbi Doug into the bakery, which was called Tom Bombadil's. To the women behind the counter, Doug said, "Hey, gimme a chocolate glazed. And she'll have . . ." He looked at me with his eyebrows raised.

"Uh," I said. "Maple, I guess."

"Maple," he repeated.

I sat down at the table in front of the window, and one of the women dumped a maple-iced donut in front of me on a piece of waxed paper.

"So how are the Millers?" he asked. He mimed someone swinging a baseball bat. "They're still obsessed with the—"

"The softball, yeah," I said. "Yeah, Rachel's still playing softball. Nate's going to Emory. They're good."

"Emory," he said, nodding approvingly.

"Yeah. Um, so, if you don't mind my asking, why did you quit? Not that this"—I looked around the bakery—"doesn't look great and everything, but . . ."

He had the expression of a man who'd had this conversation way too many times already. I said, "Actually, never mind."

"No, no," he said. "It's okay. Being a rabbi was just a bad fit. I wasn't happy. So I couldn't make anyone else happy, either."

"So now you make people happy by selling them donuts."

He smiled. "There you go. So. I believe you wanted to discuss accountability."

"Oh. No. I don't want to dump my problems on you."

"It's okay," he said. "It seems to be an important subject for you."

I nodded and took a bite of my donut. It was pretty good. Maple-y. I like maple. "You really think accountability's the cornerstone of a civil society?"

Doug took a bite of his chocolate glazed, which left little icing crumbs in his beard. "Did I say that? Yeah, well. It's certainly something we all struggle with, isn't it?"

I shrugged. "I guess nobody likes getting in trouble," I said.

"Well," he said. "I think it's more than that. People aren't always accountable to themselves, either, you know? They have this fragile, ah, what's the word? A fragile self-narrative. Where they imagine themselves as the hero. Of everything, pretty much. But you know how many people are really the hero?"

I shook my head.

"Not many. Not many. But no one wants to be confronted with that, right? You're just a regular schmo who screws up? It's painful. People like to avoid pain." He called to the counter, "Can I get a coffee over here?"

"We ran out of regular an hour ago!"

"Blech. I'll take the decaf, that's fine."

I mulled it over. It wasn't that what he was saying was wrong, exactly; it just didn't apply to me. Except for one thing: I was avoiding telling my mother the truth because I knew telling her would be painful. For both of us. And again, it wasn't my fault.

One of the counter ladies brought him a paper cup of coffee. "So," he said to me, after he'd stirred in a packet of fake sugar, "why are you so interested in the subject?"

I decided I had nothing to lose by telling my life story to a random ex-rabbi and seller of donuts. Maybe this is why Nate likes going to therapy; you get to spill your guts and it doesn't really matter if the other person still likes you afterward. I said, "I may have let my mother think I got into a college I didn't actually get into."

"You may have," he said. "Interesting. And why did you do that?"

I scowled at the table. "It seemed like the best option at the time. Can I get a coffee, too?"

"Ask at the counter," he said. "The best option, or the easiest?"

I got up and went to the counter, where the woman handed me a cup of coffee and pointed me toward the milk and sugar. "Take your pick," I said as I doctored my coffee. "But it's not really the point right now. She thinks it, and I have to make her unthink it."

"So what's keeping you from just telling her the truth? You think she'll be disappointed?"

I sat back down at the table. "It's a little worse than that," I breathed. "I didn't get in anywhere else, either."

"Oh," he said. "Well, shoot."

"It wasn't my fault!"

He gave me a look that said, *Sure, kid.* "Okay. So . . . what? You bungled your SATs?"

"No. Just take my word for it. Somehow my applications got messed up, and the result was I didn't get in anywhere."

"Your applications."

"Yes."

"Got messed up."

"Yes."

"You know," he said, "there's this river in Egypt—"

"I am not in denial!"

"Okay," he said soothingly. "Okay." He puffed up his cheeks and blew out a breath. "It's just. Just."

"You don't believe me," I said.

"Well . . ."

"This won't work if you don't believe me," I said. "Take my word for it. It wasn't my fault."

He frowned. "What was your name again?"

"Mischa."

"Right," he said. "Mischa. So weren't we just talking about accountability?"

"Yes," I said. "And this is why. If I act like it's my fault, then I'm covering for the person who actually screwed me over."

"And that person is . . . who?"

"That's the problem. I don't know."

He chewed his donut for a while. "This is quite a situation. Do you . . . Forgive me, but do you often feel that other people are trying to 'screw you over,' as you put it?"

I narrowed my eyes. "No. Actually. Take my word for it; I'm not paranoid."

"Okay," he said. "So you're not paranoid." He took a long

drink of coffee, probably because he didn't know what else to say.

"So what do I tell my mother?"

He crossed his arms and nodded thoughtfully. "What do you think you should tell her?"

"If I knew that, I wouldn't be asking you in the first place!"

He sighed. "If you told your mother what you told me, how do you think she'd react?"

I shoved my coffee away. "She wouldn't believe me, either." I pushed my chair back and got up. "This has been super helpful, thank you."

"Just wait," he said. "Listen. Just tell her the truth. You didn't get in, period, full stop."

"But she'll want to know why!"

"Tell her you don't know why. What are you going to say? The boogeyman kept you out of college?"

God, coming out of his mouth, it did sound incredibly stupid. If I hadn't seen the transcript with my own eyes, I wouldn't have believed it, either. No one was going to believe me, because the whole situation was unbelievable. I imagined my mother's face turning some unnameable shade of purple as I told her the dog ate my transcript.

"You're going to have to tell her sometime," he said. "Just come out and say it. 'Mom, I love you, but I didn't get into Cornell.' Was it Cornell?"

"No."

"Well, where was it?"

"Revere," I said. "Paul Revere."

"Oh my."

"Uh-huh."

"You know, though," he said. "There are other schools. You could apply someplace else. There are always other options."

"Yeah." I sighed, not bothering to explain why, in fact, there were no other options.

As a final offering, Rabbi Doug gave me a box of donuts to take to my mother's office. "You know," he said. "The first part of being accountable is admitting the truth to yourself."

"Yeah," I said, taking the donuts, because I needed whatever help I could get. "I'll keep that in mind."

I walked the rest of the way with my giant box, like a prisoner going to the gallows. With donuts. I pulled a powdered sugar out of the box and ate it while I walked.

When I got there, Margaret, the secretary, jumped up to greet me. "Mischa!" she said. "Well, this is a surprise."

"Yeah," I said. "Hi. Is my mom here?"

"She's in the conference room," she said. "But you can go on in. I'm sure everyone would be glad to see you."

"Oh, no," I said. "No, no. I'll just wait. Why don't I sit at her desk until she's done?"

"No, no," she said, beckoning me onward. "Just go ahead."

"But—"

She pulled open the conference room door. "Norah," she said. "Look who's here!" And then she shoved me inside.

"Mischa!" my mom called. "What are you doing here?"

My mother was at the oval conference table with her boss and about six of her coworkers, people I'd known since I was in diapers. They stared at me in surprise, like I was some rando who just crashed their meeting. Which I was.

"I brought donuts," I said weakly. "Surprise."

"Oh, wonderful," my mother's boss said, rising to her feet and reaching out for the box, which I gave her without protest. "We were about to take a break anyway."

"Lucky timing," I croaked.

I fell into a chair next to my mother while everyone fell on my donuts like ravenous beasts, or like underfed pro bono lawyers. "Mom," I said quietly. "I really need to talk to you in—"

"So, Mischa," my mother's boss said. "Congratulations about Revere. You know, I've been reading up on it more. They really do have a great internship program."

"Yeah," I said. "I've heard that." My mom squeezed my hand under the table.

"So I've been talking to their career-services office about setting up a program here for some of their students."

"An internship program?"

"Yes! Give the prelaw students some experience. What do you think?"

"I. Uh. So. At Revere?"

"Right! Your mother volunteered to coordinate it on our end."

"She did?"

"She's so proud of you. You must know that. Anyway, we'd love to have you here. It's great experience."

I said, "Uhhhhhhhhh."

"We're embarrassing her," someone said.

"Ha ha ha," I said. "Ha."

"Mischa?" my mom said.

"I LOVE DONUTS!" I said, reaching for another one and shoving half of it in my mouth, while my stomach reminded me that three donuts in ten minutes was really a lot of donuts. I choked it down anyway.

"We're also thinking of endowing a small scholarship there," my mother's boss went on. "For students interested in social-justice law. Five hundred a year, so nothing huge. We're talking about naming it after you and your mom. The Abramavicius Award."

I grabbed another donut. "That's. Wow. That's. Something," I said. "Wow."

My mom said, "Mischa?"

Four donuts in ten minutes was really, *really* a lot of donuts. "I think I need some water," I said.

"I'll get you some from the kitchen," my mom said.

"I'll go with you," I said.

In the tiny Legal Helpline kitchenette, my mother got me a mug of water from the sink. I took a long drink, which really did not make my stomach feel any better, and stared at the mug. On the side was an image of a man on horseback, carrying a lantern.

"Oh, no," I said.

"I just got that one," she said. "It's part of a set." She turned the mug in my hands so I could see that the other side said PAUL REVERE CLASS OF 2022.

"I should get going," I said.

"But," she said.

"I just came to give you the donuts. As a thank-you. To everyone. For the gift card."

"Okay. How are you getting home?"

"Metro," I said.

"If you stay another two hours, I can drive you. You can sit at Eleanor's desk. She's out today."

"No," I said. "I should be getting home. I just. Say bye to everyone. Okay? Thanks. Yeah."

On my way down the street, I thought: *I am going to vomit.* And then I thought: *I am really going to vomit.* And then: I vomited. Onto a shrubbery. It was an unkind thing to do to a shrubbery. I felt really guilty about it. So, so guilty.

Afterward, I wandered back into Tom Bombadil's, because my stomach did not feel equal to the pressures of mass transit. Doug was behind the counter, yelling at people about lumpy glaze. "Hey," he said. "How did it go?"

"I'm going to sit here," I said, pointing at a chair. "And then I'm going to leave."

"Whoa," he said. "What happened?"

"Give me a ginger ale," I said.

He filled up a cup from the dispenser and set it in front of me. "Do you want to talk?" he said.

"No."

"Do you want another donut?"

"Doug," I said. "I never want to see another donut again as long as I live."

CHAPTER TWENTY

THAT WEEKEND, I CONSIDERED RUNNING AWAY FROM HOME. The only hitch was that I had nowhere to go and nothing to do when I got there. I was too uncoordinated to run away and join the army—I'd probably shoot myself in the foot the first day. I had almost no money saved up. I had no useful job skills, and my only work history consisted of a lot of babysitting and three summers checking people in at the front desk of the Y.

I was like Robbie the robot vacuum. We both had a very specific skill set. (Robbie could suck up dirt. I could suck up to teachers.) Beyond that? We could do nothing.

I woke up on Sunday morning bizarrely early because someone had texted me and I'd forgotten to put my phone in airplane mode before I'd gone to sleep. It was from Leo Michaels, of French club fame.

I was really starting to dislike him.

The text said, *Can you pick up the madeleines for the meeting this afternoon?*

You aren't seriously texting me at—I checked the time—*6am about this.*

Sorry, he said. *Didn't realize how early it was. I just got back from a run. So can you?*

I'd forgotten that we were meeting at Leo's that afternoon. I rubbed grit out of my eyes and stared up at my ceiling. I did not want to pick up madeleines, and I did not want to spend my afternoon in a French club meeting. I said, *Sorry, I'm sick. I can't make it.*

We're supposed to be getting ready for the summer abroad fair, and you already missed the last two meetings, he said. *Can I drop off some of these posters so you can work on them?*

I really can't.

Mischa, unless you are literally dying, you have to do this.

No, I thought, *in fact I don't have to do this.* I typed, *I think it might be mono. It's probably contagious.*

Fine. I'll just leave them on your porch.

I tossed my phone to the foot of the bed and fell back against my pillow. I felt a little bad about missing another meeting, but not bad enough to actually go. The longer I thought about it, the less bad I felt. What did they need me for? I was supposed to be making posters about three different summer programs, in Paris, Toulouse, and Grenoble. I'd never been to any of those places. It was ridiculous. The whole thing was ridiculous.

My phone was buzzing again, so I picked it up and looked at it. Leo was saying, *What's your address again?*

I couldn't help it. I texted, *818 Fraser Ave, Great Falls,* which is not my address. It's Meredith Dorsay's address. *Make sure you come right now, and knock really loud or I might not hear you.*

I would pay for that, I knew, in a bunch of different ways. Maybe I could blame it on the mono. I was delirious.

I decided to get up.

My morning ritual, ever since I'd gotten my rejections, was to start the day by probing the spot in my brain that kept the information about my college-less future. *I am not going to college,* I reminded myself. *I can't go to college, because my transcript is a mess, and my letters of recommendation are worse. There is nothing I can do about any of these things.*

And I waited for that horrible pang of despair. But this time it didn't come.

I probed some more: *All my hard work has been for nothing. Soon, I really will have to tell my mother. Everyone in my life will know.* I poked a little harder: *I am a complete, unmitigated failure.*

But I felt . . . nothing. Because one other thought had crept in, perhaps part of some self-preservation instinct that wouldn't let me wade too long through the pits of despair, and it was this: *If I have nothing left, then I have nothing to lose.*

Now that made me feel something. A little tingle, somewhere in the vicinity of my heart or my lungs, deep in my chest. I knew it wasn't technically true: I still had some things—my health (for the moment, at least), my mom, a place to live, and the rest of the basics. But all the things I'd been working my butt off for, those were all gone, and if those things were gone, there was really no point in continuing to work for them, which meant I could essentially do whatever I wanted. Here was my new truth: I was no longer Mischa with ten million things to do, Mischa the hardworking, Mischa the perfect. I was Mischa the untouchable. Mischa the underdog. Mischa, destroyer of worlds.

That last one may have gone too far, but only just.

I sat up in my bed. I could walk away from Blanchard and never come back, and that idea certainly had its appeal. More reasonably, I could stick around just long enough to get my diploma and then sign up for the summer term at the local community college.

But that seemed too logical. Too much like the desperate next step of Mischa the perfect, and being Mischa the perfect had proved to be both unsatisfying and, ultimately, a waste of time. I looked at my phone. It was six in the morning on a Sunday, not a normal time for me to be up, and I knew my mother would be asleep for at least another four hours. I pulled the Mischa Abramavicius Bucket List back up. But the only thing I really wanted to do was the thing I'd been too chicken to write down in the first place.

I got up, brushed my teeth, and put my shoes on. I got in the car, and I drove away.

Not *away* away. I knew where I was going.

I parked in Nate's driveway; his parents had left the garage door open in their hurry to leave for whatever sports thing Nate's sister had that day. I gently knocked on the front door, but there was no answer. Of course there was no answer. Nate didn't get up at seven on a Sunday for anything. I mashed my face against the glass inset in the door, and the catch popped open—his parents must not have shut it all the way when they left. I gave it an experimental push, and the door swung open the rest of the way, leaving me to stare at the Millers' slate entryway.

I don't normally go into people's houses uninvited. It's rude and super creepy. But Nate wasn't the type to care, and anyway, I was just going to sit in the kitchen and wait for him to wake up. I'd make myself a pot of coffee. I'd find something to read.

I'd just just finished pouring my first cup of coffee when I heard a noise from the living room, and my heart plummeted because maybe not everyone in the house was gone except Nate. Maybe his dad was home sick, and I wasn't exactly sure how to explain why I was in his kitchen, making coffee in my pajamas. Why hadn't I gotten dressed?

Then I remembered the worst thing Nate's dad could do was toss me out of the house. I felt a little bubble of laughter come up my throat, and I stuffed my fist in front of my mouth to stop it. I heard the noise again; it was coming from the living room. It was a faint snore.

I stepped into the doorway and saw that Nate had fallen asleep on the couch.

He had one arm propped behind his head, and I guess he'd gotten hot in the night because his T-shirt was in a ball on the floor. His mouth was open, just barely, and every third or fourth breath came out like a sigh. His Zen Buddhism book was on top of his chest, with Post-its sticking out from its pages; also, one of them was stuck to his shoulder.

Now even in my not-perfect state, I knew that watching someone sleep is, like, number one on the list of creepy stalker behaviors, but I didn't think going back into the kitchen felt quite right, either. So I sat down on the arm of the couch by his feet, and I touched his wrist and said, "Nate."

He sucked in a breath and opened his eyes. "Mischa?" he said in this groggy, croaky voice that was probably the sexiest thing I'd ever heard. He rubbed sleep out of his eyes and sat up against the arm on the other side, setting his book down on the floor.

"I'm sorry," I said. "The door was open and . . ." I shrugged and plucked the Post-it off his shoulder. "I made coffee."

He left off rubbing his eyes and looked at me. "What happened to your hair?" he asked, which was when I realized that I'd forgotten to brush it on my way out the door. I did my best to smooth it out with my hands.

"Did you have a fight with your mom? Did you tell her?" He sat up a little more. "Are you having a nervous breakdown? Because if you are, it's okay. I know all about those."

"No," I said. "None of that. I just . . ."

"You just . . . ," he prompted. "You wanted my mother's expensive imported Kenyan coffee?" He gave a lopsided smile. "You wanted to catch me naked and asleep?"

I looked down at the blanket that was tangled around his hips. "You aren't—"

"Nude on my mother's Bauhaus sofa? No." He let the blanket fall enough for me to see the waistband of his boxers. "Sorry to disappoint."

I looked away, but I knew I was blushing.

"So you aren't warring with your mother, in the throes of a psychological meltdown, or hoping to see me without my pants. Give me that coffee." I handed over the cup I'd made myself and he took a sip and then made a face because I take three sugars and he only takes one. "Someday you'll drink your coffee like a grown-up." He drank another sip and shook his head.

"You could make your own, you know."

"Too much trouble. Anyway, I was just shocked awake by

a girl who broke into my house to ogle me while I slept. I'm traumatized."

I got up from the arm of the couch. "You want me to leave. I'm sorry."

"No," he said, setting the cup on the coffee table. "I don't want you to leave. I'm babbling because I'm half-asleep and you're in your pajamas and I figure if I keep talking long enough, at some point you'll interrupt me to tell me why you're here."

I fiddled with the ends of my unbrushed hair. Perfect Mischa would have had a lie close at hand. *I needed some government notes.* Or maybe: *I was in the neighborhood visiting someone else, and I wanted to pick up that book I loaned you last week.* But not-perfect Mischa said, "I woke up this morning and realized I could do whatever I wanted."

"You wanted to hang out at my house at seven in the morning?"

I picked up the coffee again. Maybe he was right. Maybe it was too sweet. "I wanted to tell you . . ." I faltered again.

"Should I put my shirt on for this? This sounds serious."

I growled because I didn't know what to say. Perfect Mischa would have had a quotation handy. Something poetic. Something romantic. Neruda, or Tennyson. Or at least I would have timed the moment better. I would have been wearing deodorant, for one thing. But I was not going to chicken out and do my little "there's someone I like" dance again. If he said no, he said no, but I was not going to die from it. The world would keep going around the sun. I would be sad, and then I would get over it. Apparently, getting over things was something I could do. I screwed my eyes shut and said, "I am in love with you. I have been in love with you for a long time, actually, and I didn't want to say it and mess things up, but now everything's so messed up anyway, so I'm saying it. I love you. I love you. I love—*oof*."

And I was cut off by the force of his mouth meeting mine. My eyes popped open, and his were staring back at me, our lips in this awkward locked position, my mouth half-open because I'd been talking and his lips sort of between mine and against my teeth.

I'd just bared my heart. And now we were staring at each other like a pair of goldfish, his lips puckered, my cheeks puffed out. I started to laugh, and he leaned away and wiped his mouth on the back of his hand. "That was terrible," he said, but when I opened my mouth to reply somehow, he said, "Just, shh."

I closed my mouth. He took the coffee out of my hands and put it back on the table. And then he kissed me for real.

He leaned in so slowly I had to reach for him, and then his lips were so, so soft, and then I tried to pull him closer by his shirt, and then I remembered he wasn't wearing one and I was just running my hands over his bare skin, which was smooth and warm. "Say it again," he whispered between kisses. "Please."

"I love you," I said, which earned me two arms around my back, pulling me closer. "I love you," I said again, and he lay down again, pulling me with him, tucked in between his body and the back of the couch. "I love you," I said, and his lips moved to my neck, whispering, "Yes, yes, yes."

It was sometime later that we finally came up for air. My lips were tingling, and his hair stuck straight up from my fingers running through it.

I felt a little weird then, because he hadn't exactly said anything back. Maybe he made out with everyone who said they loved him, because he was unfailingly polite that way. Or maybe he was just a horndog.

He gave me a lazy smile and said, "So, for a long time, huh?"

I nodded. We were both under the blanket, and I picked at the edge.

"How long is that, exactly? Since last week? Last month?"

"Since always," I said. "I've loved you since always."

"Hmm," he said, running a finger along the edge of my jaw. "Not since always. I would have known that."

"Why would I lie?"

"You don't even remember. Do you?"

"Remember what?"

"I kissed you," he said. "The third week I knew you, I kissed you."

"You never kissed me!"

He laughed. "See? You don't even remember. We were watching a Ray Harryhausen marathon on TV, and halfway through *Sinbad and the Eye of the Tiger* I kissed you, and you patted me on the shoulder and went to make more popcorn."

I blinked a few times. I remembered that day. But it was right when I'd first met him, and he'd been dating Pete Neilson and just broken up a few days before.

"I thought you were gay," I admitted. "Anyway, it was on the cheek! It didn't count."

"I was fourteen," he said, looking me dead in the eyes. "It counted."

I touched the cheek in question, as if I could still feel his kiss there, like it'd been waiting all this time. I'd lain in my bed that night, touching it just like this and wishing it had been real somehow. But I'd dismissed it, because he'd been with a guy, and I hadn't understood what that meant.

"You never said anything," I said. "Not a word."

"I made a move. You turned me down." He shrugged. "I don't force my attentions on people who don't want them."

"But I *did* want them. I tried to tell you. I told you there was someone I liked."

"You never said that was *me,*" he said.

"You're always asking people out. I thought if you wanted things to go that way—"

He laced his fingers through mine. "You were always talking about other guys. You spent all of sophomore year talking about Jim's *hair.*"

"I was trying to get over you," I said.

"Well," he said. "What a lot of time we've wasted. Hang on. I'm still wasting it." He sat up, pulling me with him, and put a hand on either side of my face. "I love you," he said. "Sorry for not saying it earlier."

I kissed him hard enough to knock us both off the couch.

CHAPTER TWENTY-ONE

AFTER A COUPLE OF HOURS ON THE COUCH, MY MOUTH WAS feeling pleasantly numb. I leaned away for a little air. "Hi," I said.

"Hi."

He kissed me again. And then we jumped because there was this loud beeping followed by the roar of a vacuum as Robbie the robot unhooked himself from his charging station and started making his rounds of the room.

Nate leaned his forehead against mine, and we laughed. "I hate that thing," he admitted.

"You could just vacuum yourself."

"Let's not get carried away."

"Could you turn it off?"

"I don't actually know how. It's on some kind of pro-grammed schedule."

Robbie bumped my foot, which I lifted off the floor. "Could you just move it to another room?"

Nate smirked. "Hang on." He scooped up Robbie—still vacuuming—shoved him into the bathroom, and closed the door.

"Will he freak out that he can't get back out again?"

"It's a vacuum, Mischa, not a dog."

My stomach started to growl.

"Coffee wasn't enough, huh?" he asked.

"I guess not. Are you hungry?"

"Starving," he said. "I really want sushi. Is that weird?"

"It's not weird, but I'm not sure where we're going to find a Japanese place open at ten in the morning."

"I think that conveyor-belt sushi place over in Fairfax opens at eleven." We'd been under the blanket, and he pushed it off himself and got up, running a hand through his hair. "By the time I get dressed and we drive over there, it'll probably be open."

I sat up. "I don't know," I said. "Sushi's kind of . . ."

"Delicious?"

"Expensive."

"Oh, I'm totally buying. I've got some pre-Emory money from Grandma burning a hole in my pocket."

"Pre-Emory money?"

"I don't know. She sends me a check; I don't ask questions."

"I'm in my pajamas," I reminded him.

"You can borrow something of Rachel's," he said. "You're about the same size."

"I'm like three inches taller than her. Anyway, she'll kill me!"

"She has so many clothes, she won't even notice."

···

I felt kind of bad poking through Rachel Miller's closet un-invited, but I also really didn't want to go for sushi in my jam-mies. "There's a lot of glitter in here," I called to Nate, who was brushing his teeth in the bathroom. I pulled off my paja-mas and tried to put some little tank top on. It wouldn't even reach my belly button.

"Aim for the back," he said. "That'll be the stuff my mom buys her that she never wears."

I scrounged around and pulled out a blue dress and held it up to myself.

Definitely not my size. I checked the label. Not going to happen.

"Nate," I said. "I can't wear these."

He came in through the doorway. "Maybe I can help you find—oh."

I crossed my arms in front of my bra.

"Hi," he said.

"Hi."

"Hi."

He coughed and turned around to face the wall. "You are half-naked in my little sister's bedroom."

"Hey," I said. "There's a subject for next Thursday's ther-apy session."

He said, "No, no. It's fine. This is not at all awkward and totally my fault."

"I could wear something of your mom's, maybe."

"Okay, now you're not helping."

"I have to wear something, Nate."

"Maybe I have something." He went into his room and

came back with a blue T-shirt and a pair of shorts. "My grandma just sent me the shirt, and the shorts have a drawstring."

It was, of course, an Emory T-shirt. I slipped it on over my head. The shorts were kind of a weird length, but they fit well enough. It was strange wearing Nate's clothes, like, oddly intimate in some way. They smelled like Nate's laundry detergent. I felt a little like he was hugging me. "Do I look okay?" I asked.

"You look perfect," he said.

I felt myself blush, just a little.

He said, "Seriously, though, you are going to brush your hair, right?"

Kurenai Sushi is one of those places where there's a big conveyor belt and the food goes around on little plates—color coded by price—and you have to grab it as it goes by. I'm not sure why it's so much fun to catch your food like that; maybe it harkens back to our hunter-gatherer days, I don't know. But every time I grabbed a California roll as it whizzed past, I felt a little jolt of victory.

"Hey!" I said. "Tempura!" I grabbed the plate and set it in front of me on the shiny red table. "And I'm wearing your drawstring shorts, so, like, I can pretty much eat forever."

Nate had given up on his spicy tuna and was smiling at me.

"What?" I said.

"Nothing," he said. "I'm just glad you're happy."

"I am," I said. "I am happy."

He came around to my side of the booth and slid in next to me. "I have a thought," he said softly into my ear.

"Is it a good one?"

"It's a very good one. If I were Peter Pan, I could fly with this thought. You want me to share it with you?"

"Pixie dust," I said, stuffing tempura into my mouth. "You need a happy thought and pixie dust."

"Not this time," he said. He pulled me a little closer and whispered into my ear, "Come to Atlanta with me."

I jerked away. "What?"

"Come to Atlanta with me. You don't have to go to community college here. You can go there. And maybe transfer after a year."

"But. Where will I live?"

"In an apartment. With me."

I dropped one of my chopsticks. "And we will pay for this apartment how?"

He shrugged.

"You think your parents are going to pay for it?" I asked.

"They were going to have to pay for the dorm room."

"I don't know . . ."

"Just think about it. We'll go to class. We'll come home. We'll eat tempura."

"I'll have to have a job," I said. "To pay for the tempura. And the classes. And my half of the apartment."

He shrugged, like this was no big deal, to move to Atlanta and get a job. "So you'll get a job."

I put my chopsticks down and pressed my face into his chest. "You'll be embarrassed of me."

"What?"

"You'll be at Emory all day, and then come home to your loser girlfriend."

"You're not—"

"I am. I am, Nate. If you liked me before, it's because of the person I was. And I'm not that person anymore."

"What, because you're not going to a fancy college? I don't care about any of that," he said in my ear. "I never cared."

I closed my eyes tightly, wishing it were true, but not understanding how he couldn't care. "Come on," I said.

He ran his nose along the edge of my jaw, and my breath hitched. "You think I care what college you're going to? You think that's all you're worth to me? That has nothing to do with who you are."

"It has everything to do with who I am! It's who I chose to be."

"Mischa—"

"No, listen."

I stopped to watch a dragon roll go by. I didn't know how to explain this. It barely even made sense to me anymore. I tried to remember what it had been like to be Mischa a few weeks ago, before I started waking up and doing the "I'm not going to college" mantra.

"Here's the thing," I said. "I used to get up every morning knowing exactly who I was and what I had to do." I waited for him to interrupt me, but he just looked at me expectantly. "I went after every brass ring someone put in front of me. And I was really, really good at that. And now that's over. I have no idea who I am now."

"Mischa," he said. "You are brilliant and funny and sexy as hell. And you're a really great friend. And you're all those things no matter what."

"I don't know," I said. "I'm not the same. I don't feel the same."

"Hey," he said. "That's okay, though. Changing is okay."

"I just wish . . ."

"What do you wish?"

"I don't even know. I wish this never happened? I wish I'd known it was going to happen, so I could've done things differently."

"What would you have done differently?"

"I would have had fun," I admitted. "More fun, I guess. I wouldn't have joined twenty clubs I don't care about and studied every minute."

"Fun," he said. "Well, that's easy enough. Let's have fun."

"What do you mean?"

"Tomorrow. Let's skip school. You and me. And we'll do whatever you want. Anything. All day, it's your party."

I closed my eyes. Suddenly everything on the Mischa Abramavicius Bucket List looked kind of stupid and out of my reach. Swimming with moon jellies in Palau? How was I supposed to get there? "I don't even know what I'd pick," I said.

He gave me a squeeze. "I guess that's your homework tonight."

CHAPTER TWENTY-TWO

NATE GOT TO MY HOUSE AT SIX O'CLOCK THE NEXT MORNING, which I'm pretty sure is the earliest he's ever been up. I called the school, did my best Norah Abramavicius impression, and told them I thought I had mono. Then I left my mom a note telling her I'd gotten a ride to school from Nate, climbed into Nate's car, and drove away.

We pulled into the nearest Starbucks drive-thru a few minutes later, where Nate ordered a cappuccino and I got a hot chocolate with a shot of espresso.

"So," he said while we were stopped in the line. "What's on the agenda?"

I handed him my phone. I'd gone through the Mischa Abramavicius Bucket List and picked out the local highlights and put them in a separate memo.

"This is some list," he said, frowning.

"It was everything I could think of within driving distance."

"Mischa," he said. "I think you're missing the point of this exercise."

"All those things are fun!"

"Individually, yes, but all together? It's like a marathon." He handed me back my phone. "You don't always have to be an overachiever."

I looked down at the screen. "I don't know what to cut," I said sadly.

"Tea at the Ritz?"

"I've always wanted to go," I said. "But I could never justify spending the money."

"Kayaking the Shenandoah? How are those things supposed to go together?"

"I have varied interests!"

He pulled through to the window and picked up our drinks, stuffing a dollar into the tip jar. "You don't have to check things off a list," he said as he pulled into an empty space and lifted the lid of his cup; I could see they'd forgotten the nutmeg, but he didn't complain about it. "Just pick one thing. What's your fantasy day? If you had all the time and money in the world?"

"I don't know. I don't know how to pick."

"Mischa," he wheedled. He took my cup out of my hand and held it out of my reach.

"Give me back my hot chocolate!"

"Just answer the question!"

"Fine! I want to put on an Alexander McQueen evening gown with an asymmetric hem and go to the opera and sit next to Ruth Bader Ginsburg. I want her to drop her purse, and I'll pick it up, and she'll say, 'Young lady, no one has ever picked up a purse in such a dashing and considerate way, why don't you come back with me to my house for hot fudge sundaes, and also I shall give you an internship and write you a letter of recommendation on the back of this copy of the Constitution that I carry around with me, and also your earrings are heaven.'"

Nate stared at me with an expression of alarm. "That's a very specific fantasy."

"You asked."

He laughed and gave me my drink back. I was making him nervous, but I wasn't sure why. Maybe he was afraid I really was about to have a breakdown. He said, "Why stop there? Maybe the two of you could go skydiving together. I bet RBG loves extreme sports. I mean, just look at her."

I felt my grin spreading across my face. "Oh my God," I said. "Nate. Skydiving."

"I was kidding," he said. "I don't think Ruth is really into extreme sports. Like, at all."

"Not her. Us."

"Skydiving? You're not serious," he said. "Ha ha."

"I'm serious," I said, pointing at my eyes. "This is my serious face."

He waved me off. "How about this: let's go to Paris."

"I don't have a passport."

"Fine. New York, then."

"I don't want to go to New York. I want to jump out of an airplane."

"And what, precisely, do you think that will do for you?"

I'd read about skydiving once. It takes approximately five

minutes to hit the ground: about thirty seconds of free fall and then another four minutes of floating once your parachute opens. I said, "I'll get to fly."

I pulled out my phone and started googling.

"Mischa," he said. "You don't have to do this."

"I know I don't. Oh! There's a Groupon."

"You are not going skydiving with a Groupon. That's not a good idea."

"It's 30% off!" I said, bookmarking the site.

"There are some things worth paying full price for," he said, pulling the phone out of my hands. "You don't get a cut-rate brain surgeon. Or jump out of a cut-rate airplane."

"It's fine," I said. "They have three and a half stars on Yelp."

He took me by the shoulders, but before he could say anything, I said, "Please don't ask me not to do this."

"That's a double negative."

"Nate," I said. "Please."

He pulled me into a hug. I said, "You don't have to come."

"Of course I'm coming," he said. "Someone has to drive you. And pick up your remains afterward."

We got to the Loudoun Skydiving Center an hour later, which had last-minute openings since it was Monday. I handed the guy at the front desk my ID, fifty-five dollars of babysitting money left over from spring break, and my phone (so he could scan the Groupon), and then he handed me a clipboard with the world's longest release form.

I read the list of various things the LSC would not be legally responsible for: death, dismemberment, paralysis. Oddly enough, there was a line in there that they were not responsible for any bad outcomes due to "malicious intent."

"What does that mean?" I asked the desk guy. "Like, if someone pushes me out of the plane without a parachute?"

"It's just a standard disclaimer."

"Does that often come up? Malicious intent?"

"We've never had anyone die," he said. "Mostly the worst that happens is some puking. Did you bring a change of clothes?"

"Uh," I said. "No."

"Try not to puke," Nate said.

"You too," I answered.

"Oh, no," he said. "I'm here. I'm being supportive. If you puke on yourself, I'll get you some paper towels. If you become dismembered, I'll find your missing limbs and help you get them reattached. But I am not jumping out of a freaking airplane."

"But—"

"Mischa, my entire sense of well-being is predicated on the fact that I have become very good at enforcing my boundaries. I do not want to jump out of a plane. Therefore, I will not do it."

I smiled, even though I didn't much like the idea of going up in the plane by myself. "Okay," I said.

"Okay," he said.

While we were waiting to watch the safety video, I pulled out my phone, which had six texts from Leo, which I instantly deleted, plus one from Jim, which I kept but didn't read, and one from Emily that said, *Are you really sure you want to give up on this?*

Yes, I answered.

Do you really have mono? she asked.

I'm at the doctor's right now, I said.

No you're not.

A woman walked in from the next room, and the man at the desk handed her the clipboard with my information tacked to it. "Miss Abrama . . . ah . . . ah . . . ," she said, looking over my paperwork.

"Abramavicius," I said. "That's me."

"I'm your partner," she said with a grin.

I'd signed up for the tandem jump because you don't have to do any training. There's just a five-minute safety video, kind of like what you watch before you play laser tag. Then you go up in a plane, someone who knows what they're doing hooks herself up to you, and you get shoved out the door at eight thousand feet. It's basically idiot-proof; you don't even pull your own parachute cord.

My partner was a woman who looked like she was around fifty. Her hair was about a third gray and tied around her head in a braid like Heidi. She had blue eyes and a really bad sunburn.

"Jill Shoenborn," she said, shaking my hand. "I'll be pulling your cord today."

"Nice to meet you," I said.

"Don't worry," she said. "I've never lost anyone yet. You're probably the youngest jumper I've ever had, though. Shouldn't you be at school?"

"Uh," I said. "That's a very long and complicated story."

She chortled. "Of course it is. Just don't tell me, please. If the truancy officer comes poking around, I don't want to have to lie. Anyway. I think you're the last one this morning, so we're going to go watch the safety video; then off we go!"

I followed her into a little dark room, where two men in their forties were clutching each other's hands and looking nauseated.

"You don't have to jump," one of them said to the other.

"I want to," he said. "That was the deal."

"Yeah, but I didn't think you'd really do it."

I went and sat down next to them. Nate, who was not planning on jumping out of anything, hovered by the door.

"Have you done this before?" I asked the first guy, who looked slightly less like he was going to puke.

"Nope," he said. "This is my post-chemo adventure. This one agreed to go with me back when he thought I might die."

"Don't tell her that!" To me, the second guy said, "I never thought he was going to die."

"So why are you jumping?" the first man asked me. "Daredevil? Lost a bet?"

"No," I said. "Nothing like that. It just . . ." I thought about the real reason, because I hadn't really considered it too carefully before.

When I was around ten, I got out of bed one night because I couldn't sleep. I found my mother downstairs watching some special on PBS; I have no idea what it was about, but there were a bunch of skydivers jumping out of a plane holding hands in a ring, and while they fell through the air, Pachelbel's Canon played in the background. They were over the mountains, and you could see this whole landscape beyond them, while they just floated together like a team of synchronized swimmers barreling toward the earth. "Can I do that?" I'd whispered.

My mom had shut off the TV. "Over my dead body," she'd said.

After I'd gone back to bed, I'd thought about those skydivers. What was the air like when you were falling through it so fast? Could you breathe it? Did it have a taste?

I knew there wasn't going to be any stirring classical music playing, but I still wanted to know. And, okay, I also wanted to know what it would feel like to have my mother tell me not to do something and then to do it anyway.

"It seemed like a good idea," I answered. "Also, I had a Groupon."

They chuckled. "And your beau?" Guy One asked, nodding toward Nate. "He's not jumping?"

"He didn't think it seemed like a good idea."

"Sensible kid," Guy Two said.

"I said you didn't have to jump."

"And I said I promised."

Then the front-desk guy came in and started the video, which showed the process and gave some warnings, like don't try to fight off your partner when they're harnessing you in, otherwise you might fall out of the plane without a parachute, and that would be bad. Mostly, it seemed like my job was not to screw things up for my partner, who was the person doing the actual jump.

"So basically," I said to Jill, "you do the work, and I just hang on like a barnacle."

Jill seemed to like that analogy. "Okay, little barnacle," she said, clapping me on the back. "Let's go find our ride."

Nate walked us out on his way to the landing area, which was a field next to the airstrip, where we would land

and then have sandwiches, because our jump fee included lunch.

"I love you," he said fiercely. "Don't get smushed."

"I love you," I said. "Technically, I think I'd get crunched, not smushed. On account of my skeletal structure."

He kissed the spot between my eyebrows. "You say the sweetest things."

"Ah," said Guy One. "Young love."

I huddled next to my fellow jumpers—who turned out to be called Bob and Matt—on the plane. Matt was staring straight ahead with wide-eyed alarm. "I changed my mind," he said. "I'm not this supportive."

I was also feeling, suddenly, like maybe this was not my best idea. The sky was rushing past us in a blur. I looked at Jill and said, "What happens if we don't jump?"

"You'll jump," she said. She was toward the front of the plane, along with Bob's and Matt's co-jumpers, whose names I'd already forgotten. "Everyone always does."

"Not everyone," I said. "There must be some people who chicken out."

"I have a 100% success rate," she said. "Everyone jumps, and everyone lives."

"Lives?" Matt repeated. "As in, does not die? As in, that was a thing we should have talked about before we signed up for this?"

Bob said, "I told you, you don't have to jump!"

"Maybe there's a compromise," Matt said. "Like parasailing. Or we could go jump up and down on a trampoline."

"Barnacle!" Jill called. "We're up first!"

"Okay," I said. "Okay. Okay."

I sat very, very still while she hooked my back to her front. Then they opened the door.

It was suddenly very, very loud and windy, and I was very aware that there was a hole in the plane, and that seemed like a really bad thing.

"I don't know," I said. "I really don't know."

"Sit on the edge here," Jill said. "Then just keep leaning forward until you're out."

"Out?" I repeated. "*Out?*"

She put her mouth right by my ear. "I believe you can do this."

I sat down on the edge and leaned forward just the tiniest amount. I was about to turn around and ask Jill if someone else could go first when she gave me the tiniest little push with her chest. And then I was hurtling face-first toward the earth.

My next thought was something like this: [insert primal scream here]

After that it was more like: *I AM GOING TO DIE.*

And then: *I am going to throw up, and then die.*

And then: *I should probably open my eyes.*

The wind was almost solid against my face, and behind me I could feel Jill's heartbeat hammering against my back. It was like looking out an airplane window, except without the airplane (or the window). Underneath me the ground was cut up into square pastures and blocky forests, with tiny farmhouses in between. The air was cold and moving fast enough that it felt like I was eating it instead of breathing it, like I was moving through frigid water.

Then I felt Jill tap me on the shoulder, which I knew meant

she was going to open the chute. I heard the parachute fly open, and we jerked up into the air, and then we slowed way, way down. The air wasn't as cold. The incredible whooshing sound that filled my head cut off, and it was just silent.

Then I looked out instead of down, and it seemed to me that I could actually see the curvature of the horizon. I thought, *Huh, the world really is round.* And of course it's not like I didn't know that. We all know. We've seen pictures. But somehow seeing it was something different. I was low enough now to see cars on the highway, with little tiny people inside them, driving to and fro, like little ants moving things around. I realized that I, too, am a tiny ant. I live on this marble-shaped planet with seven billion other ants, and every one of us is convinced that our problems, our lives, are somehow eternal and insurmountable, but look! You go up a mile or two, you look out at the horizon, and you can see what all our struggles are worth. They have exactly as much meaning as we give them, and not one bit more.

My tummy fluttered from the height and the fall and the realization that there was no ground underneath me. The soles of my feet tingled like they were missing the feeling of dirt and gravity. I didn't feel like I was flying, not really. What I felt was very small, and very insignificant, and very free. All my problems were down on the ground, and I was up here. And maybe I could leave some part of myself up in the atmosphere, above all my piddling little problems, and it could look down at me from time to time and laugh at my foolish little ant-self.

The ground was starting to draw close, and I remembered that I was supposed to land with loose legs and run, to keep from falling on my face. I bicycled my legs a few steps and fell over with an "oof."

Jill unclipped us, and I sat up next to her.

"So?" she prompted.

But I was looking up at the sky I'd fallen through. Bob and Matt were a few hundred feet up, floating the rest of the way to the ground with their co-jumpers.

"I don't know," I said, because I wasn't sure what to say.

"That's okay," she said. She patted me on the shoulder and went off to help Bob out of his harness because he'd landed and seemed to be tangled up in his ropes.

Matt turned to Bob and said, "Never get cancer again."

Bob said, "I promise," and then they both laughed, because it was such a stupid, ridiculous, heartfelt promise, and they hugged and then went off to the picnic table behind us to drink sparkling cider and eat sandwiches.

From a few feet away a voice said, "It's very blue."

I looked over toward Nate, who lay on the grass nearby and was also looking up at the sky. "How do you feel?" he asked.

"Small," I said. "And big."

It took a long time to drive home from the airstrip. "It's so quiet out here," I said, craning my neck to look out the window at the acres and acres of open space as we drove by.

"I used to go up to camp in Pennsylvania when I was a kid," Nate said. He drove with one hand on the steering wheel and the other resting on my knee, with a kind of casual possessiveness that thrilled me. "It was like this there."

"Was this in middle school?" I asked.

"Elementary," he said. "I stopped going after sixth grade."

"Soccer?"

"Yeah. Oh, and math tutoring." He laughed dryly. "I got a

C– in algebra in seventh grade and had to take it over again in the summer."

"I didn't know that."

"It's not exactly something I brag about."

I leaned back against the door so I could look out the window again. "Nate," I said. "I don't know what I'm going to do."

He smiled at the road. "You can still come with me. I didn't just make that offer because I wanted you to put your tongue in my ear."

"I know you didn't," I said. "It just seems kind of like an act of desperation."

I watched his Adam's apple bob as he swallowed, and then realized that maybe that had been kind of a mean thing to say. "It's not desperate," he said, "to make yourself happy."

"I know that," I said, lacing my fingers through his. "That's not what I meant. It's just, going from being Mischa the student to Mischa the girlfriend doesn't seem like it's going to solve my problem."

"The problem where someone hacked your transcript and screwed you over?"

"Not that problem," I said. "I meant the other problem. Where I've defined my whole life around this one little pinprick of my personality. I need to be more than that. I'm just not sure how."

"Mischa," he said. "You've always been more than a pinprick." He signaled right and started moving over onto the shoulder.

"What are you doing?" I asked.

"Pulling over."

"I figured that part out. What's wrong?"

He pulled the car over and put the hazard lights on. "What's wrong is that I can't kiss you and drive at the same time," he said. "Not without dying, anyway."

He put his arms around me and hauled me into his lap so that I was jammed between his body and the steering wheel, which caused me to honk the horn with my butt. His hands traced up and down my thighs. I said, "You mentioned something about kissing me."

"I did mention that," he said. And then he did.

CHAPTER TWENTY-THREE

WHEN I GOT HOME THAT EVENING, MY MOTHER WAS ANKLE-deep in a bottle of vermouth.

Now, three-dollar-mojito-guy (aka my father) notwithstanding, my mother doesn't drink. That bottle of vermouth has probably been in the pantry since the Clinton administration. She has a glass of champagne every year at the office Christmas party, and a glass of red wine every Valentine's Day (why, I don't know). But beyond that, the only alcohol in the house is used for cooking.

So I was surprised to find that she was actually pretty drunk.

"Mom?" I asked. Which was the shortened version of *Why are you potted at five in the afternoon on a Monday?*

"Mischa," she said. "I thought you were going to Nate's after school."

"I was. I did," I said. "I mean, I was with Nate, but I'm home now."

She set her tumbler of liquor down on the kitchen table, where she had a TV dinner and a notepad and a pen in front of her. Upon closer examination, I saw that she'd written a list of names, marked up with crosshatches and asterisks.

"Are you making a list?" I asked.

"I am making a list."

"Of?"

"Contacts."

"Contacts. Like, men? Like, for a date?"

"No. Not for a date." Her eyes were not entirely focused, like she was half in the room with me and half someplace else. Drunklandia, I guessed. "For a job."

I sat down. "For a job."

"Yes. It seems I have been furloughed."

"Furloughed? That's like when they make you take vacation and then don't pay you for it. Right?"

"That's a furlough," she said. "Ten points for Gryffindor." She finished the rest of her drink.

"But why?"

"The normal reason. Not enough money to pay everyone. So starting next month, everyone has to take five days of unpaid leave every month. Until November."

I sat down very hard. "But that's like a 25% pay cut."

"Fifty points for Gryffindor!"

"Mom. Stop doing that."

"I suppose it could be worse," she said. "It was either this or they fired two people."

"Jesus. What are you going to do?"

"I'm going to apply for another job," she said. "Either another full-time thing or someone who'll let me freelance on top of Legal Helpline to make up the difference."

I picked up the notepad and read down the list of names. It was not a long list. I recognized a few of the entries as people who had started at Legal Helpline and then moved on to bigger, higher-paying jobs.

"What if you can't find anything?" I asked. "Could you . . . I don't know. Borrow money against the house? To last until November?"

"The last thing we need is more debt," she said.

"More debt?" I said, because I didn't realize we had that much. I know she puts stuff on the credit card sometimes, but only when we have an emergency.

"Never mind," she said. "It's fine. It's fine. Everything's fine."

That was two fines too many. "What exactly isn't fine? Like, are we in a bunch of debt here?"

"No," she said. "I said it was fine."

"What aren't you telling me?"

She poured another drink.

"Come on. What is it?"

She said, "I put this year's Blanchard tuition on the credit card."

"You what?"

"I didn't have a choice. We couldn't manage it."

"We managed it before." When she stared into her glass, I said, "We did, didn't we? Manage it?"

She breathed heavily. "They cut back your scholarship. After freshman year."

I sat down in the chair next to her. "I'm confused."

"They're still covering most of it. But the part we have to pay is higher."

"Why didn't you tell me?"

"Tell you what? I wasn't going to pull you out."

"So you've been putting my tuition on the credit card for *three years*?"

"Not all of it. But some of it. Mischa, I didn't have a choice."

Back in AP Econ, Mr. Tanen had told us that compound interest was the most powerful force in the universe. I said, "What's the rate on that card?"

"Seventeen percent."

Holy hell.

I looked into the bottom of my mother's glass, which was now empty again. I picked up the bottle and moved it to the other end of the table. When she gave me an irritated look, I said, "Grandma didn't escape from Communism so you could mess around."

"Very funny," she said. But it wasn't. What Mom was telling me was this: We had a big chunk of debt that was growing bigger by the day. We were going to have to live on 75% of her not-quite-enough salary. And, oh, right! She was expecting to pay tuition bills in a few months. On that point, at least, I could correct her. If only I had the guts.

"Mom," I said slowly. "What if I didn't . . . what if I didn't go to college right away? What if I took a gap year?"

"No." she said. "No, you are not taking a gap year."

I paused. "What if I don't want to go just yet? What if I wanted to work, or travel—"

"*No.*"

"But—"

"No. So help me, we have worked too hard for too long to lose that kind of momentum. It's bad enough that you're . . ."

"It's bad enough that I'm . . . what?" I echoed, knowing perfectly well what she meant.

"Nothing," she said.

"You're a bad liar when you're drunk," I said bitterly.

"It's a global economy, Mischa."

"Would you stop saying that?"

"Oh, I hoped things would be different for you."

"You're ashamed of me."

"I never said that."

"You didn't have to."

"Do you not understand?" she said. "Do you get that this is what it's like for everyone? Why do you think I sent you to Blanchard? So you could find a way out of this! It was our way out!"

Our way out, she was saying. Not just mine. Maybe she'd been hoping that once I graduated from Harvard or wherever, it would open up networking opportunities for her, too. Maybe it would have, if I'd gotten in. "Oh, that's nice. You thought you could use my great big brain to get us a better life. More money. Fancier jobs. Well, I'm sorry I wasn't up to the task."

"Oh, stop with your tantrum. We both wanted things to turn out differently. We both wanted more."

"Would you stop saying 'we'? Did it ever occur to you that maybe I was more than just an extension of you?"

"Of course you are," she said. "I never said—"

"You did say it," I said. "You've been living it. For the last eighteen years."

"Would you prefer that I didn't care what happened to you?"

"Sometimes I think it would be better if you didn't."

"Right, because it would be so *wonderful* to have a mother who didn't care if you ended up dead in a ditch."

I pointed a finger at her. "And that's the problem! Right there! There's a billion possibilities between Ivy League and dead in a ditch. But you don't see that, do you? It's either one or the other. I'm either the golden child or I'm *worthless*."

"You're being ridiculous!"

"No," I said. "I'm not."

Before she could reply, I went to my room and slammed the door.

I pulled out my phone and went through the pictures of Jill and Bob and Matt and the plane we'd jumped out of, and I thought about how my problems had seemed so tiny and ant-like. The problem is, though, that you can put an ant in front of a mirror and show it that it is an ant. It can understand, to the depths of its soul, that it is an ant. But it can never stop *being* an ant.

I opened Google and typed, *What is the meaning of life?*

The first answer was: *Crush your enemies. See them driven before you. Hear the lamentations of their women.*

I ran a hand over my eyes. I typed, *What is the meaning of life -"Conan the Barbarian"*

This was only slightly more helpful. The first link was an article about Buddhism and how attachment causes suffering, and the end of attachment leads to enlightenment. But that didn't answer my question. I typed, *Why am I here?*

I got the number for a suicide hotline.

I closed Google and called Nate. "What is the meaning of life?" I asked, in lieu of a greeting.

He laughed a very, very long time.

"Is that your answer?" I asked.

"Yes," he said. "That's my answer. What's up? I thought we had fun today."

"I did have fun. It was fun."

"Why do you sound like that, then?"

I didn't really want to explain about my mother's financial catastrophe, because this was not the kind of thing Nate understood. To him, money was just money. You spent it, you made more, and you always assumed it would stay where you put it. I said, "If I was having a nervous breakdown, would I know?"

"Yeah," he said. "You definitely would. Are you?"

"I'm not sure. I'm trying to make sense of the person I've been for the past eighteen years, and it's not working. Google said something about how striving leads to expectations and expectations lead to suffering. Maybe that's my problem? That was your problem, right?"

He was silent for a minute. "My problem was other people's expectations. Not mine."

Yes, I could see that. My mother's expectations were definitely the source of several of my problems. In fact, I could probably write a list of the problems those expectations had caused. But my mother wasn't the only one who had weighed me down that way. "So what are *your* expectations?" I asked.

He chuckled. "If I say, 'I expect you to come to my house and take my clothes off,' does that count?"

"Nate."

"Fine," he said. "Let's see." There was a long silence.

Eventually, he said, "I want to go to college and learn some stuff. I want to meet some cool people and go to some parties and maybe take a class that turns out to be so interesting it changes my life, and then I can somehow parlay that life-changing thing into something I can use to support myself."

"That's kind of vague," I said, frowning at the phone.

"Well, I gave you something specific and you rejected it. That still stands, by the way."

"So you just want to have fun and do interesting things and then die," I said.

"Isn't that what everyone wants to do?"

"No," I said. "It isn't what I wanted to do."

"What did you want to do?"

"I wanted to be the best. At—at something. At everything."

"Why?"

"I don't know. To prove I deserved to be alive? To prove I mattered? I don't know."

We stayed on the line for a while without talking. Finally he said, "Do you think there are people who don't deserve to be alive?"

"What? No. What do you mean?"

"I mean, if there's some person who's too poor or too sick or too, I don't know, disabled to do what you're talking about, do they not matter?"

"That's not what I'm saying," I said.

"It kind of is," he said. "When I was so sick I couldn't leave the hospital for five weeks, I'd like to think I still deserved to be alive."

"Of course you did. That's not what I mean. I just mean, I should have to do the best I can with what I have. That's all everyone does."

228

"So you think you should have to do more than other people because you're better."

"No! Stop putting words in my mouth."

"Well, what is it, then? You think you deserve more? I don't get what you're after, Mischa." His voice was strained, and I realized he was really angry. I don't think, in all the years I've known Nate, that I've ever seen him really mad. Everything rolls off him. But he was mad now. At me.

"You're being unfair," I said.

"I don't think I am," he said, and then he hung up.

I stared at the phone in my hand. Nate had hung up on me. NATE had hung up on me. Maybe this was how things were going to be, now that we were together?

I texted him and said, *I'm sorry.*

It was a long time before he texted back. He said: *Are you actually sorry, or are you just saying that because you don't want me to be mad?*

For Christ's sake. *I don't want you to be mad.*

Do you even know why I'm angry?

Not really.

I stared at the three little dots that indicated that he was typing. He typed for long enough that I figured I was going to be getting an essay-length description of why he was mad at me. Instead, when the text finally came through, it said: *I am hanging up on you again.*

CHAPTER TWENTY-FOUR

I WAITED FOR NATE IN FRONT OF HIS LOCKER UNTIL THIRTY seconds before the first-period bell, at which point I accepted that he wasn't coming. While I jogged to class, I sent him a text saying, *Are you at school today?*

My phone pinged and I jumped, but it was just another group text from Penny Ford in Students for Sober Driving.

Now, don't get me wrong. I hate drunk driving as much as anyone. It's a terrible, terrible thing. But I joined SSD for one reason only: it's a thing I could list on my resume that only involved two series of meetings per year, one before homecoming, and one before the spring formal. We did two things: we put posters up around the school telling everyone not to drive drunk, and we raised money so we could call Lyfts for anyone who was drunk anyway. The money for Lyfts was a really great idea in theory, but the reality was that pretty much everyone either came to these things in a limo or had enough money to get their own Lyft, so we'd been holding on to the same two hundred dollars for the past three years.

I was in charge of posters, which had become somewhat more odious after last year, when Penny had called a vote where it was decided that we could not use poster designs from previous years, because everyone had already seen them and would therefore not pay attention. I had to make ten: two for the cafeteria, two for the wall by the front door, and six others to go in various bathrooms, which would probably be defaced within a few days.

Despite the fact that we didn't really do anything, we still had to meet every week in the spring to get ready for formal/graduation season. We'd talk about our mission (drunk driving = bad) and see if we had any new ideas (nope). Then Penny, who was the president, would get in a fight with Brian, who was the treasurer, because Brian wanted to have a bake sale to raise more money, even though we'd never used any of the money we already had. Then someone would cry. Then we'd eat pizza.

The text said, *Meeting today at four. Please remember your supplies!*

The last thing I wanted to do was make posters. In fact, what I really wanted to do was walk into an airport and get on the next plane I saw, never to return.

I can't make it, I texted back.

Mischa, you've already missed the last two meetings.

Crap. Had I? I didn't even know. I scrolled back through my texts from Penny; there had been a couple of others in the last few weeks. I'd been ignoring her. Probably I should have felt bad about that.

I'm sick, I said.

I just saw you five minutes ago and you looked fine. And don't even TRY telling me you have mono.

Look, I texted, *I'm really sorry, I just can't do it this week.*

YOU MADE A COMMITMENT, was the reply.

I'm sorry, I said.

I'm going to go to Ms. Johnson about this. Ms. Johnson was our faculty adviser. She taught Latin and coached the girls' golf team, and she nearly always seemed to wear the expression of the recently Botoxed.

Fine, I said. *She can't make me stay in SSD, though.*

Wait, you're quitting?

Was that not clear?

I can't believe you.

By then I was in calculus, and Mr. Bronstein was giving me the death glare, so I stowed my phone without answering. I'd quit. I'd told Penny I'd quit. And that, I decided, was the end of it.

I had no word from Nate when I checked my phone after class. None after French. I was on my way to look for him in the dining hall when Ms. Johnson saw me passing and called me into her classroom. Lists of Latin declensions lined the walls, along with blown-up pages of *Winnie-the-Pooh* translated into Latin. *Winnie ille Pu.* Ms. Johnson was eating a salad out of a plastic box on her desk while staring at a huge paper day planner. Every day had its own square, which was filled with notes in her tiny cursive. "Is everything okay, Mischa?" she said. "I've heard you've been missing a lot of the SSD meetings. Anything you want to talk about?"

I wasn't sure how Penny had managed to talk to her so quickly.

"Did Penny email you?" I asked.

"She was in my last class," she explained. "She expressed some concerns."

Oh, ha. Concerns. I'm sure Penny was REALLY concerned about me. My welfare was probably keeping her up at night.

"I just decided I'm kind of overcommitted right now," I said.

"It's important to honor your commitments, though. And you have been in this club a long time. We've really come to depend on you."

"Yeah, I understand that. It's just that I—"

"I know you're probably frustrated about your"—she dropped her voice—"college situation."

She said "college situation" the way one would discuss some embarrassing medical condition. Like head lice, or hemorrhoids.

"Um. I didn't realize you knew about that."

"Well, you know how small this school is," she said. "Word gets around."

"Okay."

"My point is," she went on, "that even when things are bad, it's really important to keep up your routine. For your mental health."

"My mental health. That's very important. To you."

"Of course it is, Mischa, and also, you did commit to this club, and you're leaving a lot of people in the lurch."

"I'm uncommitting," I said.

"You're—"

"Quitting. I'm quitting."

I'd already said as much to Penny, but apparently she

hadn't relayed this part of our conversation to Ms. Johnson, because she looked surprised. And that's hard to do with a face full of botulism toxin. Her eyebrows almost went up and everything.

"You know that means you're going to have to take SSD off your resume," she said.

"Oh, gee!" I said. "I never thought of that. Maybe this will go on my permanent record."

"There's no need for you to take that tone."

"See, I think there is a need. Listen. I've been in this club for three and a half years? And I can tell you this, after three and a half years in this club, there's not one person in it who cares about drunk driving. You know why it exists? So we can say we're in a club. Have you not noticed that everyone in it has a leadership position? For God's sake, I'm the vice president in charge of media outreach. Do you know how stupid that is?"

"Your position is very important—"

"I MADE POSTERS. Making posters is not a leadership position!"

"Mischa."

"Listen. I quit. Do you need me to put it in writing?" I took the pen off her desk, tore a Post-it note off her pad, and wrote *I QUIT* in big block letters. Then I stuck the note in the middle of her planner.

Inexplicably, by the time I got to the dining hall, I was crying.

Not *crying* crying. My face was still normal-looking. It was like my tear ducts had just switched to the *on* position, and water was running down my face like a faucet. I wiped my eyes on the back of my arm, and then someone stuffed a wad of napkins in my face.

I followed the hand to the arm to the shoulder to Nate, who, when I didn't take the napkins, wiped my face himself.

"You didn't answer my text."

"I left my phone at home," he said. "That's not why you're. Uh."

"I'm not crying."

"Of course you aren't. So that's not why your face is leaking. Is it?"

I shook my head. "I hate my life," I said. "Also, I quit SSD."

"Oh. Good."

"I'm also quitting the band boosters, the French club, and student government."

"You'll have a lot of free time," he said.

"Yeah," I said. "I bet it'll be great."

He nodded toward the line of students waiting to be fed. "What did you want. A bagel? I'll get you a bagel."

"Yeah. Okay."

"You'll eat a bagel?"

"I'll eat a bagel," I said, and then I went and sat down as far away from everyone else as I could. Nate reappeared three minutes later with a pumpernickel bagel and a little thingy of cream cheese.

"Where were you going, by the way?" I asked.

"What?"

"When I saw you. You were leaving."

"Oh. I was going to look for you," he said, smearing cream cheese on my bagel because I wasn't doing it. Watching him do it made me get choked up all over again. "Because you weren't here."

"Where were you going to look?"

"I hadn't decided yet."

"You weren't worried," I said. He finished with the cream cheese and put the two halves of the bagel together. "Were you worried? You were worried."

"Yeah. I was," he said, putting the bagel on the plate and pushing it toward me. "Hey. So. I think I overreacted last night."

"I think I was a jerk," I said.

"No, I mean, yes, but you were also kind of right. You are smarter than most people. Why shouldn't you expect more of yourself?"

"I didn't mean I thought I was smarter than *you*."

"Mischa. You are smarter than me."

"That's awful. I don't think that."

He handed me half the bagel. "Eat," he said. "Look, it's the truth. Maybe not in everything, but on the aggregate, you're smarter. It just is what it is."

"You're better at people, though. And you're more observant. And other things, too. Lots of other things."

"This is true."

I wiped cream cheese off my face with my tear-stained napkins. "So does this mean you're not mad anymore?"

"Not really."

I sighed. *Not really* was not exactly the same thing as *no,* but I'd take it. We ate a few bites of our bagels, and then Nate said, "You know what I hate?"

"Pre-ripped jeans? Pocket squares? Tighty-whities?"

"Not sartorially. I hate how everyone has to rank everything all the time. Like, remember when you were a kid and you had your first best friend, and your second best friend, and your third best friend?"

I suddenly remembered that Jim had told me to call Caroline, and I hadn't done it. She'd stopped texting when I never wrote back about DOC. "I never had a third best friend. But yeah, I know what you're talking about."

"It's like, somewhere along the way, someone taught us that that was how you put people in boxes. This is the third-smartest person, the second-fastest runner, and the seventh-best dresser."

"There's not a lot of room for nuance," I said.

"Exactly! And the stuff that can't be ranked doesn't matter. I hate that."

I was silent because, up until recently, that ranking system had done a lot for me. I was the smartest. The best at math. The fastest essay writer. The biggest vocabulary haver. I said, "You are my first best friend, though."

He stopped chewing his bagel and frowned at me, not a real frown, with the downturned mouth, but with his forehead. "Just your friend?"

"Now, *that* I hate," I said. "There's no *just* about being friends. Why is that a *just*? There's no *just*."

"Why does it sound like you're breaking up with me? Didn't you . . ." He coughed. "Didn't you want to be my girlfriend?"

God, I was always making him feel bad lately. "That is what I want. Right now, it's pretty much the only thing I want. It's just . . . I want you to promise you won't stop being my friend. No matter what happens."

"Like if we break up."

I swallowed down my discomfort at how easily he said those words. "Yeah."

He pulled me into a hug and kissed the side of my face. "I promise," he said. "I promise. But you have to promise, too."

I closed my eyes. "I promise. I promise, no matter what."

CHAPTER TWENTY-FIVE

THE NEXT MORNING, I WAS ON MY WAY TO CALCULUS WHEN I saw Shira coming the other way. "Mischa Ab-ram-AAAAH-veech-us," she sang, and then spun around to walk next to me. "Good morning."

"Hey, Shira," I said.

"Did you know," she went on, "that you have the same last name as the Ukrainian trade minister?"

"Actually, he's Abromavicius—"

"But he's not Ukrainian!"

"Yeah, I—"

"I googled it. Your name."

"I gathered that." Then I frowned. "Hang on, why are you so . . . obviously sober? Now. Here."

"I'll show you," she said. She held up her phone so that I

could see the screen. It took me a minute to realize I was looking at a plane ticket.

"Accra?" I asked. "You're going to Ghana?"

"I'm going with Bebe for three weeks after graduation, to
stay with her aunt," she said. She was kind of vibrating all over
like she'd had way too much coffee. "It's my graduation pres-
ent from my parents. They just told me last night. I've been
begging to go with her since sophomore year!"

"Wow," I said. I wondered if Emily was going, too, but it
seemed kind of rude to ask. "That's amazing."

"Her aunt's so great, too. I just can't believe I'm really
going." She showed me a picture on her phone, of her and
Bebe and a woman who must have been Bebe's aunt in front
of the Washington Monument.

"Congratulations," I said. "Three weeks. That's incredible." Then, since the situation seemed to call for it, I gave her
a hug. It was a one-armed hug, but still, I think it counted; I
never know quite how to hug other girls, because our boobs
always seem to get in the way, so I end up doing this thing
Caroline calls the Christian side-hug. Shira looked a little surprised, but then she hugged me back with two arms, because I
guess she doesn't care about boobs being in the way. Then she
snapped my bra.

"You know," she said, after I'd extracted myself from her
embrace, "you are actually a nice person."

"Um. Thank you?"

"I don't think I said it before, but I'm really sorry about
what happened to you."

"Shh," I said.

We were walking by the office. Mr. Pelletier was giving service hours to Derek Logan for wearing a hat in the building

to cover his really unfortunate haircut. Beth Reinhardt was on her phone, shouting, "He is *so* into me." And over all this noise, I heard someone saying, "But Dartmouth has the best study abroad programs," and looked up to see Caroline talking to Jim, who looked distinctly like he wished he was on another planet.

"It's not too late," Shira said. "There was totally more we could have done with your transcript."

"Shira," I said. "No."

"See, I was on Blanchard's server last night—"

"You *what?*"

"I just wanted to check some things. I feel like we got really close last time, and I thought—"

"Would you be quiet?"

I bumped into someone coming the other way. Unfortunately, it turned out to be Amy Gregston, and on her other side was Meredith Dorsay. "Watch where you're going, Michelle," she said. Then, seeing Shira, she added, "What, are you guys going to get high in the bathroom together? Jesus, when you self-destruct, you really go all the way."

Shira said, rather loudly, "Why don't you shut up, you overprivileged block of cream cheese."

I had a coughing fit into my fist.

Meredith said, "*What* did you call me?"

I was thinking that maybe it was time for Shira to go back in her shell for a while, but she said, "Five words from her and I'm already bored." She turned to me and said, "I'm gonna go find Bebe. Think about it, okay?" and then she was gone.

Meredith glared. I smiled and said, "She doesn't like you." Then: "I don't like you, either."

CHAPTER TWENTY-SIX

I WAS IN ENGLISH THE NEXT DAY WHEN BEBE, WHO WAS SITTING in the row behind me, sent me a text. It said, *Holy crap.*

What?

When was the last time you checked Instagram?

I barely used it at all anymore. It'd been cool when I'd first gotten my own phone (not until ninth grade, which was about five years later than everyone else I knew). I'd posted pictures of every random thing I could find: the time I accidentally wore two different shoes to school; quotes I'd highlighted in books; the trip Nate and I took to a pumpkin patch on Halloween, when he'd dressed a scarecrow up in his coat and hat and emailed a picture of it to his parents with a ransom note. I hadn't posted much lately, though. I'd thought about putting the pictures of my skydiving escapades on there, but then it would be obvious I'd skipped school.

She said, *Pull it up. Now.*

I tried to, but it kept giving me an incorrect password error. I typed it three times, and then told Bebe, *My password's messed up, I have to change it or something.*

You've got to be kidding me.

What?

Does your mom follow you?

I turned around and looked at Bebe, but she was staring at her screen, so all I could see was the top of her head, like, for her, the Mischa she was talking to existed inside the phone and not three feet in front of her.

Yes. She does.

OK. We have to get out of here. Say you have a paper cut.

What?

Say OW.

When I didn't respond, she slumped down in her chair and kicked the bottom of my seat, hard.

"OW!" I said out loud, to which Ms. Parker replied, "Mischa?"

"Paper cut," I said, stuffing my right index finger into my left fist. "Can I run and get a Band-Aid? It's bleeding."

"Sure," she said before going back to whatever she was doing.

As I got up, Bebe's hand shot into the air. "Can I walk her down? I need a Motrin from the nurse."

At that Ms. Parker scowled. But she waved Bebe out and said, "Fine."

I shut the door behind us and said, "What is it?"

Bebe grabbed my arm and pulled me down the hall into the bathroom, before flashing me her phone.

"What is this?" I asked, looking at a picture I'd never seen before. It was a selfie of me with my sleeve rolled up and my arm held out, with a party going on in the background. People were drinking out of red Solo cups and dancing. "This isn't my page."

"Yeah, only it *is* your page."

"I don't even know these people!"

"Mischa, look at what the people behind you are doing."

I blew up the screen with my thumb and forefinger. The girl behind me was laughing into the face of the boy opposite her, who was getting ready to inject something into her arm.

"What—" I said. "Is that heroin?"

"Well, he's not giving her a flu shot," she said.

My eyes went to the caption next to the picture, where Mischabella16 had written, *Waiting my turn* 😉*! Don't wait up,* @*NDA123!*

"Oh my God," I said. "Oh my God."

"Who is NDA123?" she asked.

"It's my mom," I said.

"Her Instagram handle's NDA? As in *non-disclosure agreement*?"

"Not that kind of NDA. It's her initials. Norah Deborah Abramavicius. And she's tagged. Oh my God."

"You need to delete it," she said. "Use my phone. You have to log me out first."

"Right," I said. "Right." I logged off Bebe's account and then on with my own. Or tried to. "It won't let me log on," I said. "It's not accepting my password."

"Reset it."

I clicked on the "forgot password" link and entered my email address.

That email address doesn't have an associated user account, it said. My eyes went up to meet Bebe's. "What do I do?"

"Someone must've gotten into your account and changed the default email address," she said. "It's not just hacked; it's completely hijacked."

"Meaning whoever did this can post whatever they want, and there's nothing I can do."

"That's what an account hijack is, yeah."

I stared at the picture, feeling the panic starting to take over. "Can we call the Instagram people? Get them to reset everything?"

"It'll take too long," she said. "There's no phone number for them, you have to email, and it could take days."

"So what do we *do*?"

Bebe shook her head. "This isn't my area." She took the phone back and started texting. "We need Emily. I'm sending her the link."

A few seconds later the phone buzzed. I read Emily's reply over Bebe's shoulder: *Need my computer. Meet me in the art room in five minutes.*

Bebe and I snuck down the hall, past the classrooms, which were full of students going about their normal, boring days and waiting for the bell to ring. I was about to go past Señora Ruiz's Spanish room when Bebe snagged me by the arm. "Stop," she hissed. "Mr. Pelletier."

He was at the other end of the hall, but he was checking his phone and hadn't seen us yet.

"There's nowhere to go!" I whispered, because the only doors in the immediate area were all to classrooms, and they were all occupied. But if Mr. Pelletier saw us, he'd ask us what we were doing, and then he'd either give us hours or send us back to class. Either way, that was more time that Instagram post was going to be sitting up there, taunting my mother.

"In here," Bebe said, and she pulled me into Señora Ruiz's room.

She must have been teaching Spanish I that period, because sixteen kids who looked almost prepubescent turned their faces toward us. "Beatriz?" Señora Ruiz said. "¿Qué tal?"

"Ummm," Bebe said.

I glanced at the window in the door behind us; Mr. Pelletier was still coming our way, but he hadn't passed the classroom yet.

"Hola, estudiantes nuevos," Bebe said, tugging on her braid and trying to look like she meant to be there. "So as you might know, I'm the president of the Spanish club."

Silence.

"Right," she said. "And, um, we have a meeting next Thursday at three, and I wanted to extend my personal invitation to all of the beginning Spanish students. We're really excited to expand our membership."

Silence.

"Oookay," she said. "So if anyone's interested, maybe I can get your email addresses? Maybe we can pass around a piece of paper?" She edged toward Señora Ruiz. "I forgot to bring paper," she murmured.

"Muy mal preparada," Señora Ruiz said, handing her a piece from a drawer of her desk.

"Lo siento," Bebe said. She passed the piece of paper to a kid in the first row, and it silently went around the room while about three people put their names on it. Bebe glanced at me;

I was watching the door, but Pelletier still hadn't gone by the room. I shook my head.

"Ah," she said. "So. The other thing. Uh. We're learning a song! For the meeting. And I'm going to teach it to you. Right now. Yep. I'm going to do that."

"Cuál canción?" Señora Ruiz asked, clearly amused.

"Right. What song. What. Song. Sorry. Estoy un poco nerviosa."

She pulled out her phone, went to YouTube, and started playing one of those videos where they show the lyrics on the screen in real time. A second later the strains of a love ballad began to pour forth from the phone's tiny speaker.

I glanced at the screen. "Seriously?" I whispered.

"It's all I could think of!" she whispered back. "You're going to have to sing it with me."

"What?"

"Why else are they going to think you're here?"

"But I don't know Spanish!"

"It's phonetic! Just read the lyrics!"

"But—"

Then she started to sing. "Bésameeeeee. Bésame muchooooo. Como si fuera esta noche la última vez . . ."

I had not known, until that moment, that Bebe Tandoh is completely tone-deaf. Unfortunately, I am not much better than that. Particularly when singing in a language I don't know, to a melody I'm not really 100% sure of. I knew my mom had a cover of this on an old CD, but it was like a jazz remix. Diana Krall, maybe? It hardly mattered.

I gaped at Bebe in silent horror while she really tried to sell it, and what she lacked in tonal accuracy she made up for in volume. One of the freshmen said, "That's so embarrassing." Bebe slung an arm around my neck as we sang, "Mirarme en tus ojos . . ." I put a dramatic hand to my forehead because why not.

"¡Canten con ellas!" Señora Ruiz ordered, perhaps out of pity, and she began to sing along, the freshmen reluctantly joining in on the chorus. "Bésame, bésame mucho . . ."

Finally Mr. Pelletier passed by our room and hurried down the hall, as if he'd suddenly seen something much more interesting and picked up his pace. "Bebe," I muttered. But she was into it now and hitting some high note. "Bebe," I repeated.

"Right," she said, trailing off. "So that was our song. So, come out on Thursday. We'll have, like, snacks and stuff."

"Thanks, everybody," I said, and then I opened the door and we went back out.

"Wow," I said.

"We never speak of that again," she said. "Let's find Emily."

We found her in the empty art room two minutes later, her laptop already set up on one of the tables. "Took you long enough," she said.

Bebe and I exchanged a glance. She pursed her lips at me. I said, "I had to. Um. Pee. I had to pee. Sorry."

"Mischa," Emily said. "Never mind. While you were peeing, I was working on your Instagram page."

"You rehacked it?"

"Well, no. First I reported your account as hacked, but you know, that can take days to get resolved, so I had to do something else."

"What do you mean?" I asked. "What did you do?"

"Think about it this way. Instagram is a business, right? So what's the number one thing any business wants?"

I said, "To make a profit?"

Without missing a beat, Emily said, "What's the number two thing any business wants?"

"Uhh."

"Not to get sued," she said. "I reported the picture as a copyright violation. And, um. I had some friends report some of your other pictures, too. The point is, in another day or two your account will be suspended pending investigation, and hopefully by the time they realize you weren't posting stolen pictures, they'll also have realized that you were hacked, and fix it."

"Or I'll get arrested for violating the Copyright Act!"

"Yeah, *probably* that won't happen. But I did deal with the more immediate problem, which was keeping your mom from seeing it."

"How exactly did you do that?"

"I hacked *her* Instagram page."

"*What?*"

"Her password's your birthday. It wasn't that hard. Anyway, all I did was unfollow and block you, so even if someone tags her on another picture before your page comes down, she won't get any notifications or anything. She'd have to be specifically looking for your page."

"Which you said you hardly use anyway," Bebe said. "So she probably won't go looking."

I slumped onto one of the art stools, and Bebe sat down next to me. "Thank you," I said. "Eeesh." I rested my forehead on my arms. "I just don't understand. I thought this was over! Why would someone bother messing with me again? It wasn't enough to ruin my academic prospects, now they want me in jail?"

"I don't think they wanted you in jail," Emily said.

"Mischa," Bebe said. "They tagged your mom."

"They wanted to get me in trouble with my mom?"

I thought about the picture. It was supposed to be of a Blanchard party. "They wanted her to pull me out of school?"

"That's my guess," Emily said.

"Is there any way to figure out who did it?" I asked.

"Unlikely," she said. "Unfortunately. But let's have a look."

Emily pulled the picture up on the computer. On the big screen, it was a lot more horrifying than it had been on Bebe's phone.

"Well, obviously it's fake," I said. "I don't even know any of those people."

She blew the picture up, and then again, and then again. "Oh, it's definitely photoshopped," she said. "I just want to see how."

"Does it matter?"

"I want to know if the person who did it was any good."

She put a finger to a subtle line between my face and the background. "Here's where they spliced it," she said. "You can see where they cut you out and pasted you in front of the party."

I recognized the shot of me; it was from last spring, right after the SGA election. Caroline had ordered temporary tattoos for all of us, and I was holding my arm out so she could put the giant *VP* in flowery script on the inside of my forearm. I'd been laughing, we'd all been laughing, because we'd won and it was a fabulous thing to list on our college applications, and we were so, so happy. I'd posted the picture last May with a caption that said, *abramaVICTORY!*

"Ew," said Emily. "Someone is not good at Photoshop."

Bebe pointed to the periphery between my face and the background. "See how it's all pixelated at the edges?" She glanced at Emily. "This is a student job."

"Probably," Emily agreed. "Oh, hello." She blew up the screen some more. "There's a piece of paper on the table here. It's got writing on it."

"Can you go to 800%?" Bebe asked.

"I'll try. It's going to be blocky." She clicked. "Huh. That should really be blocky."

But it wasn't. What was on the piece of paper was a line drawing of a cat with its legs sticking straight in the air and *X*s over its eyes. Over the cat was a crudely drawn knife, on which someone had written "curiosity."

"Curiosity killed the cat," I said. "Someone put that there for me."

Emily said, "Oh, no. Someone put that there for us."

"For you?"

"Whoever put this there knows two things: that you're poking around, and that you have help."

"We're being warned," Bebe said.

"We're being warned," Emily agreed. "How delightful."

CHAPTER TWENTY-SEVEN

GOING BACK TO CLASS AFTER THAT WAS NOT FUN. EVERY TIME I saw someone I knew, I thought, *Is it you? Are you the one doing this to me?* Caroline said hi to me, and I just about knocked her head off. "What is wrong with you?" she asked, and I wasn't sure if she meant what was wrong with me in general, or specifically at that moment. She flashed me this look that made me feel awful, because really, she hadn't done anything wrong.

"Nothing," I said. "I'm sorry. Bad day."

"Whatever," she said

"Caroline," I said, but she was already walking away.

When we got out of French, there was a crowd of people blocking the hallway and steadfastly refusing to move.

"What is this?" I asked Jim, who's a head taller than me and had a better vantage point. "Can you see anything?"

"Yeah," he said. "There's two rent-a-cops up there with a German shepherd. Looks like they're doing a locker search."

"A locker search?"

"Looks like."

In all my years at Blanchard, I couldn't remember them ever searching lockers before.

"What are they looking for?"

"Jeez, Vicious. They have a dog. What do you think they're looking for?"

"Right," I said, because they only needed a dog to look for either drugs or explosives, and if they thought there were explosives in the building we'd all have been evacuated already. "Did they find anything yet?"

"I've been standing here exactly as long as you have."

"Oh. Yeah." Leaving Jim behind, I pushed through the crowd to where Nate was standing with the rest of his English class. "Hey," I said. "News?"

"Someone said there was a tip called in," he said. "But I don't know if it's true or not."

"I wonder who called," I said, checking my phone to make sure I didn't have any messages from my mother. Just then the dog started to whimper and paw at a locker. A murmur went up around us.

"Uh-oh," Nate said.

"Do you know whose locker that is?"

He shook his head. "Somebody who's about to have a really bad day."

The security guard opened the door of the locker, and the dog jammed his nose into the interior. The man, who was built like the side of a barn and blocked most of my view, started digging through a pile of discarded sweatshirts before pulling out a ziplock bag. I couldn't see what was inside it, but next to me, Nate said, "Yikes."

The guard said something to Mr. Pelletier, who was standing next to him, and he looked out to the crowd.

On the other side of the hall, Shira Gastman pushed her way to the front of the group of students that was huddled there.

"Ms. Gastman," he said blandly. "We need to have a conversation."

"That's not mine," she said. "I know it's not."

"Let's discuss this somewhere more private—"

"No! It isn't mine! I'll take any drug test you want. It isn't mine."

Some sounds of amusement were made near me, because the idea that Shira would come up clean on a drug test was a joke. I heard someone say they were surprised she'd never been caught before.

"We should do something," I whispered to Nate. "We know Shira's clean."

In my pocket, my phone buzzed. It was Emily. The text read, *Say nothing.*

I looked up and saw her on the other side of the hall, standing next to Bebe with a hand on her shoulder like she was restraining her, which was ridiculous, because Bebe could easily rest her chin on top of Emily's head. They were having a quiet argument. Bebe looked like she was on the verge of punching Emily in the mouth.

I texted back, *What? She's about to be arrested!*

I watched her text me back with one hand, the other still settled on Bebe as if she was pushing her down to the floor. *Say NOTHING.*

Emily, what the hell?

Wait until the crowd clears and meet me back in the art room.

I looked over my phone at Nate, who had been reading over my shoulder.

In my ear, Nate said, "She's right."

"But we can clear her!"

"No, we can't. All we can do is go down with her."

Back in the art room, Emily sat with a hand on either temple, like she was trying to hold her brain in. Nate and I sat opposite her. Bebe paced angrily in front of the table, glaring at her. "You are seriously cold sometimes, you know that?"

Emily dropped her hands. "If you had intervened, what would have happened?"

"I could have told them it was planted!"

"*Think,* Bebe! We have no evidence of that. If we get in the middle of this, suddenly we're the ones having conversations with Pelletier and those rent-a-cops. Maybe they want to have a look at our emails." She leveled a look at me. "Or they start checking our social media accounts."

I put my hands over my mouth, and Nate rested a hand on my shoulder. "This is going to be okay," he murmured.

Emily had her laptop open and was typing. I'd never seen her look so grim before.

"What are you doing?" I asked.

"Deactivating Shira's Ophelia email."

"She wouldn't put anything in an email," Bebe said. "That's what TalkOff is for."

"It's not worth the risk," she said. "They might make her unlock her phone, and God only knows what she has on there."

"Jesus," said Nate.

"It's done," Emily said. "We can reactivate it once this is over." She looked to me. "If they ask you for your Instagram handle, *tell them you don't have one.*"

"But what about Shira?" Bebe said. "You're so busy trying to cover our butts you're completely forgetting about her!"

"Listen," said Nate, in his soothing Nate voice. "All Shira has to do to prove she's clean is pee in a cup. She can clear herself."

"She can clear herself of using," Bebe said. "Not possession." She sat down in the other chair. "If they try to say she was selling it, she's screwed."

"They can't prove that," I said.

"Mischa," Bebe said. "We don't know *what* they can prove."

The bell rang out in the hallway, which meant we were all officially late for class. I felt a brief impulse to get up and run, like a baby duck chasing its mother.

I said, "I just don't get it. Why would someone want to mess with Shira? All she does here is stare out the window—Wait." I pressed my palms down into the table. "Wait. Yesterday Shira was talking to me in the hallway, and she brought up my transcript."

"She brought that up in the hallway?" Emily said incredulously.

"She was kind of jacked up about her trip to Accra," I said. Emily flinched a little, like this was the first she was hearing about it. "Um. She was kind of going off about that, but then she brought up the transcript and said she thought there was more you guys could do, and she'd been on Blanchard's server again." I exhaled. "And then Meredith Dorsay ran into me."

"Meredith."

"Yeah," I said. "Wait. It wasn't just Meredith. It was Amy, too. Amy Gregston."

"Wonky English Grade Amy?" Nate asked.

"Yes! And they were together at the mall, too, a few weeks ago. Shoot. Why didn't I think of this earlier? It's Meredith. It's Meredith, and this is because of me. She found out Shira was helping me, and first she did the Instagram thing and then this. A bag of joints in the locker, everyone believes it, and Shira's out of school the next day."

"They probably won't expel her this close to the end of the year," Emily said to Bebe's horrified face. "They'll just graduate her early. Get her out of the way so she doesn't embarrass the school, and try to keep a lid on it. They've done it before."

"What?" I asked. "When?"

"Sophomore year. Do you remember Neil Hickman? Some teacher walked in on him selling ecstasy in the bathroom six weeks before graduation, but he was already in at Northwestern, so they just kind of disappeared him for the rest of the year."

"Did they ever tell Northwestern?" I asked.

"Not sure. But he started there the next fall. My guess is they didn't."

That almost made me feel a little better, because the last thing I wanted was for Shira to end up in the same boat as me. Still, though. I felt myself starting to shake with rage. Meredith had heard us. Meredith had done this. And that meant that she had been the one behind my transcript hack, too. There was my proof. It had always been her.

I imagined twenty thousand ways to murder Meredith Dorsay and make it look like an accident.

I pushed back from the table and got up.

"Mischa!" Nate said. "What are you doing?"

"I'm going," I said, "to have a conversation with Meredith."

Emily said, "No, you can't do that, Mischa."

"This is overdue."

"Are you stupid?" Emily said. "She's just going to deny everything!"

I stopped at the door. "I want her to deny it to my face," I said. And before anyone could forcibly stop me, I pushed the door open and stormed into the hallway.

Meredith was in French this period. I hated that I knew that. Why did I even know that? How much of my brain was taken up knowing useless minutiae about people I barely cared about?

I tapped on the door of Madame Henri's classroom, and then stepped inside.

"Pardon," I said, in my tightest accent. "Ils doivent s'adresser à Meredith Dorsay au secrétariat."

Madame Henri nodded at Meredith, whose mouth had popped open at the sight of me, and who followed me out into the hallway.

"What do you mean, they need to talk to me in the office?" she asked.

"Just follow me," I snapped.

"Why would they send *you*?"

I went around the corner without answering. "If you don't tell me what's going on, I'm going back to class," she hissed.

I'd wanted to have this conversation somewhere more private, but it was either here or nowhere, so I spun around and said, "What you did to Shira was low."

"You think I ratted out Shira? Why would I? Everyone in this whole place knows her story. I'm surprised they never caught her before."

"Are you actually going to look me in my face and deny this?"

"Deny *what*?"

"What you did to Shira. What you did to me!"

She stopped short. "Excuse me?"

"I know what you did with the transcripts. And it's going to come out."

"What I did with the . . ." She trailed off. Her eyes flared with understanding, but I couldn't tell if she was faking the expression or not. "I see what this is. You screwed up and got rejected from everywhere good, and you're too entitled to admit it was your fault. You need a scapegoat."

"No," I said. "I saw what you did to my transcript. *I saw it.* Don't deny it. And how many of your own grades did you go in and change? Did you bump that freshman English grade up to an A? I bet you did."

"You are pathetic," she said. "I can't believe you. We live in a meritocracy, Michelle. You get what you earn. I earned my place at Harvard. And now you're trying to blame me because you couldn't hack it."

"I hacked it. I hacked it fine."

"Oh please. You show up with your 'poor little me, my mom drives a Honda' sob story, as if we're supposed to feel sorry for you? Your mom's a lawyer. You aren't some underprivileged kid from the street. Your dad's not in prison." She hesitated. "He's not, is he?"

The truth was I had no clue where he was, but I said, "No."

"Just own the fact that you got rejected. Have a little

dignity." She wrinkled her nose at me. "I'd rather go to community college than take a spot I hadn't earned."

"I did earn it," I growled.

"No," she said. "You didn't. But I did. And it's not because I *cheated*. It's because I'm smarter than you." She shoved by me to go back to class.

"Meredith," I spat.

"No," she said angrily. "Get out of my face."

It was only after she'd left that I realized what I'd done: I'd told Meredith flat out that I thought my transcript was hacked. Which meant that in approximately ten minutes, everyone in the entire school would know.

I was twenty minutes into AP Government when I got a note to go see Dr. Marlowe.

CHAPTER TWENTY-EIGHT

RICHARD MARLOWE, WHO HAD BEEN THE HEADMASTER OF Blanchard since before I was born, looked like a cross between Harry Potter and Santa Claus. He had a well-kept beard and tiny wire spectacles, and always, always wore a sweater vest over an oxford shirt.

I hadn't seen the inside of Dr. Marlowe's office, having never been in any kind of trouble. It was larger than strictly necessary for a one-person office, with a desk that faced a fireplace that I suspected, by its cleanliness, was never used. Four windows ran along the length of the room, looking out at the grounds. The leaves of the maple outside the window threw dappled shadows onto the walls.

I sat across from Dr. Marlowe at his desk and played with a ragged edge of a fingernail.

"So," he said. "Mischa. I hear you're having some problems with the college admissions process."

I stared at the bust of Shakespeare that sat on the corner of his desk. It was so cliché. So obvious sitting there on his oversized mahogany desk. On the wall there was a fake antique map of the world, with the Mediterranean at its center and a lot of writing in Latin.

Hic sunt dracones, I thought.

"Here be dragons," I said out loud.

"I beg your pardon?"

I shook my head. "I tried to make an appointment with Ms. Pendleton," I said. "But she hasn't been in for weeks. Is she sick?"

He opened his desk drawer and closed it again without getting anything out. "I'm afraid Ms. Pendleton is no longer with Blanchard."

"She's no longer here. Did she quit?"

"I'm not at liberty to discuss the details of her departure," he said. "But certainly anything you wanted to tell her, you may tell me."

I opened my mouth and shut it again without letting anything out. I was aware that anything I said to Dr. Marlowe would be relayed to my mother.

"What exactly have you heard?" I asked.

He chuckled, softly, at nothing, because nothing was funny so far as I could tell. "Did you tell Ms. Dorsay something about your transcript?"

"No," I said instinctively. "Why?"

"You know those files are extremely secure," he said.

"I'm sure they are."

"Even the teachers don't have access to them," he said. "Did you know that?"

"No," I said. Then I frowned and said, "Hang on, how do they put their end-of-year grades in, then?"

"They forward them to Mrs. Hadley, and she inputs them."

"And what if Mrs. Hadley makes a mistake?"

"Well, then you would know when your report cards go home at the end of the quarter, wouldn't you?"

"Yes," I said. "I mean, of course."

"Ms. Abramavicius," he said, and I was a little unnerved by how easily he pronounced my name, when we'd never spoken in person before, and every other teacher in the school had fumbled it at least twice. "I can't have you spreading rumors that impugn the good name of the school. Do you understand that?"

"I never said anything to Meredith," I lied. "She hates my guts. Ask anyone."

"Hmm," he said. "I also understand you are not happy with the colleges that have accepted you. You plan on attending Paul Revere, is that correct?"

That, too, must have come from Meredith, either directly or indirectly. He hadn't bothered to check with Revere about my status, because they would have told him I'd been rejected.

"That's right," I said.

"It's hardly a bad choice, Mischa, though I can certainly understand why you're disappointed. I must admit that, given your record, I'm a little surprised about the decisions of some of your other colleges, but sometimes these things can be a little capricious."

"Capricious. You think so?"

"Hmm. And your list of extracurriculars was not quite what one would hope, for colleges of this caliber."

"My extracurriculars. You think that was the problem?"

"I think you had a list of very good schools. You're not an athlete, a legacy, or an underrepresented minority. Your grades and test scores were excellent, but there are many such candidates. I think it's likely that your portfolio simply failed to distinguish itself."

Without thinking, I blurted out, "What about my letters?"

He blinked twice. "I beg your pardon?"

"My letters of recommendation. What about those?"

"Those are confidential, so I'm not at liberty to discuss the contents of those," he said. "However, I've read your letters, and I can assure you, your teachers thought very highly of you."

He met my eyes levelly. I could detect no lie, which meant that my real letters must still exist in Blanchard's computer somewhere. I wondered how I could get them.

"If you are unhappy," he said, "I would suggest one of three courses of action. You may accept your place at Revere, and then consider transferring."

My eyes cut to the window. I said nothing.

"You may take a gap year, get some better experiences to line that list of extracurriculars. Some work abroad, perhaps. And then apply again next year."

If he'd seen my file, he knew that I was there on scholarship and had as much chance of working abroad as he did of sprouting wings and flying out the window. "Or?"

"Or, if you want more options for next fall, you could apply to some schools with rolling admissions."

I nodded. That much I'd already considered. And discounted, because my recommendation letters were a shambles, and I had no way to ensure that my transcript wouldn't be messed with again.

"So you see," he said. "You really do have a number of adequate options. Things are hardly as dire as they may seem right now." He handed me a business card. "If you or your mother have any concerns, please feel free to email me directly. I can also recommend a private college admissions specialist, if you wish."

I took the card and pocketed it, then got up, because I knew a dismissal when I saw one.

"Thank you," I said. Then added, rather robotically, "I feel much better now."

"Of course, Miss Abramavicius."

At the sound of my name, I turned back again and asked, "What's going to happen to Shira Gastman?"

He sighed and shook his head, as if Shira had long been a thorn in his side, he'd expected this turn of events, and was disappointed nevertheless. "I'm afraid I'm not at liberty—"

"To discuss it," I finished. "Of course. Thank you, Dr. Marlowe."

"Mischa," he said. "I wouldn't be too hard on Miss Dorsay. She's really under a terrible strain."

"Meredith? What do you mean? She's going to Harvard."

"I would just give her a wide berth for the moment," he said. "For both your sakes."

I closed the door behind me.

• • •

I had a text waiting for me from Emily. It said, *Did you really expect her to admit it?*

I deleted it without answering. I was mad at Shira for talking about my transcript in the middle of the hall. I was mad at myself for mouthing off to Meredith and getting hauled into Dr. Marlowe's office. And I kept mulling over what he'd said about her. That I should give her a wide berth. Was it because he knew she was pissed at me? Or had he heard something else?

My phone buzzed again. Emily, again. *It no longer matters whether you want to pursue this or not,* she said. *We have to find out the truth.*

I replied, *Isn't that what we've been trying to do? Ineffectively?*

We need the transcript files.

Go ahead and get them, I said. *Just leave me out of it this time.*

I need your help.

When I didn't answer, she said, *Mischa, please.*

I sighed. *What do you suggest?*

We're going to have to steal Mrs. Hadley's phone.

Right, that's simple.

I didn't say it would be easy, she said. *I just said we had to do it.*

I had to wade through a bunch of people to get to my locker. Government was over now; everyone was going home. I looked for Nate, for Bebe, for Emily, but didn't see anyone. I wondered if they'd gone back to class, or if they were still in the art room.

How is Shira? I asked.

Suspended. Until further notice.

Did they have her take a drug test?

No.

Isn't that strange?

Yes.

Do you still think it's Meredith Dorsay?

. . .

. . .

Yes.

CHAPTER TWENTY-NINE

THERE ARE FEW THINGS LESS FUN THAN BEING STUCK IN A sealed cardboard box with another person.

I decided this after spending two hours stuck in a cardboard box with Emily Sreenivasan. Seven thousand, two hundred seconds. The box smelled like coffee breath (both mine and Emily's), Emily's vanilla body wash, and the extra-strength antiperspirant I'd used so I wouldn't have pit stains in my mug shot if we got arrested. Also, I was really regretting the coffee, because I'd had to go to the bathroom for the last hour. I shifted my body as much as the space would allow, which was not much, to try to give my bladder some breathing room.

The box had contained not Mr. Pelletier's mother, killed in a fit of oedipal pique, but 122 reams of paper, which were now inside Mr. Pelletier's office, stacked to look like a giant paper Stonehenge so everyone would think they'd been moved as part of a clever senior prank. However, even without the paper inside, the box was not big enough for two people. I wished we'd cut some extra air holes.

While the box was cramped, smelly, and bathroomless, it was not dark. This was because Emily, whose legs were slung over my knees, her back slumped in the shape of a *C*, was playing Donut Destroyer on her phone with the sound turned off.

I pulled out my own phone and texted her, because we could not talk and risk being overheard by the office staff who were milling around a few feet away. *I can't believe you're playing that now.*

What, she texted back. *This is boring. What are you doing?*

Cat pictures, I said.

Really?

Yeah. This one's super fat and he's smiling.

Hey, switch with me, she said. We switched phones, and she thumbed through a few images while I lost the rest of her game.

Just then a group text came through from Bebe. *Mrs. Hadley is at her desk,* she said.

Where are you?

Across the hall.

It was Friday. This was very significant because on Friday the office staff always dresses down, and on dress-down Fridays Mrs. Hadley always wears jeggings. Which was significant because jeggings have no pockets. Which was significant because when one has no pockets, one keeps one's cell phone in one's purse. One supposes.

Our plan had four parts and involved breaking three laws. They were minor laws, I told myself. Hardly illegal. Probably misdemeanor-level. I'd suggested to Emily that we google it just to make sure, and she'd actually swatted me in the back of the head.

"Don't google that! Have you learned nothing?" she'd asked. "Do you know how easy it is to find someone's search history? You might as well stand on the street corner and shout, *I AM ABOUT TO COMMIT A FELONY!*"

"We aren't though, are we?" I'd asked. "Just to clarify."

"Mischa," Bebe had said. "Grow a spine."

Emily texted, *Nate?*

Yeah, he said. *We should go fast if we're going at all.*

Shira?

Shira was the linchpin of our plan, which was a problem because she wasn't supposed to be on campus at all. She'd snuck in with us before the office staff had come in and was currently hiding in a janitorial closet in the art wing. She was also the one of us with the most to lose, because she was technically trespassing (that makes four laws—oops), and she was going to briefly have to come out of hiding.

Okay, Emily texted. *I'm going to conference everyone in. Everyone will be able to hear everyone else. No chitchat.*

She connected everyone via conference call.

Go, she texted.

We had to hit our first marker before the bell rang, because otherwise the faculty would notice that Emily and I were missing. I heard the click of Bebe's shoes on the wood floor as she walked into the office; she was wearing skinny jeans and a pair of strappy sandals with three-inch heels, one of which was primed to snap off. She would be holding a venti Starbucks passion tea, a drink so vividly pink it could stain any fabric. Any second, Mrs. Hadley would be wearing it.

"Hey, Mrs. Hadley," Bebe said breezily. "I'm supposed to pick up a copy of my—"

She was cut off by a crash, which would have been Bebe's post-heel-snap fall, and a yelp, which was the sound of Mrs. Hadley being bathed in pink tea.

"I am SO sorry," Bebe was babbling. "It's my shoe—I'm sure it'll wash out of that sweater if you rinse it right now."

"Pink tea?" Mrs. Hadley was saying. "Who drinks *pink tea?*"

"It's part of my detox—"

"Never mind," she said. "I'd better go wash it."

Mrs. Hadley shuffled off to the front-office bathroom. I heard the creak of the door, and then Nate's voice. "You don't want to go in there. Unless you're a plumber."

"Why are you using this bathroom?"

"It's the closest to my locker." I imagined him clutching his stomach. "I think I had some bad sashimi last night."

"You need the nurse."

"I'll get there eventually," he said, and then proceeded to make vomit sounds and slammed the door in her face.

The sounds of Mrs. Hadley's footsteps receded as she made her way to the next nearest girls' bathroom, which was down at the other end of the hall.

Shira, Emily texted. *Wait two minutes.*

I watched the seconds tick by on my phone. At precisely 8:03 the fire alarm went off.

Shira, Emily texted. *Go home.*

I'm gone, she said. *Good luck.*

Bebe said, *I love you.*

Shira said, *I know.*

There was a lot of noise outside as the office staff griped, shoved papers out of the way, and left. Someone forced Nate out of the bathroom, where he groaned and threatened to puke some more.

We waited until everyone was gone, and then Emily pulled a box cutter out of her pocket and proceeded to slice the tape that Bebe had used to seal us inside.

"Aren't you worried Shira will get caught for pulling the alarm?" I asked. "Someone told me they put some kind of dye in those things that shoots out on your hand if you pull one."

She snorted. "She didn't pull it, sugarplum. The first rule of minimizing your footprint: never go digital when you can go analog."

I'd been trying to hold the flaps still while Emily cut, but at that I dropped my hands. "Wait. You don't mean she set an actual fire?"

"Just a small one. Very well contained." She chewed on her lip. "I hope."

"You *hope*."

She bobbled her head in what might or might not have been a nod. "Well, you know, Shira's a little cranky today."

"Well, that's comforting. So what if the fire department shows up before we're done?"

"We'd better hope they don't," she said, pushing the flaps of the box open and stepping out, pulling her backpack out after her and slinging it over her shoulders.

I got out after her, grabbed my own backpack, and then fell over, because my body seemed to have permanently taken to the fetal position. "Ow," I said. "Ow."

"Ow. Ow."

"New plan," I said. "Call a chiropractor."

"That's junk science," Emily groaned, hunching her way toward Mrs. Hadley's desk.

"It's fine," I said. "My insurance wouldn't cover one anyway."

Mrs. Hadley's purse, as we'd hoped, was underneath the desk, left behind during the fire alarm. Emily pulled it out and started rifling through it.

"Is it there?" I asked. "Please tell me it's there."

"Got it," she said, fishing out the phone. I stuck a flash drive into the computer and typed in the password, then pulled up the transcript database.

Please enter access code, it prompted. I heard the phone ding with the incoming text message that would contain the code we needed.

"No no no no no," Emily said. "There's a key lock on the phone."

"What?"

"She locks her phone! She's an eighty-year-old woman who lives with cats! Why does she need to lock her phone?"

"You didn't think about this?"

"No!"

She was attacking the screen with her thumbs. "It's a number," she said. "Probably four or six digits."

"Try her birthday," I suggested, less than helpfully.

She stopped typing and shot me a look. "I'm afraid I forgot to send her a card this year."

I pulled open the top drawer and sifted through its contents.

"What are you looking for?" She was still typing random combinations of numbers. "What if it's her social? UGH."

I hit pay dirt—the card the rest of the faculty had signed

for her last birthday. I showed it to Emily, who said, "That would be helpful, if it had a DATE on it."

I scanned the card. Mr. Bronstein had written in one corner *Happy seventy-fifth!*

"Maybe it's the year," I said. "Try 1943."

She typed it, then slumped. "That's it. We're so late. We're 200% screwed."

She entered the second password from the phone into the computer. "We're in." She opened up the IGradeBook software and pulled up the database.

"Here we go," she said. "Okay. Here's the database." She tapped the screen with her finger. "Blanchard Grades. And—wait. There's a second one. Blanchard University Admissions."

I frowned. "Why would they have two different sets of data?"

She opened the admissions database. "It looks like this is simplified," she said. "It's just end-of-year grades, plus the first-quarter grades from this year."

"Couldn't they just extract those from the regular database?"

"They could," she said. "Maybe they're doing it this way to make it easier on Mrs. Hadley. I don't think she's the most tech-savvy person on campus."

She opened the first database and pulled up my record. "There you are. Does that look right?"

I scanned it, A after A after A. "Yeah, that's right. Except . . ."

"What?"

I pointed to a field on the far right of the screen, called "RANK." "Why is my rank so low?" Mine was 118. "Isn't that class rank?"

"It sure looks like it," she said. "But what's that one?" She pointed to the next field, which was "PFC AMT."

"It's a test-score aggregate?" I suggested.

"I'm not sure," she said. She sorted the database by RANK. Meredith suddenly became number one.

She ran her finger from the PFC AMT to the RANK. "They're inversely connected," she said. "The higher the AMT, the lower the rank. That makes sense, if it's a test score. Maybe there's something to do with the AP scores? Or, like, it's SATs, SAT IIs, and APs all together somehow."

She went back to Explorer and typed, *PFC AMT formula.* "Maybe I can figure out how they're calculating it."

No results.

I scowled, trying to think of what test we'd taken on which Meredith had done so well and I'd done so poorly.

She cleared the search and went back to the database. "Doesn't matter anyway. It doesn't seem to affect the grades. See? Here's Meredith." She pointed at the top entry. "B+ in freshman English. Right?"

"Yeah," I said. "That seems accurate."

"It looks like the grades in the main database haven't been messed with," she said. She clicked over to the college admissions version, which was a lot easier to scan through since it wasn't broken out into quarter grades. "Here you are again."

And there was my messed-up transcript, in all its unholy glory. "That's what I saw at Revere," I said.

She opened Meredith's. The freshman English grade had suddenly turned into an A.

I thought of Meredith, with her little tiny smile, telling me she was smarter than me, when all along, she'd been cheating.

I wanted to claw her face off.

I muttered. "That smug little—"

We heard the footsteps of burly firemen outside the door. "Back in the box," she hissed, and we dove back inside, Emily pulling the flaps shut just as the doors opened.

We heard the firemen walk the perimeter of the room.

"This one's clear," one of them said.

"Someone left the computer on," the other one said.

Emily whispered something under her breath. A prayer, maybe, that they wouldn't notice what was glaringly up on the screen and get suspicious, because there was no way a staff member would have left those files open and walked out of the room.

"Let's go," the other one said.

We waited until we were sure they were gone before we jumped back out of the box.

"We don't have much time left," she said. She bolted back to the computer and typed a few things I didn't see. "I want to check Amy Gregston, too, but this is faster."

"What are you doing?" I asked.

"I'm making a new database," she said. "Using the final grades from both. I want to compare them without having to go one line at a time."

"You think someone else has changes?"

"I think it's possible."

She hit enter, and a new page opened up.

"This has the final grades for all the seniors across all sub-jects for freshman through junior year," she said. "It's set up to flag any changes between the two databases."

"Right," I said. "There's Amy."

"Hang on—I haven't sorted it yet." She clicked to sort it by her flag.

We stared at the screen.

"Holy *crap*," she said.

Her flag was either a 0 or 1, and she'd sorted it so that the 1s—the people with changes—were all at the top of the screen. The entire screen was full of row after row of 1s.

"That can't be right," I said. "You must've done that wrong."

"I didn't do it wrong."

"You must have. That's too many people."

"Mischa—"

"Emily, that's too many people!"

"It's not wrong," she insisted. "Whoa. How many is that?"

I scanned the list, counting in my head. "Nineteen," I said.

She let out a low whistle.

"Meredith wouldn't have done all that. She doesn't even *like* nineteen people."

"It must have been a ring," she said, scrolling down the list. "Some kind of a grade-changing ring. Jesus Christ."

"How many of these people had grades that went up?" I asked.

"Sixteen," she said. "And three went down. Including you." She read the other two names off the list. "David Chu and Lisa Mann."

"I don't—" I started, and then I stopped, because I'd just read the next name on the list.

Nathaniel Miller.

"No," I said. "No."

The bottom went out of my stomach. I stared at the name, waiting to see it morph into something else. There were two Nates in our grade. Maybe it was Nate Oberman. He was a tool. Nate Oberman would totally do something like this.

But this wasn't Nate Oberman. I recognized Nate's creative writing and journalism electives. It was him. It was our Nate. My Nate. "No," I said again.

Emily was stone-faced.

"You're not surprised," I said.

"Are you? Nate didn't have the grades for Emory. You must have wondered about it."

I squirmed inside, because honestly, I had. Nate was one of the smartest people I knew. He wrote beautiful essays—when he turned them in—but he could barely do math to save his life. I knew he'd gotten a C– in precalc last year, because I'm the one who got him through it at all. I glanced at his grades. Apparently precalc wasn't the only math class he'd had problems with.

"There's no way he was in on this," I said.

"Mischa," she said. "Look at what's in front of you!"

"But he was helping us! Why help us, if he knew he was going to get caught?"

She shook her head. "Nate is . . ."

"No," I said. "No, I know him. He wouldn't do this. Why would he?"

"Maybe because he got scared," she said. "He must have known he didn't have what it took to get in there. Maybe he got worried he wouldn't be able to handle it, and he wanted out."

"I don't believe that," I said. "That's a load of crap."

"The evidence says otherwise," she said.

"Stop copying the database," I said.

"What? No!"

"Emily—"

"Mischa, pay attention! Do you not get it? There are nine-teen people on this list. Sixteen people who got a spot that should have gone to someone else. Three people who got shafted."

When I said nothing, she said, "You do remember that you're one of those people, right?"

"Believe me," I said. "I haven't forgotten."

There was a rumbling out in the hallway—the students coming back into the building.

"We have everything copied," Emily said, pulling the flash drive out of the computer and logging off. "Time to go."

"Don't do this to him," I said. "Emily, he didn't do this."

"If we don't get out of here, we're going to get caught!"

We both stopped and looked up, because the voices were now a whole lot closer than they had been thirty seconds ago.

"Are they *running*?"

"We need to get out of here," I said.

"I'm glad you caught up to that," she said. I followed her to the door. There were people there. People who were about to see us coming out of the office.

Mrs. Hadley was one of them.

We figured this out just as she opened the door and saw us. In the office. She saw us in the office. I thought, *Those orange prison jumpsuits are super ugly, and also my mother is never going to forgive me for this.*

"Hi, Mrs. Hadley," Emily said, her expression suddenly brightening. "We saw Bebe outside, and she told us about your sweater." She shrugged out of her backpack and unzipped it, pulling out a Target bag. "I just bought this last night, but then I realized it's a petite, and I don't wear petite, and I thought . . ."

She handed Mrs. Hadley a white cardigan with kittens em-broidered on the pockets. Mrs. Hadley took it, a little reluc-tantly. "Oh," she said. "I couldn't."

"Oh, please take it," Emily said earnestly. "Bebe feels awful, and I was just going to return it anyway."

She ran a hand over one of the tiny ginger kittens. "You girls are so thoughtful," she said. "Thank you."

"Anytime, Mrs. Hadley," Emily said smoothly.

"You'd better get to class," Mrs. Hadley said. "I wouldn't want you to be tardy."

"You're absolutely right," Emily said, and pulled me out into the hallway. "Contingencies," she said to my raised eye-brows. And then she disappeared into the throng of students flooding the hall on their way to class.

CHAPTER THIRTY

I JOINED THE CROWD OF PEOPLE ON THEIR WAY TO FIRST PERIOD.
My head was kind of cottony. A ring. There was an entire ring
of people at Blanchard with changed grades. People had used
it to get into places like Stanford and Yale and Harvard. And
they'd used it to keep me out.

Nate had been one of them. That's what the evidence
showed.

Would Nate really do something like that? It went against
everything I thought I knew about him.

But I'd seen his name on the list.

On my way into class, he texted me: *Did you get it?*

I stuck my phone away, riddled with doubts and guilt.

Emory, I knew, was Nate's dream school. He had family
in Atlanta and was dying to go down there to be closer to his
cousins and aunts and uncles, and he loved the city and the

campus. He'd been talking about going there since sophomore year, and he'd been so, so excited when he'd gotten the letter. But I'd seen his math grades. Emory wouldn't accept those. They just wouldn't.

Nate must have known that.

He found me after class. "You didn't answer me," he said. "I had to text Emily. She said you got the database."

I stared fixedly at the floor. "Is that all she said?"

"Ye-es," he said slowly. "Why? Did you guys end up making out in the box?"

"No," I said. "We didn't make out in the box." I rubbed my eyes. "We found nineteen people with changed transcripts." I looked up at him, waiting for a twitch, a grimace, something that would indicate that he'd known anything about this at all.

But he just said, "Whoa. That's. Whoa. So, Meredith Dorsay?"

I wasn't sure whether he meant that Meredith's transcript was changed, or that Meredith was the one who had changed it, which had been the prevailing theory until about an hour ago. I said, "Meredith was one of them. Yeah."

He said, "And you."

"Well, obviously, me."

"Anybody else we know?" he asked.

I hedged. His eyes were troubled, like you'd expect, but the fact was that Nate was a terrible, terrible liar, and if he'd known something was wrong with his transcript, it would be all over his face. And it wasn't. "Nobody interesting," I said. "Look, let's talk tonight. Okay?"

"Are you all right?"

"Yeah," I said. "I think maybe I was just in that box too long. I'm feeling—I don't know. Claustrophobic. Or something."

I texted Emily on my way into class. *He didn't know,* I said. *I'm sure of it.*

There was no response.

Emily, come on.

Again, nothing.

We're going to have to talk about this sometime!

Finally a text came through; it was a selfie of Ms. Ishikawa, the computer science teacher, looking thoroughly pissed, and a caption that said, *EMILY CAN'T COME TO THE PHONE RIGHT NOW BECAUSE SHE IS IN CLASS, MISCHA ABRAMAVICIUS. WHAT CLASS ARE YOU SUPPOSED TO BE IN?*

I stashed my phone without answering.

On my way to lunch I got a text from Shira. It was a selfie of her at Panera, in front of an entire chocolate cake with a fork stuck in it. It said, *Suspension not so bad!*

It was a group text, and Bebe responded, *Save me some of that cake.*

Shira replied, *Not bloody likely.*

When I got to the dining hall, Caroline was sitting alone with a bowl of tomato soup and a cheese sandwich, and it occurred to me that, unlike Meredith, unlike Nate, she'd actually earned her spot at college all on her own. I wondered if she knew that, at Blanchard, that made her special.

I was still feeling a little numb, but I didn't really want to be alone, and Caroline was kind of a safe space. She was pure, somehow, untouched by either cheating or cybercrime.

"Hey," I said. "Mind if I sit?"

Caroline looked at me. I was aware that I'd barely spoken

to her in weeks, and she was probably mad about that. I said, "I can go, if you want."

"No," she said. "It's okay."

I picked the crust off one edge of my sandwich while she watched. After a minute she said, a little hesitantly, "I decided on Columbia. By the way."

"Oh," I said. "Wow."

"It's okay," she said. "I don't expect you to be happy for me or anything."

"I am," I said. "Happy for you. I'm happy for you. I think Columbia's great. There's the city. With the bodegas. And the cats."

"Yeah," she said flatly.

"Look," I said. "I'm sorry. I know I haven't been the greatest friend."

"Maybe we should just change the subject."

"Okay."

She yawned and rubbed the heels of her hands into her eye sockets with a groan.

"Are you okay?" I asked.

"Yeah," she said. "I'm just tired." She looked it, I realized. Her posture was abnormal—slumped, I guess—and her hair looked like she'd forgotten to brush it in the back. In short, she looked pretty much like I felt. Which was bad. It was bad.

"Up late?"

"Yeah. We had a practice AP in Latin today. I was studying."

I laughed, because suddenly that struck me as really funny, taking a practice AP. "It never ends, does it?"

"Nope. It never ends. Well, I guess I'll die someday."

"Yeah."

"Yeah."

"That probably shouldn't seem like such a relief," she said.

I sat up a little and looked at her again. She really didn't look so great. "Seriously, are you okay?"

"Yeah. I'm okay. Or I will be, in about four hours."

"You're sure."

"I'm sure."

I ate a spoonful of my soup. It was not hot. Probably it had not been hot for some time. "Why do we do this to ourselves?"

"What else are we going to do?"

"I don't know," I said. "Move to a commune? Turn on, tune in, drop out?"

"Smoke some dope?" She laughed. "That didn't turn out so well for Shira Gastman." I showed her the picture of the cake on my phone. "Or maybe it did," she said.

I put the phone away and ate a corner off my sandwich. "Hey, if you hadn't gotten into Columbia or Dartmouth, what would you have done?"

"Um. Gone to UVA, probably. Or someplace else, I don't know."

"What if you hadn't gotten in anyplace else?"

"Hey," she said gently. "Revere's not so bad. You know my step-cousin who went there? He's totally in law school now. He loved it there."

"I'm not talking about me," I said, even though I kind of was. I was also thinking about Nate. I was thinking about what it must feel like to know your dream is out of reach because of a couple of math grades. If that would make you do something you normally wouldn't.

"Do you want to get together to study for that quiz in government on Thursday?" she asked.

I set my sandwich back down on my plate. "Actually, I hadn't been planning on studying for that."

"So, what, you're just giving up? On everything?"

I shrugged and ate my soup. It tasted a little too much like the inside of a tin can and that worried me, but I kept eating it because it was in front of me and I was hungry. "Listen," I said, "you know Sisyphus? Guy with the boulder? Cursed with having to roll it up a hill for all eternity and stuff?"

"Sure."

"You ever wonder why he didn't just . . . stop . . . pushing the boulder?"

"Well, he couldn't. That was the curse. He was in hell, that was the whole point."

"Yeah," I said. "But what were they going to do, make him push an even bigger boulder? What was stopping him from just sitting down in the dirt and saying, 'I am not pushing any more stinking rocks up this stinking hill.'"

Caroline scowled. "I can't remember. I'm pretty sure there was a reason, though."

"But what if there wasn't? What if someone just told him to do it, and he just kept doing it because it never occurred to him he had a choice?"

"So in this analogy," she said, "you're Sisyphus. And the boulder is—"

"High school, yeah."

"And you're just . . ." She made a flourish with her spoon. "Giving up."

"Yes."

"And you think nothing's going to happen to you."

"I think nothing *worse* is going to happen to me," I corrected her.

"Mischa," she said, "things can always get worse."

Bebe found me at the end of the day; she was still limping on her broken shoe. I guess it would have been a giveaway if she'd had an extra pair with her that day. That we'd had an extra kitten sweater with us had been bad enough.

"Hey," she said. "I heard, you know. Stuff."

"Yeah," I said. "We found stuff. It was . . ."

"Stuff."

"Yeah. It was stuff."

"So we're going to Emily's now. Emily and me. To analyze the stuff. Are you coming?"

"I don't know," I said. "Do you really think Nate was in on this? You know him. Can you imagine him lying about something this big?"

"I'm not really sure," she said. "I haven't analyzed—"

"The stuff."

"Right." She started walking toward the doors, and I followed.

"Emily thinks so," I said. "Occam's razor, right? If it looks like there was a grade-changing ring, there was probably a grade-changing ring."

"That's not how Occam's razor works. We haven't even thought about the other possibilities."

"Which are?"

"Not sure yet. But say it's true. There was a ring, and Nate was in on it. Does it change anything?"

"Of course it does!"

She stopped short and turned toward me. "Would you really cover this up to protect Nate? You would just . . . not go to college. For him."

I exhaled slowly. "No. I guess not."

"Glad we got that straight." She started walking again—tiptoe, *click,* tiptoe, *click*—in her broken-down shoes.

When we got to Emily's, she already had both databases open, one on each of the two monitors that were set up on the desk in her basement.

"I feel like I'm missing something," she said as Bebe and I went to sit next to her. "Sixteen people with grades that went up. Sixteen people with nothing in common. They aren't friends. They aren't necessarily applying to the same colleges. They don't play the same sports. A lot of them don't even like each other."

"Maybe they didn't know who else was involved," I said. "Maybe, like, there was one central person changing the grades."

"I considered that," she said. She pulled out a piece of paper on which she'd drawn a web, connecting the sixteen people to one another. "But there isn't one person who's friends with everyone else, and it's not like they could be bribed, because all these people are super rich."

Bebe turned to look at her. "All of them?"

"Yeah," Emily said. "Look at the list. These are the sixteen people who had their grades tampered with."

Bebe pointed at the RANK field. "What's that?" she asked.

"Class rank," I said. "But it seems to be influenced by test scores, too. We're not really sure how it works."

Emily pointed at the PFC AMT field. "Near as I can figure, it's SATs plus some kind of number made from AP scores? I don't know. We couldn't find a formula. . . ."

Bebe nudged Emily out of the way and scrolled up and down the screen. "Are you guys completely out of it?" she asked. "Did you even look at the range?"

I looked at the numbers again. I hadn't actually been paying that much attention. "What?"

"One fifty to eighty-eight thousand? What kind of test score does that? Even if it's an aggregate, that doesn't make any sense."

"We were a little busy not getting arrested," Emily said. "We didn't exactly have time to analyze—"

"You saw what you expected to see," Bebe said.

Emily glared at her, but Bebe continued as if nothing had happened. "Now, where am I?" she muttered, scanning down the list. Her rank was somewhere in the middle.

Tandoh, Beatrice. RANK: 62. PFC AMT: 3000.

"It's a dollar amount," she said. "Parental Financial Contribution Amount."

"How can you possibly have figured that out?" Emily asked.

"It's the only thing that makes sense with this big a range," she went on. "My parents give seven hundred and fifty dollars to the school every December. Over four years, that's three thousand bucks." She scanned down to the bottom of the list, where the last half a dozen people had numbers under five hundred. Mine was one fifty. "I'm guessing your mom didn't donate much to the school," she said.

"She paid the tuition," I said.

"These are gifts to the annual fund," she said. "It's not part of the tuition."

"I didn't realize that was required," I said.

"It's not," she said. "It's a tax write-off."

"Apparently it was a little more than that," Emily said.

"Wait," I said. "Wait. So RANK is—"

"It's a fundraising rank," Bebe said. "It's the rank of whose parents gave the most money to the school. It's got nothing to do with class rank."

Bebe and Emily looked at each other over my head. "Tell me you're not seeing this," Bebe said.

But we were. Because now that we had the lists side by side on two different monitors, we could see exactly who the sixteen people with baked transcripts were.

It was the top sixteen ranked students.

Emily sat back from the desk. "Oh my God."

"Money makes the world go round," Bebe said.

"There was no grade-changing ring," I said. "But wait. Are you saying it was someone at the school?"

"No," Emily said. "Mischa, it *was* the school."

I felt strange.

When I was a little eighth-grader in my navy blue suit, I'd come to Blanchard for my tour and my interview, and Ms. Whitman, the admissions director, had offered me a plate of cookies and talked to me for forty minutes about what I wanted out of high school and where I hoped to be in ten years. Afterward she'd said to my mom, "She's very articulate. Any school would be lucky to have her." My mom had been so proud. I'd been so proud.

Emily was still talking. "Someone in the administration,

at least. Someone high enough to care where the money was coming from."

"No," I said, because the logical part of my brain was still telling me this didn't add up. "No, that doesn't make any sense."

Emily shook her head over my objection. "They're socially engineering their student output so that the kids with the most money go to the best colleges. If I'm right, with these new transcripts, the entire top 20% of the class is now the kids of major donors."

"I understand why they would bump up people's grades," I said. "But why bump mine down so much? Why write those fake recommendation letters?"

"What were your SAT scores?" Bebe asked.

"1580," I said. "And I had 5s on four AP tests last year."

"That's why," she said. "They didn't want to risk you getting a spot they wanted for someone else. So they cut you off at the knees."

"I don't understand, though. What does the school have to gain by me getting in nowhere?" I pointed at Lisa Mann. "Lisa still got into Chapel Hill. That's what Shira said. I don't think they'd have taken her with a D in trig. And David's going to Johns Hopkins."

"I'm not sure," Emily said. "It doesn't make sense. But there are only two possibilities: either they really hate you, or someone screwed up."

"But that would have to be Ms. Pendleton," I said. "She's the one who sends these out to colleges. And she's been gone for weeks."

"She was definitely in on it," Emily agreed. "But someone higher up was pulling the strings. What does the college counselor care about fundraising?"

"Who do you think it was?" I asked.

"I don't know. My money's on Pelletier."

"Why him?"

"The Lexus," she said. "Plus he's a schmuck."

"That would be nice," Bebe said. "We turn him in to Marlowe and the whole thing's done in an hour. I bet he was the one who framed Shira, too. It makes sense; he was the one running the locker search."

"Wait," I said. "He was there that day, when Shira was talking about the transcripts in the hall—he was yelling at Derek Logan about that stupid hat. Pelletier must have heard us. So can we prove it was him?"

"Check the metadata," Bebe said. "It'll tell you who created the fake records."

"They would have masked their IP address," Emily said. "No one would do something this illegal and leave their fingerprints on it."

"Just do it," Bebe said. "The Instagram was a hack job, too."

Emily pulled up the metadata for my fake transcript. It looked like this:

```
Abramavicius, Mischa
Record Added: January 7, 2018 8:47 p.m.
Record Last Modified: January 7,
2018 8:47 p.m.
Created by: Administrator
Changed by: Administrator
IP Address: 107.32.24.1
```

"Well, that's helpful," I said. "Who's Administrator?"

"Could be anyone," Bebe said. "We'd need to check the IP

address, and to do that we'd have to look at every staff computer on campus."

Emily smirked. "Or we could check this," she said, pulling a folded piece of paper out of her pocket. It was a list of IP addresses. A long list.

"Where did you get that?" Bebe asked, incredulous.

"I went after school to get my phone back from Ishikawa, but she wasn't there, so I checked her desk." She gave us a smug smile. "I found this in her top drawer."

"Why would she have it?" I asked.

"She does tech support for the staff," Bebe said, scanning down the list. "Oh," she said, her face falling. "So much for that idea."

IP: 107.32.24.1 Assigned: R. Marlowe.

CHAPTER THIRTY-ONE

My mother was in front of her computer when I got home, her laptop sitting open on the kitchen table like she'd been paying the bills online, except I didn't see any bills around, or her checkbook register, or anything else like that. She looked at me, a long look that spoke of disappointment, like the time she caught me stealing five dollars from her purse to buy candy when I was six.

She pushed back from the kitchen table and watched me for a good long minute.

I thought: *She knows about Revere.*

There were a limited number of people who could have told her, though. And I couldn't figure out why they would have.

"Hi," I said.

"Sit down," she said. I sat. She turned the computer to face me. "I want you to explain this," she said.

It was my Instagram page.

I'd thought it would be down by now. According to Emily, it should have been down by now. But there it was, still live, and either Mom had noticed the block or someone had told her to take a look at it. Either way, this was bad.

What she was looking at wasn't the picture of me at the party, though. It was a letter. Some long diatribe about the unfairness of life, about how every college I'd applied to had rejected me, and about how I was bound to get revenge on the good people of the Blanchard School, whose fault this all was, in some unspecified way. The letter got increasingly strange and disjointed the longer it went on, deluded, paranoid, enraged. There were oblique references to fire. And then I said I was going to kill myself.

"I didn't write this," I said. "Someone made this entire thing up and then sent you the link. My page got hacked a few days ago. I tried to report it."

Without speaking, she took two folded pieces of paper from next to her laptop and slid them toward me.

I unfolded them.

To Whom It May Concern:

It is only with grave reservations that I
write this letter. On the one hand, Mischa
is a very bright student, as her test
scores attest.

No. *No.*

"*You searched my room?*" I asked.

"Mischa," she said. "Did you get into Revere? If I ask you to show me your acceptance letter, can you do that?"

I swallowed. "No."

"Did you get in anywhere you applied to?"

"No," I said. "I didn't. That part's true. Someone hacked my transcript and my letters—"

"Mischa, stop."

"It's true!" I pulled out my phone. "Call Emily Sreenivasan. She'll tell you."

"She's friends with that girl who got caught with the drugs, right?"

"Shira was framed! How do you even know all this?"

"So you've been lying to me for the last month. About Revere."

"I didn't want to," I said desperately.

"But you did. I've been burning myself to the ground for four years to send you to Blanchard, so that you could lie to me about this? When were you planning on telling me? When I dropped you off for orientation?"

"Mom—"

She slammed her fist down on the table. "NO. This is not okay."

"What? That I didn't get in anywhere? Or that I let you think I had?"

"You lied. You LIED to me."

"But that's not really what you're mad about," I said. "Is it? It was bad enough that your daughter got rejected from everywhere good, but now you have to tell everyone that I got in NOWHERE."

"Damn it, Mischa."

"You're not mad. You're ashamed."

She jammed a finger toward the computer screen. "And

you're going to fix all this by setting fire to your school? Killing yourself?"

"No," I said. "No. I didn't write that. The person who hacked me put that up there."

"How can I possibly believe anything you say to me?"

"Because I'm your daughter! Because the only reason I didn't tell you about Revere is because I knew how disappointed you'd be! I thought if I could fix everything, apply someplace else, it wouldn't matter. But I haven't been able to—"

"Mischa," she said. "If you really thought your transcript had been hacked, why didn't you come to me in the first place?"

I stopped short. "I don't know," I said. Which was another lie. I hadn't told her because I didn't think she'd believe me. Because telling her meant I'd also have to tell her about all my rejections. And I couldn't handle it.

"Go to your room," she said.

"But—"

"Now."

"What are you going to do?"

"Mischa. I don't know what I'm going to do." She closed the laptop. "I suppose you've figured out that you're suspended."

I gaped at her. "From Blanchard?"

"Yes."

"Because of that Instagram post?"

"Yes. Apparently someone from the school found it. You can't threaten people at school and expect nothing to come of it."

"But I didn't—"

"Mischa. Go. Now."

···

I went into my room and shut the door.

My phone rang in my pocket, and I silenced the ringer before my mom heard it. I was surprised, actually, that it hadn't occurred to her to take it away, especially if she thought I was lighting up the Internet with homicidal blog entries.

It was Emily. I picked it up and curled up on the floor between my bed and the wall.

"They're going to expel Shira," she said.

"What? No," I said. "No, you said—"

"They aren't going to graduate her early, even. They're just tossing her out."

"Is she okay?"

"What a stupid question."

"Sorry."

"Bebe's hysterical. She won't even talk to me."

"Why won't she talk to you?"

"She thinks this is my fault, because it was my idea to help you. They're using Shira to shut us up."

"But if they've already kicked her out, what else can they do?"

"Can you really think of nothing? Mischa, they're sitting on a distribution charge. If they go to the cops, Shira goes to jail."

I had nothing to say to that. Shira, in jail. Over a bag of joints that hadn't even been hers. I couldn't believe it.

"They can't come after me or Bebe directly. My mom's on the board, and Bebe's family has too much clout." She coughed, like maybe some part of her wanted to cry, but some other part wouldn't allow it. "I'm surprised they haven't tried to come after you yet."

I screwed my eyes shut. "Oh. You don't know." I texted her a link to my Instagram page.

"Great," she said. "You might have led with this. I can't believe they haven't suspended your account yet."

"It's too late anyway," I said. "My mother already saw it. Someone sent it to her, and I'm suspended from Blanchard."

"Who sent it? Marlowe?"

"I don't know. She wouldn't say."

"Hardly matters," she said. "Damn it. Damn it!"

"What are we going to do?"

"We have to get this database into the hands of someone who can do something with it," she said. "Now."

CHAPTER THIRTY-TWO

I SNUCK OUT OF THE HOUSE WHEN MY MOTHER WENT TO HER room to lie down. I left a note—just in case she checked on me—telling her I was coming back, I was sorry for lying, and I was not going to set anything on fire.

I realized that probably none of this would sound very comforting to her once she woke up and found the note next to my phone, which I'd left so she wouldn't be able to call, and so she'd know I was unreachable. Also, from everything I'd learned from Emily, I didn't want to take a chance that someone could use the GPS on the phone to track me.

Nate picked me up, and after we drove back to his house I sat on his bed with Emily, who had driven over and was playing Angry Birds in a much angrier way than had originally been intended.

Here is a list of people who refused to look at Blanchard's transcript database: The police (after laughing their heads off), who referred us to the FBI. The FBI (after laughing their heads off), who referred us to the police. The *Washington Gazette*, who did not laugh their heads off but told us that if we sent them the database, they'd put it up on the board, and one of their reporters might give us a callback. Someday.

After we'd made our useless phone calls, Nate went out to pick up some dinner. Emily eventually shut off the game and sat staring at her lock screen, which I could see from where I sat was a picture of her, Bebe, and Shira, with splotches of paint all over their faces and hair, laughing hysterically, arms around each other. On the windowsill, Maury's empty eye sockets had been filled with orange gumballs, making him look even creepier than usual.

"A paint fight?" I asked, pointing to the picture on Emily's phone.

"It was Holi," she said. "The temple has a big festival."

"It looks like fun."

"It was fun." She sighed and tossed her phone onto the bed. "You're an only child."

"Yeah."

"Do you hate it?"

"No," I said. "I—I guess I never really thought about it."

"No," she said. "You wouldn't. I hate it. I've always hated it."

"They're your sisters," I said. "Bebe and Shira."

"They're my sisters. Only they aren't. Bebe and I went to preschool together—did you know that? But she and Shira, well. I can't compete." She swallowed hard and wiped her eyes on the back of her wrist.

"You should say something to them," I said. "Once this is all over."

"It's too late," she said.

"How is it too late?"

"Look, in like six months we're all going different places."

"Yeah, but you're still going to be friends, right?"

She shrugged. "You really think you're still going to be friends with Nate this time next year?"

"Yeah," I said, more than a little defensively. "I do."

She shook her head. "You just think that because you're in love with him."

"No," I said. "That's not it. Being friends is important. Maybe more important."

She took a deep breath and stared at her phone some more.

I said, "I want you to fix Nate's transcript. I mean, if we actually find someone who will even look at the database, I want you to fix it so that he's not on the list anymore."

She put the phone down and looked up at me. "What?"

"Just make both versions of his transcript match. You can do that. Can't you?"

"Of course I can, but—"

"Look, it's not like we thought before. He wasn't in on it. This wasn't his fault."

"That's not the point!"

"If it was Shira or Bebe, you'd do it."

"No," she said. "I wouldn't insult them like that."

"That's a glib answer."

"No, it's not," she said. "Mischa, do you not understand the scope of what we've found out? Dick Marlowe's been the headmaster at Blanchard for thirty years. That's *hundreds* of people who either took a spot they didn't earn or got screwed out of one they did. And that's if you think that Marlowe was the person who instigated this. What if he wasn't? The school's a hundred years old. This could have been going on since it was founded, for all we know."

"I know, and all that's going to come out! But so what if we fix this for Nate first? He's only one person!"

"Once I start messing around with the data, the school can just say the whole thing was faked. Our evidence is tampered with."

"But you can't just throw Nate under the bus," I said.

"I'm not throwing Nate anywhere. He landed under the bus on his own."

"That's not fair."

"How is it not fair?"

"Because he—"

"Nate had a crappy childhood," she said. "Lots of people have crappy childhoods, way worse than having nagging parents who make you go to too many soccer practices and six-day tutoring. He's not worth more than everyone else just because he's your boyfriend."

I couldn't think of any way to argue back. I wanted to tell her that Nate *deserved* to go to Emory. But that wasn't a rational argument, and Emily wasn't going to listen to that. I slumped down onto the floor, leaning against the side of Nate's bed. "Well, I guess it doesn't matter anyway. Since no one will help us."

When she didn't answer, I turned to see her tapping her fingernails against her temple.

"What are you thinking?"

"I'm thinking," she said, "that we need two things. We need someone with a connection. And we need Marlowe to incriminate himself."

"I don't know anyone with connections," I said. "And if Marlowe's behind the Instagram hack and the drugs, he's never talking to either of us again."

"No. He's not talking to either of us. Not on purpose, anyway."

"Nate?"

"Everyone at that school knows you and Nate are joined at the hip. No. There's only one person at Blanchard for whom Richard Marlowe will come panting. And she's not going to want to help us."

"I'm not following you," I said.

"Think, Mischa. Think about that list. Think about who is paying Richard Marlowe's Christmas bonus. Think about who he handpicked to get into Harvard." She smiled grimly. "Think about who has the connections to get this into the press by tomorrow morning."

No. "She's not going to help us. Not unless she thinks she doesn't have a choice."

Emily said, "So we don't give her a choice."

Nate came back a few minutes later with a bag of Chinese takeout, which he set on his desk. Emily grabbed a spring roll and started eating it, and then handed one to me.

I took a bite. "Meredith Dorsay," I said, "is not going to help me."

"She's not helping you," Emily said. "And you aren't going to be the one asking. At least not at first."

"You're going to go?" I said. "No offense, but you aren't exactly the most diplomatic person."

"I'll go," Nate said.

Emily winced, just a little. I wanted to cry, just a little. More than that, maybe.

"You?" I said. "I don't know . . ."

"It makes the most sense," he said. "I've known Meredith since we were two. Our parents know each other. She'll listen to me more than she will to Emily."

"Are you sure?" Emily said. "When you went to talk to Beth Reinhardt—"

"That was different," he said. "All I have to do is go tell Meredith the truth. I can tell the truth." I flinched a little, remembering the part of me—the small part, but a part nonetheless—that had doubted his honesty. Nate checked the time on his phone. "It's not that late yet. I'll go see if I can get her to come over."

Nate left, shutting the door behind him.

Emily said, "Tell him. Tell him now."

"No," I said. "Emily, I can't."

"If you don't tell him now," she said, "he's going to find out when we show Meredith the database. Tell him now. It's better from you than from me. Go." She motioned toward the door. "*Go.*"

I followed Nate out into the hallway, jogging to catch up to him.

"Nate," I said, pulling him into the Millers' guest room. A queen bed with a navy comforter took up most of the room. I shut the door behind us and locked it.

"I'm flattered," he said, nodding at the bed. "But I think that will have to wait."

"No, listen. I have to tell you something."

"I have to go," he said, kissing the top of my head. "I have to go talk to Meredith."

"Nate!" He stopped halfway to the door. "You're on the list," I said quietly.

His hand, which had been reaching for the doorknob, dropped to his side. "What?"

"You're on the list. Your transcript is on the list."

He ran his fingers through his hair with one hand, while the other drew into a fist in front of his mouth. I could hear him suck in a breath, even from across the room.

I watched him go into his head, like he wasn't even in the room anymore. I don't know what he saw, but it wasn't me. I watched the reality of what I was telling him sink in.

He hadn't gotten into Emory. Not really. It was all fake. His transcript. His admissions letter. And if we succeeded, if we got Meredith to help us, Emory would find out what his grades really were. There was a very good chance they'd pull their offer. And he'd have to explain all this to his parents.

"Your math grades—" I started.

He cut me off with a wave. "How many?"

"What?"

"How many grades did they change?"

I swallowed. "Four," I said. "All your math grades, except Algebra I."

He made this terrible wheezing sound from his chest. Then he kicked the wall, hard enough to leave a dent. "Damn it," he said. "God damn it." His hands went over his face, and he let out one racking sob and then another. Then he slid down the wall to the floor.

I did this, I thought. I was the person who was hurting him.

"I feel the floor," he was whispering. "I feel the wall. I hear Emily playing that stupid game. I smell my mother's laundry detergent. . . ."

"Nate," I whispered.

"Sit next to me," he said. "Please."

I did. "Closer," he said, then: "Closer." I pressed myself hard enough against his side so that it was almost painful.

"Too close?" I asked.

"No," he said. "God. God. God."

"I'm sorry," I said.

He was counting under his breath. I didn't know what to do, so I just sat there with my shoulder cutting into his. When he got to thirty-four, he said, "Why didn't you tell me? Why didn't you tell me earlier?"

"I—I thought I could get Emily to change the record. To make it look like it was supposed to."

He lifted his tear-soaked face from his hands. "You what?"

"I thought I could get her to make your records match," I said. "I thought if she did that, you wouldn't show up on the list anymore, and nobody would ever have to know that it happened, and Emory wouldn't find out, and you wouldn't find out, but she doesn't want to do it, but if I keep talking to her maybe there's a way—"

"Mischa," he said, his breath shuddering, "stop."

"She can change it," I said. "I can convince her. I know she really likes you, and she'll do it if you ask, you just have to ask her, Nate. You'll still get to go. To Emory, I mean. They won't have to find out."

I watched him breathe for a minute. He was counting his

breaths. I counted them with him, silently, because I didn't know what else to do.

Quietly he said, "Is that what you think of me?"

"I don't. What?"

"Four years. We've been friends for four years. And you think I want to cheat to get into college?"

"No," I said. "No, it's just, you're already in there. You're already in, and I know you want to go, and you should go, because who cares how you did in geometry? It doesn't matter, Nate, it shouldn't matter, because I know you."

"How much?" he asked. "How much money did my parents give the school?"

"What difference does it make?"

"Mischa!"

I swallowed. I could tell him I didn't remember the number, but I figured I'd lied to him enough already. "Sixty thousand dollars," I said.

He swore and let the back of his head bang against the wall. Then he started to laugh. "They don't quit, do they?"

"Your parents?"

"Yeah. They couldn't get me to play their game. So they played it with Blanchard instead."

"You don't think they knew about this, do you? That the school would change your grades?"

"I don't know. Maybe they thought . . . I don't know what they thought. Damn it. God damn it."

I was losing circulation in my left arm, but I didn't say anything. I didn't tell him everything would be okay.

"What are we going to do?" I asked.

"Well, I'm going to talk to Meredith," he said. "Just as soon as I remember how to stand up."

"What about Emory?"

He closed his eyes. "Well, I imagine I won't get in." He sighed. "I can't feel my arm anymore."

"Sorry," I said. I scooted away about half an inch, and he flexed the fingers of his right hand to get the feeling back.

"What am I going to do with all those sweatshirts?" he asked, shaking his head.

"How many do you have? Like, seven?"

"Nine," he said, laughing sadly. "I have nine. Who has nine sweatshirts from the same school? Ugh. Maybe I'll sell them on eBay. Or burn them."

"They're a poly blend," I said. "I don't think they'd burn. They'd probably just melt."

He turned his head to look at me for the first time since he'd sat down. He gave me the saddest smile in the world. "Thanks for the warning."

"Nate," I said, leaning my head against his shoulder. "If it were just me, I'd tell Emily to forget it. Just delete the whole thing and pretend we'd never seen it."

"I'm not going to let all this happen to you and Shira just so I can keep my Emory letter," he said. "Don't be stupid."

"I just wish—"

"I know," he said. "I wish it, too."

CHAPTER THIRTY-THREE

AN HOUR LATER THE DOOR TO NATE'S BEDROOM CREAKED OPEN and Meredith stepped in, followed by Nate.

She said nothing. I said nothing. Emily held up Maury and said, "Gumball?"

Meredith said, "No." She sat down on Nate's desk chair, leaving Nate to join Emily and me on the bed. "Can we cut to the chase? If you have proof that my transcript was changed, I want to see it."

Emily had already extracted Meredith's fake transcript from the database and printed it out, and she handed it over.

Meredith put her face very close to the paper. "I see no difference," she said.

"Oh come on!" I shouted, before I remembered that Nate's parents and sister were all down the hall, and I really needed to shut up.

"The freshman English grade," Nate said. "We all know you didn't get an A."

"I should have," she muttered.

"And yet you didn't," Emily said. "Funny how that works."

"So you're saying there are more like this," she said.

"A lot more."

"Who?" she asked, eyes narrowed. Emily pulled out a handwritten list of names and handed that over, too. I wondered why she didn't just show Meredith the actual database, but then it dawned on me that Emily didn't trust Meredith to get her hands anywhere near the data.

"And you're saying these people were all inflated?"

"Most of them," she said. "Mischa was dropped. So were David Chu and Lisa Mann."

"But they both got into college," she pointed out.

"Right. They weren't dropped as much as Mischa. But they were dropped, just enough to keep them out of the top 20% of the class."

"Because their parents didn't donate money to the school."

"That's the gist of it, yeah."

"And mine did."

"Do you know how much your parents gave Blanchard over the last four years?" Emily asked.

"We don't talk about money," she said. "It's tacky."

I snorted. Emily simply waved her off and said, "Eighty-eight thousand dollars. On top of your tuition."

"That's a lot of money just to change a B+ to an A," she said.

"Yes. It is."

"And you want me to help you because . . ."

This was the part where we bluffed, because up until now we'd only told her the truth. The lie was that we had any way, any way at all, to actually do anything with the information we had.

"Because it's the right thing to do?" Emily said. "I thought Lisa was your friend."

"We're friendly," she hedged.

"Let me spell it out for you," I said. "We're going public with this, either on your terms or ours. If you play along, you look like a hero. You're a whistle-blower, and everyone loves those. You did the right thing even though you had something to lose."

"And if I don't?"

"Then you're the girl whose parents bought her way into Harvard."

When she sat silent, I said, "Didn't you say you'd rather go to community college than take a spot you hadn't earned? I guess it's time to put that to the test."

She scowled. I could see the gears turning. I didn't think she knew we were bluffing. Finally she said, "If I help you, I want one thing. I want the story to go out with my name on it. Alone. I was the one who figured all this out. I want all of the credit."

"You piece of—"

"You can have it," Emily said. "Who will you send it to?"

"Margot," she said. "My cousin. She's at MSNBC. If I give her the story, she'll make sure it runs."

"Keeping it in the family," Nate said.

"If I send it to a stranger," she said, rolling her eyes, "they might not believe it. Margot will believe it, if it's from me."

This is what we'd been banking on, but that didn't make it any less infuriating.

"You're hoping that if you get all the credit, Harvard will forgive you the B+," I said.

"Gee, Michelle. I got a B+. And *you* got completely, totally shafted. But if you don't want my help, that's your call." She smirked. "I'll enjoy ordering hamburgers from you."

Nate muttered, "Crap."

I said, too loudly again, "I don't know what your problem is! I showed up the first week of school, and you decided you hated me. I was just some random person you decided to focus your ire on, or whatever. What did I ever do to you?"

"You were in my way," she said through gritted teeth.

"This is high school," I said. "Not *Game of Thrones!*"

"Oh, please. It's exactly like *Game of Thrones*. Life is like *Game of Thrones*. There are only so many spots at the best schools. Only so many jobs. You have to be on your A game every day, Mischa, or you end up like a wounded wildebeest. You have a cruddy leg, and you can't keep up, and BAM. You get culled."

"That's a crappy metaphor. Wildebeests don't eat each other."

"Fine! Pick a carnivore! Not the point!"

"Ladies," Emily said. "Nate, why don't you show Meredith that book. About the thing. Mischa—" She jerked her head toward the door. "Step out with me. Please."

She dragged me out into the hallway, shutting the door behind her.

"Are you going to tell me," I said, "that she's just another cog caught in Blanchard's machinery? None of this is her fault, and I should go easy on her?"

"Oh no," she said. "No. She's awful. But that's not the point."

"And what is the point?"

"Mischa," Emily said in a lowered voice. "We don't need

credit for this. We need the truth to come out. We need Shira exonerated, and we need you unsuspended and in college. It doesn't matter who gets the credit."

"But she'll be a hero," I hissed. "She'll keep her spot at Harvard, she'll be a hero, and she didn't *do anything!*"

"It doesn't matter," she whispered. "The ends justify the means. We don't have a choice."

"There's always a choice. We can wait for the *Gazette* to call us back. We can call other papers."

"There's still the other problem," she said. "They can say our database is a fake. We need Marlowe to incriminate himself, so everyone will have to admit that it's real."

"That's just a detail! We have enough!"

"Mischa, have you not been paying attention? Do you not understand what we're up against? We need Meredith. She takes the credit for this, we put her face on our work, and suddenly Blanchard's looking at going up against Frederick effing Dorsay and his giant Scrooge McDuck vault of cash. The Dorsays can burn this all to the ground. If it's just you and me? Blanchard's lawyers are going to *eat us alive.*"

"I'm willing to take that chance," I said.

"Are you willing to sacrifice yourself to spite Meredith?"

"I might be," I said.

Emily met my eyes and said nothing.

I blew out all my air. "I hate her," I said.

"Of course you do," she said. "Good grief."

"There must be some other way," I said.

"If you have a plan," she said, "I'm eager to hear it."

CHAPTER THIRTY-FOUR

MEREDITH SET UP A MEETING WITH RICHARD MARLOWE AT
eight-thirty the next morning, to discuss her plans for the all-
night grad party. Mrs. Richardson let Meredith into his office
at 8:15. At 8:17, Meredith helped me climb in through the
window.

"He's not going to be happy when he comes in here to talk
to me and finds you instead," she said as I hoisted my leg over
the windowsill. "How are you going to keep him from walking
back out?"

"You do your job," I said, "and I'll do mine."

She stared at me for a minute, her eyes gray, mine brown.
We were, I realized, exactly the same height.

"If you screw me over," she said, "so help me, I will make
your life a living hell."

I smiled, letting her see every one of my teeth.

And then I went to sit in Richard Marlowe's chair to wait.

At 8:28, Richard Marlowe came into his office, because Richard Marlowe would not want to keep Meredith Dorsay waiting. He was, as expected, not pleased to see me sitting with my feet on his desk.

"Richard," I said, because, no matter what, I had to sound like I absolutely owned him. "Won't you sit down?"

He was considering heading back out, because I was not supposed to be in the building, his office, or his chair. Meredith, on the other hand, could have used him like an ottoman, and he would have endured it without complaint.

"Close the door, Richard," I said.

He shut the door.

"Miss Abramavicius," he said. "You do realize you're suspended, pending expulsion."

"Oh, I realize," I said. My hands gave an involuntary quiver. I shoved them under the desk. "That was a mistake on your part, Dr. Marlowe. But let's not start off that way. Have a seat."

Very reluctantly, he sat. He didn't know it, but this was perhaps the most important victory I would win that day.

"I bet you're wondering why Meredith was the one who set up this meeting. And I'll tell you: she did it because I asked her to. She thinks I'm here for the SGA. I'm supposed to be asking you to get the board to donate more money for the graduation party. It seems we're a bit underfunded this year. I told her I could convince you to go to bat for us. Seeing as you're always such a champion for the students."

He said, "That's not why you're here."

"Correct," I said. "But before we get to that, I want to ask you a question. Have you met my mother?"

He looked back at the door again like he was thinking of leaving. It was a strange question. He said, "I've met all of the parents of students at Blanchard. Your mother included."

"That must be a lot of people, considering how long you've been here."

"Yes," he said. "It is a lot of people."

"And what did you think of her?"

Of course, Richard Marlowe would have little reason to remember my mother. The amount she'd donated to the school was a pittance; neither was she famous enough to increase the school's standing in some other way—she wasn't a playwright or an artist or a washed-up politician. Marlowe said, "I found her quite admirable."

"Really," I said. "In what way?"

"Well, her dedication to your education, naturally."

I inclined my head. "Yes, she is very dedicated. I would say her entire life has been dedicated to my education. Her time, her money. Everything."

He nodded, conceding the point.

"It really takes its toll, that kind of dedication. Eats you alive. Anyway, I'm going to make you a promise. While we sit in this room together, I give you my word—on my mother, on her *dedication*—that I will tell you no lies. And I'll also give you my word that the true things I'm going to tell you are all things you need to hear."

He raised his eyebrows fractionally. "Miss Abramavicius. I think you should go."

I tamped down the nervous churning in my gut. I said,

"Don't believe me? I'll start by telling you why I'm here. What my mother wants is for me to go to a very good college. This is also something I want." I met his eyes. "But that isn't happening, is it?"

He laced his fingers together and regarded me carefully.

"So there's one thing that's true. Here's another: the only person in this building whose welfare matters to me more than my own is Nate Miller." I waited for this to sink in and saw the moment that he remembered that Nate was on the list. "Do we understand each other?"

He nodded.

"Now, here's the last thing I'll tell you: I have, at my disposal, a copy of Blanchard's transcript database. Meaning I have copies of the transcript of every senior in this building. Including the nineteen people with two different versions."

I waited for him to deny it or argue or simply eject me from the room. Instead he said, "Where is your cell phone?"

I'd left mine at home, but I'd been prepared for the question, so I pulled Nate's phone out of my pocket. I held it up so that he could see me power it down, and then I slid it toward the middle of the desk.

"Where's yours?" I asked.

He scoffed. "You can't possibly think I would want to record this conversation."

"Humor me," I said. He reluctantly pulled his phone out of the inside pocket of his blazer and put it on the desk next to mine.

"Do you have another recording device with you?" he asked.

"I do not. And I assume you don't have some tape recorder running full-time in here like Nixon."

"No."

"Such an idiot," I said. "Right? To record incriminating conversations of himself? I mean, who does that? I wonder what he was thinking."

"Miss Abramavicius," he said. "What is it that you want?"

"Well, it's simple. I don't want your firstborn child. All I want is a kindly worded admission offer from the sort of school that should have taken me in the first place. If you give me this, you'll never have to see me again." I weighed this possibility in one open palm. "If you don't"—I opened my other hand—"I'm sending everything I have to Meredith's father."

We'd pulled this threat out of our hat, because it was a bluff Marlowe couldn't afford to call. He let out a single bark of a laugh. "You can't be that stupid," he said. "He'll bury it."

"Oh, he'll absolutely bury it. He won't want it to get out and hurt Meredith. However." I crossed my ankles. "Once he sees the shoddy operation you're running, once he finds out that your computers were hacked into by *students*—students who know about your little racket—he'll never give you another dime. No more Dorsays will darken the doorsteps of Blanchard's hallowed halls. Meredith has three younger brothers, did you know that?"

He said nothing. Of course he knew.

"That's three more students paying sticker-price tuition, three students' worth of tickets to the Christmas Gala, three students' worth of end-of-the-year donations. Not to mention the endowment you were hoping Frederick Dorsay would leave you in his will. Millions of dollars, all told, Richard. We're talking about millions of dollars. All lost. And for what?"

He said, "I don't believe you."

"Don't believe I have the database? Let me remind you

who's in it. Meredith Dorsay. Amy Gregston. Connor Orton. Michael Lawless. David Chu. Do I need to go on?"

"No," he said.

"I have to say, I'm a little confused, though," I said. "I understand increasing the grades of the kids whose families gave money. I even kind of understand dropping the grades of the students whose parents didn't give money. What I don't understand is what you did to me. Why mangle my recommendation letters? Why drop my grades to Ds, when you could have just made them Bs? How does it help Blanchard for me to get in nowhere?"

I got up from the desk and went to the window, and he turned in his chair to mark my progress. I propped myself against the windowsill, forcing him to squint, as I was now backlit.

"It doesn't," he said. "That was a mistake." He took off his glasses and set them on the desk, as if he were trying not to have to see my face in perfect focus while he explained how his school had ruined my life. "The letters and the transcript were supposed to go to Harvard and Princeton only. Ms. Pendleton made a mistake. For which she has been terminated."

"I hope you mean fired," I said, horrified.

"I mean fired," he said. "The letters were an insurance policy."

"Because my SAT and AP scores were so high."

"Yes." He put his glasses back on in one movement and crossed his arms. "You must understand the position I'm in. The position the school is in. Our tuition doesn't cover our operating costs. We depend on donations to keep afloat."

"Of course," I said sympathetically. "I understand that. You need students like Meredith to get into Harvard, so she can make more money. Perhaps she will remember fondly her alma mater, where she got her start in life, and write you a check. Maybe her children will come to Blanchard, and she'll donate even more. And they will get into Harvard. And so on."

"You're a very good student," he said. "And you should have gone to a very good college. Mistakes were made. For that, you have my apologies. However, it's easily remedied."

I asked, "How do you intend to remedy it?"

"I have been in this post for thirty years, Miss Abramavicius. I have a certain amount of . . . clout . . . with the deans of admissions at a few schools you might be interested in. Duke, for instance. I can have a spot for you there within five minutes."

I frowned. "And what do I have to do in exchange for this?"

"Sign a nondisclosure agreement," he said, "stating that you will never again discuss what we've talked about in this room. And I also want your copy of the transcript database."

I pulled the flash drive out of my pocket, held it up so he could see it, and put it on the desk next to my phone. "I'm surprised you didn't ask for it earlier," I said.

"Does Miss Sreenivasan have another copy of this?" he asked.

"Yes," I said, because I had promised to tell no lies. "But if you do what I ask, she won't do anything with it."

Marlowe walked around to his file cabinet, went through one of his drawers, and pulled out a piece of paper.

"Do you normally keep nondisclosure forms in your office?" I asked, retaking my seat at the desk.

Ignoring me, he said, "Shall I call Duke?"

I picked up the pen. I signed my name. And I said, "Make the call."

He picked up the phone and dialed, then spoke briefly to a man he called Bruce. He explained that he had a very good student who was not happy with her college choices, and he would like Bruce to take a last-minute look at my application. He would send my transcript over right away, along with an unofficial copy of my SAT scores and my letters of recommendation. Did he think he might have a spot for another incoming freshman? By all accounts, Bruce thought that he might. Marlowe hung up.

"There," he said, smiling. "That's done."

I nodded. "There is one other thing. A small matter."

"We had an agreement already."

"You'll hardly mind this," I said. "It's about Shira Gastman."

"I already told you: I'm not at liberty to discuss—"

"You found drugs in her locker and never tested her for drug use. You know she's as sober as I am."

"Are you implying that I had something to do with planting drugs on Miss Gastman?"

"I'm not implying it," I said. "I'm saying it directly. And we never did discuss the matter of my Instagram page."

"I'm not sure exactly what you're accusing me of."

I pulled out a printout of the last Instagram entry and handed it to him.

"I assure you," he said. "I had nothing to do with this. Or with Miss Gastman."

"How did you know," I asked, "that I was working with Emily Sreenivasan? I never mentioned her. How long have you known who was helping me?"

When he failed to answer, I said, "555-234-8170."

"What is that?" he asked.

"Frederick Dorsay's personal cell phone number," I said. "That's the number Meredith uses when she wants to reach him. The one he always answers." Still no response. I said, "You don't even have to admit this, Richard—tell me it was Pelletier. Or Mrs. Hadley. Or the Easter Bunny. I just want you to call it off. That's it."

He sighed. "Here's what I have to offer."

"I'm listening."

"Miss Gastman will be reinstated. Your suspension will be lifted, and I will explain to your mother that the Instagram fiasco was an unfortunate prank." He folded his hands in his lap. "And you have your spot at Duke. All is well. Are you satisfied now?"

All is well.

For a moment, I saw the entirety of what he was offering. I could take the spot at Duke. My mother would be thrilled; we'd go out for ice cream and laugh and laugh about the ridiculous misunderstanding we'd had. Shira would be off the hook, and Nate would go off to Emory. Everyone in my life—everyone that mattered to me—would get exactly what they wanted. Happy endings all around, as we all went off to our shiny, successful futures.

It made an appealing picture.

"You're right," I said. "It appears we're done here. So I'll be going home."

"Miss Abramavicius," he said, starting to get up.

But I wasn't quite done talking. "And you'll be going . . . ," I continued. "Huh. Where do they put white-collar felons around here? I don't actually know. Should I look it up for you, or do you want it to be a surprise?"

"I beg your pardon?"

"Oh, you will beg my pardon. You'll be begging a lot of people's pardons."

He loosened his tie, just enough to let me know he was taking me seriously. "What do you intend to do?"

"Me? I intend to do nothing," I said. "I'm going to go home and take a nice, hot bath and eat a carton of Ben and Jerry's. I'm not the one you have to worry about."

His eyes cut sideways. He said, "You lied to me. You've been recording this conversation."

"Nope," I said. "A for effort, though."

The door to Richard Marlowe's private bathroom opened, and out stepped Meredith Dorsay.

"Too bad you didn't ask *me* to sign something," she said, holding up her still-recording iPhone. "That seems like an oversight."

He rounded on Meredith. "If this gets out, your chances of getting into Harvard—"

"I'm pretty confident of my chances of getting into Harvard, actually," she said. Looking at me, she added, "Should I send all this to Margot now, do you think, or wait until after lunch?"

"Sorry, I can't advise you." I grinned at Marlowe. "I signed a nondisclosure."

CHAPTER THIRTY-FIVE

MARGOT DORSAY, AS IT TURNED OUT, WAS NOT AT ALL BAD AT her job. The story started off at MSNBC. And then it went on to all the major papers. Meredith was the hero of the piece. She'd taken the recording of my conversation with Marlowe, kept the most incriminating bits, and then edited me out of it.

But I did keep my word. I never spoke of it again.

Of course, I didn't have to. Everyone had already read the paper. Including my mother.

Several days after the story broke, Mom and I were back at the duck pond down the street from my house; we'd long ago used up all our peas, and the ducks had gone back into the water to swim off their lunch. We'd been silent for the last fifteen minutes, because I honestly couldn't think of anything to talk about.

"Hey," I said. "Did you know that turtles eat baby ducks?"

"Ugh," she said, making a face. "That's disturbing. Who told you that?"

"It came up," I said.

"Is that just snapping turtles, or all turtles?"

"Oh. I don't actually know. Did you want me to look it up?"

"Uh, not really."

More silence. Mom took a sunscreen stick out of her purse and rubbed it on her nose.

"Did you hear back from that guy about the part-time thing?"

"Oh," she said, handing me the sunscreen. I ran my finger over it and rubbed a little on my own nose. "Yeah. I didn't get that."

"Sorry," I said.

She put the sunscreen away and shook her head. "Is this the most awkward conversation we've ever had?"

I shrugged. "I think the sex one was worse, actually."

"I was good at that!"

"You put a condom on a banana, Mom."

"That was very informative!" she protested.

"You put me off bananas for life! You could have at least used a zucchini or something. I wouldn't miss eating zucchini."

"You can't fit a condom on a zucchini!" She held her hands about a foot apart, and I smacked them back down, not needing the visual.

"You could have used a small one!"

"Where am I supposed to find a zucchini the size of a—"

"STOP stop stop. I get it. Eesh."

She laughed a little. "So banana bread? Banana muffins?"

"It's all dead to me, Mom."

"Banana pancakes?" she asked. I shook my head. "*Wow.* Sorry about that."

"You should be."

We stared out at the ducks a little longer. They were swimming in circles, lost in their inner duck lives. I don't know what ducks think about when they're not eating. I bet they have deep thoughts.

Mom adjusted herself a little, and I thought she was going to get up, but then she said, "There's something I want to give you." She pulled the ring off the first finger of her right hand. It was my great-grandmother's wedding ring, the only thing anyone in my family had from the old country. It had gone to my grandmother when she'd died, and then to my mother when Grandma died a handful of years ago.

"No," I said, "wait. I don't really care that much about the bananas."

"This has nothing to do with bananas." She took my hand and slid the ring onto my own forefinger. "Your grandmother," she said, "would have been proud of you."

I stared at the plain gold band on my finger. I remembered Grandma wearing it when she came over to visit. I'd play with it while I sat on her lap and she read to me.

"Mom," I said, "are *you* proud of me?"

"I've screwed up pretty bad if you have to ask me that," she said. "I already said it, but I'm sorry. I'm sorry for not believing you."

"I'm sorry for not telling you right away," I said. "I was scared."

She looked at me sadly. "That's a problem. Isn't it?"

I shrugged.

She sighed. "You asked me one time what Grandma said when she found out about you."

"What Grandma said? Yeah. I remember."

"I don't think I answered you."

"No. You didn't."

She smiled. "I didn't tell her. I showed up at the house for Thanksgiving seven months pregnant. Just me and my giant belly and a pie that wasn't even homemade."

"What? Why?"

"I hate baking," she said.

"Mom."

"I was scared. That way, she found out in front of ten other people, and she had to pretend like she already knew so she wouldn't be embarrassed." She snickered. "By the time everyone else went home, she was too full of turkey to go full-throttle on me. I thought you and I were a little tighter than that, though."

Mom reached out and held my hand, the one that was wearing Grandma's ring. I pulled out my phone and opened a picture Nate had taken of me, floating down to earth in my parachute.

She looked at it, her eyebrows approaching her hairline, and said, "Huh."

There'd been a conversation about transferring me to a public school for my last quarter, but the idea of having to get used to seven new teachers and a few hundred new kids that I'd never see again after a whopping nine weeks seemed ludicrous. Blanchard's interim principal, who had been hired by the board of directors to take over from Marlowe and Pelletier, offered to graduate me early, mainly, I think, because despite Meredith's public credit taking, there seemed to be an undercurrent at school that I was the person behind everything, which made me decidedly unpopular with fifteen of the nineteen people on the list. There was quite a furor when the corrected transcripts were sent out, and Blanchard kept begging for the colleges to offer some kind of amnesty to the students they'd already accepted.

Meredith was the triumphant whistle-blower. Harvard maintained they were happy to have her.

Not everyone else was so lucky.

Nate was not so lucky.

"It's okay," he insisted. "It's what I deserve."

We were on a date, the first one we'd been on since the skydiving. It was the night of the Blanchard Senior Formal, and neither of us had any desire to go, so I'd asked Nate for the most DC date he could think of, which meant we were taking a tour of the monuments at night (which happened to also be #57 on the Mischa Abramavicius Bucket List). We'd stopped near the Jefferson Memorial and were staring out at the black slate of the Tidal Basin. A few weeks ago it would have been stuffed with cherry blossoms and tourists, but now it was pretty empty, just us and a bunch of other couples and a few panhandlers.

"It is not what you deserve!" I said hotly. "What Meredith's taking credit for is what you actually did! You knew what would happen if we released those files. We never could have gotten them in the first place if it hadn't been for you. And you did it all anyway, because you knew it was the right thing to do. They should care about that. It should *matter*."

"It turns out that matters less than my math grades," he said. He looped an arm around my neck. "Mischa, I'm not sorry, if that's what you're wondering. Blanchard was a garbage fire."

"I don't see how you can be so calm about this," I said. I wondered how much of his placid attitude was for my benefit, because he didn't want me to feel guilty. I wondered what he really let himself feel, when he was alone.

"I'll go someplace else," he said with a shrug. "I have three other schools to choose from. I'll choose one of them."

"You don't have to pretend to be so blasé. I know you really wanted to go there."

"So maybe I'll transfer next year. Nancy Roman's pretty sure they'll take me if I do well someplace else."

Nancy Roman was the college coach Nate's parents had hired after he'd lost his spot at Emory, to help him figure out what to do next. For weeks he'd refused to meet with her, convinced this was just another instance of his parents pushing their agenda on him. But I'd persuaded him not to cut off his nose to spite his face, and he'd relented.

"What about your parents?"

He shrugged. "Well, I'm sure they'd like a refund from Blanchard."

I laughed without really meaning it. "Hey," he said. "This is always how it was supposed to be."

"No. It's really not."

He squeezed my hand. I squeezed his back, a silent acknowledgment.

"What about you?" he asked. "Have you decided yet?"

I shook my head. Once my corrected transcript and letters had been sent out, I'd been accepted to five of the seven schools I'd applied to. But the idea of going, of showing up on campus in August and pretending like nothing had happened, made me a little sick.

"What does your mom say?"

"You know what she says."

"Did you talk to her about the gap year?"

"Yeah. She wasn't happy about it. But she doesn't get to choose. Not anymore."

"So all you have to do," he said, "is pick a school, announce your deferral, and decide what to do with your life for the next sixteen months."

"Yep. That's all."

"Doesn't sound like too tall an order."

I ran my fingers through the grass underneath me. In another month it would be summer. Nate would have graduated, and there would be nothing but several weeks of endless days in front of us.

"Nate," I said. "Have *you* ever thought about taking a gap year?"

He chuckled. "I don't think that's a good idea for me," he said.

"Why not?"

"Because I know myself. If I take a year off, it'll turn into two, then three, then ten. I won't be able to make myself go back."

"You think that's what'll happen to me?"

"No. But you're different."

I hugged his arm and leaned my chin on his shoulder.

"I'm going to miss you," I said. Then: "What about this summer?"

"What about it?"

"I don't know. I don't know." I flapped my hands. "Remember when I made that list of all that stuff I wanted to do? And then we scrapped it and went skydiving?"

"Well, *you* went skydiving," he said. "*I* ate a really bad chicken sandwich."

"Right. What if we did some of the other things on that list? What if we made a bucket list together, for this summer?"

"Like a vacation?"

"I don't know. Maybe."

"Us. Together. For the whole summer?"

"If that sounds bad—"

He cut me off with a finger on my lips. "Mischa," he said. "I thought you'd never ask."

CHAPTER THIRTY-SIX

A FEW WEEKS LATER, I SAT AT EMILY'S DINING ROOM TABLE with the Ophelias and Nate, playing poker and eating pretzels out of a crystal bowl. I sat between Emily, at the head of the table, and Nate, who was struggling to fend off Emily's giant fluffy cat, who kept trying to lick the salt off his pretzels. At the other end of the table, Bebe and Shira were alternately sneaking peeks at each other's cards and then pretending not to notice. Between the two of them, they had nearly wiped the rest of us out.

I was losing badly and folded before the hand could get any worse for me. Then I took a swipe of the hummus that was sitting in the middle of the table, dodging Emily's cat, who was now sniffing at the bowl.

"She won't actually eat that, will she?" I asked. "She knows she's a carnivore?"

"Sometimes she forgets," Emily said, picking up the cat and setting her down on the floor before sliding a stack of chips toward the middle of the table. "So has Nate told you about the latest drama?"

I turned to Nate, who shrugged. Bebe said, "It's the graduation speaker. It's a whole thing."

"Really? Who's the graduation speaker?" I asked.

"I can't believe Nate hasn't told you," Shira said.

"I've been a little preoccupied."

"Yeah," said Bebe. "Well, it started because Beth Reinhardt said she could get David Hasselhoff."

I covered my mouth with my hands. "No. Are you serious?"

"Yes! And then there was this big fight between the people who wanted *literally anyone* but David Hasselhoff, and Beth's friends who wanted him because he was the most famous person we could get. So Beth's people won and they booked Hasselhoff, right? But then this whole transcript scandal blew up, so Hasselhoff backed out and now no one else will do it."

"No one?"

"Nope. So then they were going to use one of the teachers, but none of them wanted to do it either, so the committee just decided not to have an adult speaker. It's going to be Meredith Dorsay, and that's it."

I frowned. "Meredith Dorsay?"

Nate put his hand over mine. "She's giving the valedictory speech."

I let out a long, slow breath.

"Mischa, everyone knows it should have been you. Even Meredith knows it. Nobody expects you to come to this thing, but—"

"Why would I come?"

His eyes cut away. "I just thought maybe . . ."

"No, I'm sorry. I just don't think I can."

"I understand. Pretend I didn't say anything."

But I couldn't pretend, because Nate was going to have to go through this three-hour ordeal, and so were Emily and Shira and Bebe and Jim and Caroline, and everyone else I'd gone through four years of Blanchard with, and I felt bad. So on the ninth day of June, I put on a dress and, twenty minutes into the graduation, snuck into the back of the auditorium.

Meredith was just being called up to the front of the stage to speak. I silently willed her to trip, which was kind of unfair because she wasn't guilty of anything other than being herself. Which admittedly wasn't a very nice person, but still.

She set her mortarboard down on the podium. And then she proceeded to give the most generic graduation speech of all time. She thanked her parents and her teachers and her friends. She recited that quotation about being the change you want to see in the universe and a few lines from *Oh, the Places You'll Go!* I wondered, briefly, if she'd bought the speech off the Internet. But it also occurred to me that maybe Blanchard had insisted that she do it this way.

At the end, she looked up to the back row. For a split second, she looked right at me. And then her eyes skated over me as if I did not exist.

But she added, right before she stepped down from the podium, "I've often wondered what the secret to success is. Is it intelligence? Wit? Charm? But I think there's one thing we forget. Life is a series of opportunities. And when you're presented with one, you have to grab it with both hands. And when you're not, you make your own." Her eyes briefly met mine.

"Thank you," she said.

There was a smattering of polite applause. I got up from my chair and left.

I saw Emily in the parking lot afterward with her parents, the Doctors Sreenivasan. She was about to get in the car when she noticed me and walked over.

"I can't believe you came to this," she said.

"Well, you know. I couldn't miss the chance to see Meredith Dorsay unironically read Dr. Seuss."

She snorted. "My parents and I are getting lunch, if you want to come."

"Thanks," I said. "I'm actually meeting the Millers later. Congratulations, though."

Flatly she said, "Whee. I have a diploma from a school whose name is synonymous with scandal and corruption."

"Hey, at least you have a good story for when people at MIT ask where you went to high school."

"Actually," she said, "I was planning to lie."

"That works, too."

A limo pulled up in front of the building, and the Dorsays—Meredith, her parents, her brothers, and Cousin Margot—climbed in. "Oh," Emily said, "the places she'll go."

The limo drove away. The parking lot was pretty full of people heading out to parties and restaurants. I balled up my program and shoved it in my purse. "Someone told me something once," I said, "about how people can't own up to their mistakes because of a fragile self-narrative. Like, they have to think they're the hero or they fall apart."

She laughed dryly. "You think Meredith has a fragile self-narrative?"

I thought about that for a minute. I wondered about the mental contortions it would take for Meredith Dorsay to believe she was the hero of literally anything.

Finally I said, "I think she's a schmuck."

CHAPTER THIRTY-SEVEN

NATE'S CAR WAS PACKED TO THE BRIM, MOSTLY WITH HIS STUFF. He was in the driver's seat, his car idling in my driveway; my mother was just inside the front door, and I was just outside it.

"I know you think this is a bad idea," I said.

She said, "Just promise me you'll still go, at the end of the year. You have a lot of good choices now."

"I promise," I said. "Come next August, I'll be on a campus buying overpriced textbooks and hating my roommate."

"Do you have enough money?" she asked.

"Is there any such thing?" I asked. "No, I'm fine. We'll be fine."

She leaned against the door frame. "We," she said. "You and Nate, you mean."

"Yeah," I said. "But we're also fine." I pointed from me to her and back again.

"Are we?"

"Nothing that happened was your fault."

"Except for the credit card debt."

"Well, that part was your fault." It wasn't like I was mad about that, though. To be honest, I wasn't really mad about any of it. We'd wanted the same things. I still wanted to go to a good college. I wanted to have a good job. I'd just been so caught up in the idea that that was the goal, it hadn't occurred to me that those things were the beginning of a very long, non-linear path. I would take classes and do badly. I would get a job and get fired. I would get another job and hate it and realize I needed to start over. And between now and then, I still needed to decide what I wanted that job, that life, to look like. I was passably good at a hundred different things. It was time to decide what I loved.

"Mom," I asked. "Did you ever think about what would make you happy?"

"Please don't start."

"I'm serious," I said.

"What makes you think I'm not?"

"Well, are you?"

She leaned in and kissed me on the forehead. "I love you, Mischa," she said, which was, I guess, as good an answer as any.

"I love you, too. I have to go."

I hugged her one last time, and then I went.

I climbed into the car next to Nate and sat my butt down on Maury, who he'd stuck in my seat while I'd been saying goodbye.

"Oof," I said, because having a plastic skull under one's nether regions was not especially pleasant. I pulled him out from underneath me and saw that he was, for the first time, without accessories.

"He's naked," I said.

"We're taking him out for a new wardrobe," Nate said. "I'm thinking a top hat and a cravat."

"He doesn't have a neck," I pointed out.

"Details, details."

I tossed Maury unceremoniously into the backseat, where he landed on top of the list we'd made of all the things we wanted to do that summer, before we ran out of time or money or both.

"Rude," Nate said. "Are you ready?"

"No," I answered. "Let's go."

ACKNOWLEDGMENTS

Very great thanks are due to Hannah Bowman, who is both my agent and the author of the terrifying college admissions formula that appears at the beginning of this book. Nobody ever told me I would need an agent with a math degree; I'm so very lucky I found one anyway.

Katherine Harrison, thank you for being my editor, for shining a light on things that needed fixing, and helping me to solve problems I couldn't work through on my own. Thanks also to the rest of the good people of Knopf BFYR for all the millions of tasks that are involved in editing, designing, proofing, printing, promoting, and selling books.

Thanks to Christopher Budd, who so graciously lent me his expertise not only in computer security and realistic hacking that does not involve people typing really fast for no reason, but also in skydiving. Thanks also to the staff at Caxton College in Valencia, Spain, for helping me with Mischa's French, and to my husband for double-checking Bebe's Spanish, and to Kate Hattemer for translating Paul Revere's motto into grammatically correct Latin. Any mistakes in the book are my own.

Thanks to my mother, who read early drafts of this book and did not hate them, and to my father, who is likely responsible for my cynical outlook. And to Paul, who snuck me into his high school job on Sunday mornings so I could use the typewriters to fill out my college applications. I'm so glad we never have to go through that again.

And finally, for my kids. Listen. Come closer. Closer. I love you, no matter what.

READ ON FOR A LOOK AT
ARIEL KAPLAN'S LATEST PAGE-TURNER,
WE ARE THE PERFECT GIRL!

Chapter One

Sometimes, when I'm lying in my bed at night, staring up at the darkened ceiling, I think that the greatest problem in the English-speaking world is that we don't understand love.

It's a lack of vocabulary, that's what I've decided. We have one word: *love.* And we expect it to mean everything, only it's clunky and imprecise and leads to misunderstandings and anger and frustration and tears.

The ancient Greeks, I think, had a better system: multiple love words, a love word for every possible occasion. If you love your friend, you've got *philia.* If you love your mom, you've got *storge.* If you love the sexy, sexy guy who sits across from you in biology, you have *eros.* And if you feel some great, cosmic, unconditional love for God or the Universe or your Fellow Man, you have *agape.*

There are others, actually, but those are the mains. So while in English we may have beautiful sentiments like "Love is love," clearly eros is not storge, unless you are Oedipus, and then you have a problem. Anyway, the specificity of the Greek system has always appealed to me.

I guess philia is probably my favorite. I don't exactly understand agape, and eros is not something I ever expect to experience myself. But philia is love for the masses. Everyone has a friend. At least, I hope they do.

My greatest source of philia is Bethany Newman, who has been my best friend since we were eight. I have other friends, of course, but Bethany is special because she looks at me and sees me exactly as I am. I really philia her for that.

I was philia-ing her a little less this morning, though, when I woke up to find her sitting on my kneecaps. She was smiling at me with a smile that was too wide to look at first thing upon waking. It was more like a midafternoon smile. An "I've already had two cups of coffee" smile.

"Ow," I said.

"The pool opens today," she replied. She bounced a little. "Did you forget?"

I kind of had, being asleep and all. Our town had splurged and installed a heating system in one of our outdoor pools, which meant it opened on the first of May instead of over Memorial Day like the rest of the pools in the area. I remembered that we'd talked about going last night, but I didn't remember agreeing to wake up at the crack of dawn for it.

"My knees don't bend that way," I said, shoving her off. "Why are you waking me up to tell me about the pool?"

"We were supposed to go shopping!" she said. "Half an hour ago! It's 11:30."

"It is not," I said, but it did seem kind of bright out. I'd set my alarm for ten. Hadn't I? I was pretty sure I had. I felt around on the bedside table for my glasses and then for my phone. "Where's my phone?"

"I have no idea. Come on, Aphra, get up."

I sat up slowly. It wasn't regular shopping Bethany wanted to do; it was *bathing suit* shopping, which is the worst kind of shopping. Bright lights. Spandex. Those hygienic liners that don't make me feel any better about trying on a suit fifty other people have already tried on, even with underwear.

I had agreed to go, though, because Bethany came to me last week with a Plan, and Bethany so seldom has Plans that I felt like I had to go along with it.

The Plan was agreed upon the night of junior prom. Bethany and I went together with a bunch of other girls, and while we were there, we saw Greg D'Agostino with a bunch of his friends from the swim team. He was in a tux, and he looked, possibly, even hotter than usual.

Bethany really wanted to ask him to dance and spent nearly the whole night trying to work up the nerve. Around 10:30, she decided to walk by him during a slow song and hope he'd take the hint.

Except by then, he'd already left.

So now we had a plan to throw Bethany's bikini-clad body in front of Greg D'Agostino until he magically notices her, falls in love (technically, in eros, but Bethany doesn't appreciate the Greek system like I do), and then . . . I'm not really sure what happens after that. I guess maybe he'll ask her out? And then they'll go out. And then Bethany will, with any luck, be able to speak more than four words to him.

This seems a little unlikely to me, but I haven't said anything because I'm sure Bethany already knows that.

I pried myself out of bed, jammed my contacts into my eyes—I swear, this is not vanity, glasses just annoy me—put on some clothes, and went off in search of my phone, which was in the hands of my little brother, who was using it to play *Minecraft*. Walnut the cat was curled up on his lap while Kit used him as a furry lap desk.

"Why are you on my phone?" I asked, pointing at the laptop he'd abandoned on the coffee table.

Without looking up, he said, "I hit my time limit."

There are parental controls on the family computer that cut Kit off after an hour so he doesn't rot his little brain. "So do something else," I said. "How did you get my phone?"

"It was by your bed."

"You can't just steal it while I'm sleeping!"

"You weren't using it."

"Did my alarm go off?"

"Oh." He looked up. "I didn't know what that was. I turned it off." He switched off his game and handed the phone to me, looking contrite, because Bethany and I row on the crew team and he knows that we usually have regattas on Saturday mornings. "Sorry. Did I make you late for your boat race?"

"I'm not mad," I said, patting his head. Kit is only nine, and I think he has the softest hair in the whole world, like the down on a baby duck. Someday he probably won't want me to pat his head anymore, so I'm getting my Kit-hair fix now, while I still can. Plus, he's the only sibling I have that I'm on speaking terms with, and I'm not willing to let a hijacked cell phone get in the way of that. "We didn't race today," I said. "Where's Mom and Dad?"

"Dad's at the store. Mom's asleep."

Both of my parents are professors at George Mason: Mom teaches English, Dad teaches medieval history, and Mom has an evening class on Fridays and likes to sleep in on Saturday mornings. This was a little late, though, even for her.

"You should wake her up," I said. "I'm leaving with Bethany."

"Can I go with you?"

"You'll be super bored," I said. "We're going shopping."

"For candy?" he asked hopefully.

"Could we do candy?" I asked Bethany. "That actually does sound better."

"No candy," Bethany said. "Suits." She leaned down and we gave him the Kit Kiss, which we've been doing since he was a baby, where I kiss one cheek and Bethany kisses the other. Probably someday he won't let us do that anymore, either. "We're going to the pool later, if you want to come."

"Can I play on your phone there?"

"No," I said. "But you can swim."

He made a face.

"I'll buy you a Fudgsicle," I said.

He made another face.

"I'll let you eat half my cookie-wich, too," I offered.

"If you let me eat the whole thing, I promise not to steal your phone again."

"Sorry," I said. "I don't negotiate with terrorists."

"You're mean."

I ruffled his hair again, saying, "The meanest."

Half an hour later, we were ensconced in a dressing room in the Wet Seal at the mall.

I stood holding an armful of Bethany's discarded bathing

suits while she stuffed herself into a one-piece with these weird spiderweb cutouts in the middle.

"That's going to give you the worst tan lines ever," I said.

She looked in the mirror. Bethany has, like, actual abs, but even she could not make this work. "This is hideous," she said. "Who designed this?"

"It's like the *Charlotte's Web* model," I said. "Only it should give you tan lines that say *Terrific!* Or *Radiant!*"

"Or *Some Pig*," she said, and we both cackled. The woman in the stall next to us made a *hrmph* noise.

"Shhh," I said. "There is no laughing while swimsuit shopping. This is very serious business."

"Serious," she said, dropping her voice.

"The fate of the world may be at stake," I said. "I mean, really. That suit could kill someone."

"The person wearing it, or the person looking at it?"

"Possibly both," I said. She was already peeling the straps over her shoulders, because we've been friends so long that nudity is no longer a thing between us. I handed her the next one, which was a blue bikini with hibiscus flowers on it. She put it on and turned to look in the mirror. "I like this one," she said. "The top's really supportive." She gave an experimental wiggle and nothing fell out.

"Looks good to me," I said.

"Here, they have one in red," she said, taking a suit with white polka dots out of the pile. "You should try it. It's on clearance and everything."

"Oh," I said. "No."

"You always wear red."

This is true. . . . I always buy a red bathing suit. A red one-piece bathing suit. I like a utilitarian approach to swimwear, which means not having to put sunscreen on locations I would prefer not to be seen touching in public.

Unfortunately, they did not have any red one-pieces at the Wet Seal that day. Bethany thrust the bikini at me. "It's your color," she said. "And it's only twelve bucks."

"Fine," I said. I put it on and then stepped out to look in the three-way mirror. There was a salesgirl out there putting discarded suits on hangers; the *hrmph*ing woman seemed to have exited the premises to find a more serious bathing suit store. I stood in front of the mirror and held out my arms to either side for Bethany's inspection.

"Oh," she said.

I poked myself in the rear. The leg holes were so tight and cut so high I looked a little like a segmented insect. "I appear to have grown a second butt," I said. "I don't think it's a good look for me."

"You need a bigger bottom," the salesgirl said. "But the top's fine. I mean, that side's fine." She pointed at my left boob.

I glanced down. Yeah. So the thing is, one of my boobs is a cup size bigger than the other. I've been informed—numerous times!—that this is very common. Very common. Also: annoying. I have discovered that if I tighten the straps on the left side of my bra, it is mostly not noticeable when I have clothes on. But in a bikini? I am exquisitely lopsided. My left boob looked great. My right looked . . . kind of sad.

"I can give you a cookie," the salesgirl said.

"I love cookies," I said. "I'm not sure that would help, though. Unless you can make all the fat from the cookie metabolize into my right boob."

She laughed. "No, I mean, it's a little insert that goes in the bottom of the cup and makes your smaller side a little bigger. It'll just even you out."

"Won't that be noticeable?"

"Nah, it's silicone," she said. "They look super natural."

"Okay," I said. "Let's see the fake boob."

"It's not a fake boob," Bethany whispered as the salesgirl ducked out. "It's a cookie."

"That is not a real distinction," I said.

The salesgirl reappeared with a little moon-shaped piece of beige silicone, which she directed me to put in the bottom of the bikini cup, plus a bigger-sized bottom.

"Wow," Bethany said. "Look at your rack!"

I looked in the mirror. I had to admit, my torso had never looked this good. There was still an awful lot of my butt on display, though.

"I don't know," I said.

"Get it," she said. "Get it, get it, and we can go to the pool later."

I poked the cookie through my bikini top. "Is this really going to stay put?" I asked. "Like, even if I go swimming?"

"It will," the salesgirl said. "Promise."

I thought, *Do you work on commission?* But I didn't say it, because it seemed kind of rude, and also because I couldn't imagine what commission she'd get for selling a twelve-dollar suit. Instead, I just stared at myself in the three-way mirror, turning right and then left, mostly checking out my chest, which did look amazing. I tried to ignore the other parts of me that looked less good. Of which there were several.

I have never, myself, sat down and cataloged my many

imperfections, but if you are a girl-person and you live in the world, people feel compelled to let you know this stuff. So I am aware that, in addition to the lopsided boobs, my shoulders are too wide (rowing crew has not helped with this) and my eyes are too small; I have a weak chin, no cheekbones, stumpy legs, and, oh yes, a big bump on the bridge of my nose, which itself is not particularly small.

Most days, none of this bothers me. I know that's a radical position, to be a homely girl who does not secretly dream of a makeover, but I truly don't. Of course, part of that is because I can do all the extreme makeovers on earth, but nothing will fundamentally change what I look like. I will look like me, but with extra makeup. Me, but a tiny bit thinner. Me, but with a new haircut.

On the whole, this is not something I mind, because knowing this gives me license not to obsess about it too much. If it's not a thing I can change, then there's no point in worrying about it, and it's not like my self-worth is tied to whether random guys want to hook up with me.

I'm actually a very secure and happy person, and I know this because I tell it to my therapist every Monday for fifty minutes.

I pushed my hair behind my ears and checked out my reflection. It was a radical act, to be the homely girl in the red bikini. It was a giant middle finger to men and the world and my fellow swimmers at the Hidden Oaks community pool.

In my ear, Bethany said, "Get it."

So I bought the bikini. And then I went to the pool with Bethany.

· · ·

The cookie in the right side of my bikini top felt kind of nasty and sweaty, but it made my boobs look great, so I tried to ignore it. We gave our passes to Shannon Garcia, who goes to school with us, and went through the locker room.

We walked out onto the pool deck. Kit, who had gone through the men's room, ran off to join some kids from his school who were playing Marco Polo in the shallow end. "Don't forget about my Fudgsicle!" he called.

"Don't run on the deck!" I called back, and we watched as he did a belly flop next to his friends, who screamed at the splash of chilly water. There's something kind of liberating about seeing little kids at the pool; they're just there to have fun and that's it.

Bethany grabbed my arm. "Ohmigod," she said. "Ohmigod."

"What?"

She jerked her head toward the guard chair. I shaded my eyes and looked up at the bronzed body of the lifeguard. I had to squint against the sun to see who it was—he was wearing sunglasses and his face was in profile. Of course, it was Greg D'Agostino, every bit as handsome as he'd been the last time I'd seen him. You know. Yesterday. I'm not sure why Bethany was acting like seeing him was a surprise, since that was literally the entire purpose for our being at the pool: to see Greg, or, more to the point, for Greg to see Bethany.

We were not the only people who had noticed Greg in his half-naked splendor. There was a whole contingent of girls sitting opposite the pool from him, in the best viewing spot. They weren't even trying to pretend not to stare. Greg was trying his best to pretend not to notice. Or maybe he really was watching the pool. Which I guess was his job.

He glanced up as we walked over and took seats to his left.

His eyes barely stopped on me or my perfect, symmetrical chest. But they went to Bethany in her blue bikini and stuck there.

I'd expected that, honestly. Bethany is legitimately the prettiest girl I have ever seen; I suspect she's probably the prettiest girl most people have ever seen. I swear to God I'm not jealous, though. I've seen the way people treat her for it, and in my opinion, it's actually better to be plain.

Bethany noticed him watching and stood up a little straighter. Which basically means she stuck her chest out a little farther.

I rolled my eyes, just a little. I couldn't see Greg's, obviously, because of the sunglasses, but his face was still pointed in our direction. I'd already spread my towel out on one of the deck chairs and sat down, but Bethany was still standing up. She cocked a hip, propped a toe on the chair, and started to spray sunscreen on her leg.

I snorted, because she'd already put on sunscreen before we left the house. I watched as she repeated the process with the other leg.

"He's still looking," she hissed. "Do yours, too."

"He's not looking at *my* legs," I said. I was already sitting on my very exposed butt and I was not getting up for anything. I pulled out my AP Euro reading, which was Dostoyevsky's *Crime and Punishment,* and dropped it on my chair. It was a big book. It went *thunk.*

"Why did you bring that? That isn't a beach book."

"We aren't at the beach, and I have to write an essay on it for next week."

She shoved the book away from me and pulled her bikini straps down her shoulders. "Do my back," she whispered. "And make it look good."

This whole business was shockingly un-Bethany-like.

"Did you get a personality transplant since yesterday?" I asked.

"Shhh. He's still looking."

"Possibly because you woke up this morning and decided to become a complete attention whore."

"Shhh!"

But I was already spraying her back. "This is ridiculous," I said. "You're going to fall out of your top."

"He stopped looking," she said. "Can you get him to look over here again?"

"Oh, Bethany!" I shouted, making a show of rubbing in the sunscreen. "Your skin is so soft!"

"Not like that," she hissed. I glanced up at Greg, who had just moved to hide a smile behind his hand.

I'd made Greg D'Agostino smile.

I pulled Bethany's straps up and sat back with my book, glancing down toward the shallow end to make sure Kit was still playing with his friends. "I've done my duty," I said. "I'm going to read now."

She took a few deep breaths, like she was psyching herself up for something, and then said, "Let's go off the board."

I blinked at her a few times and shut my book. This was another un-Bethany-like thing to suggest. "What?"

"Come on," she said. "I'll look stupid if I go by myself."

I was about to say, *You'll look stupid anyway,* but she was doing pleading Bethany eyes, which work as well on me as on anyone else. Also, it was kind of hot, and I was starting to leave sweat marks on my towel.

"Fine," I said. "I'll go off the board." I got in line behind Bethany and a couple of other girls, who were trying to get Greg's attention with flips and twists. Bethany did an elegant swan dive. I got up on the board.

Greg's eyes were still on Bethany as she climbed the ladder, flipping her shiny black hair over her shoulder.

I felt something weird.

I tried to catalog the feeling. It was definitely not philia. I was jealous. I am never jealous of Bethany, but right then, for some reason, as I stood at the end of the board with my perfect chest in my red twelve-dollar bikini, I wanted, just once, for Greg to look at me. That's it. Just for him to acknowledge that I was even there, that I existed, and that my boobs looked really, really good. I bounced my way down the board. One major jump at the end, and I catapulted myself up in the air for the biggest cannonball Greg would see all summer.

At the last second, I heard Bethany call, "Wait!" I twisted around to see what was wrong and ended up landing flat on my back.

Which caused the clasp of my top to pop open.

It occurred to me, belatedly, that there might have been a reason this suit was on clearance.

I managed to clasp it again before I surfaced, and I hoped no one had actually seen anything important. It had been a huge splash—my back still stung from it—so hopefully that had been enough to cover my nakedness.

Bethany was standing at the top of the ladder.

"What is wrong with you?" I asked.

"Nothing," she said. "Uh, are you okay?"

"Yeah." I dog-paddled over to where she was standing and pulled myself out of the water. "What were you screaming about?"

"It's just, I remembered something. Like, a reason you might not want to go off the board."

"You were the one who told me to do it!"

"Yeah, because I forgot. . . ." I pulled myself out of the pool, and she said, "Oh, no."

"What? What?"

She stared pointedly at my chest. I looked down.

I had one full-looking boob and one that looked sadly deflated.

"Oh, no," I said. "Where is it?"

We stood side by side looking down into the water. By now, some little kids had lined up and were splashing in behind me.

"I don't see it," she whispered. "Do you think silicone floats or sinks?"

"I don't know!"

"Well, if it were floating, we'd see it, right? So it must be under there somewhere." She prodded me with her elbow. "Go get it."

"What?"

I had to move out of the way of the ten-year-old boy coming up the ladder behind me. "Would you move?" he said.

"Sorry," I said.

"Just dive in and get it!" Bethany whispered.

"I don't have any goggles! You get it."

"I don't have any goggles, either, and it's your boob!"

"It's not a boob! It's a cookie! And it was your idea! You get it!"

"What am I going to do with it? I'll look pretty suspicious climbing out of the deep end with a fake boob"—I gave her a dirty look—"I mean, a cookie in my hand. Just dive in, find it, put it back in your top, and get out again."

"How long do you think I'm capable of holding my breath?" I asked, but I turned to one of the little kids in line and said, "Can I borrow your goggles?" and someone else in line ahead of me said, "OW!" and I looked up and realized one of the other little shits—kids! I mean kids!—had thrown my fake boob in his face.

"What was that for?" he shouted, picking it up and throwing it back.

"OW!" said the first kid. "I found it in the pool! It's a tan jellyfish!"

"It doesn't have any testicles," one of the other kids pointed out.

"You mean *tentacles*!"

"That's what I said!"

He threw it back and it hit the kid next to him in the stomach, who shouted, "You *suck*, Cooper!" and then pelted him back.

"Do something," Bethany whispered. "Do something, do something, do something."

"Boys," I said in my best babysitter voice. "Can I please have the . . . uh . . . jellyfish?"

"We found it!"

"I just want to check something," I said.

"You're gonna steal it!"

"I want to see what brand it is!" I tried grabbing it from the nearest kid, but now the little boys were in full-on keep-away mode, and he threw it over my head to someone else, which was when it hit Greg D'Agostino square in the chest.

And for one long, horrible second, thanks to the viscosity of wet silicone and the terrible luck I was born with, it stuck there.

"Oh, God," I said.

"Oh, God," Bethany said.

The fake boob dropped to the floor of the guard stand. Greg picked it up between his thumb and forefinger and looked at it.

Greg D'Agostino was touching my boob.

It was a lot less enjoyable than I would have expected.

I tried to decide which was worse: claiming the boob or walking away and hoping that he maybe thought it belonged to someone else. "We'll go sit down," I muttered to Bethany. "And we'll walk slowly. Just pretend it doesn't exist."

"Okay," she said. "I'm walking in front of you. We're walking. . . . We're walking. . . . Hey, do you want a Dr Pepper?"

"Not. Now."

"Right, sorry." She sat in her chair, and I sat next to her. Greg D'Agostino blew the whistle for break and climbed down from the guard stand.

He was yelling at the little boys, who were trying to get my boob back from him. "It's ours! It's ours!" they shouted.

"It's not yours!"

"Yuh-huh!"

"Do you guys want a time-out? It's break. Go sit down."

"We want the jellyfish!"

"Do I need to call your mom again, Cooper?"

"You suck!"

"I told you to sit down!"

Cooper stuck out his tongue, but Greg already had his back

to him, because he was walking around the edge of the pool. Toward us.

"Your book," Bethany whispered. "Get your book."

I grabbed *Crime and Punishment* from the foot of my chair and opened to a random page. As Greg approached, I turned the page and said airily, "I just love Russian novels, don't you?"

"American novels are so short," she agreed nervously.

"I mean, why bother? You might as well read the back of a cereal box."

"I know!"

By now, Greg was standing at the foot of my chair. I swallowed.

He said, "Hi."

"Oh," I said. "Hello. We were just discussing the merits of Russian literature. Thoughts? Opinions?" I glanced up at him. He really was beautiful. Dark wavy hair. Good muscle tone. Excellent teeth. "Revelations?"

He glanced at my book. He said, "Лично я думаю что работа Чехова немного более актуальна."

I . . . had not seen that coming. I glanced at Bethany, who I knew did not speak Russian any better than I did, and she raised her eyebrows fractionally.

He still had my boob in his hand, this beautiful, barechested, Russian-speaking boy. I wasn't sure whether this was extremely funny or extremely sad, but I guess my better nature won out, because I started laughing. I hoped Greg didn't think I was laughing at him. Bethany shot me a horrified look.

I only know one Russian phrase; my father went to St. Petersburg for a history conference a few years ago, and I convinced him that this was the only thing he really needed to learn out of his phrasebook. I asked, maybe a little suggestively, "Скажите пожалуйста, где туалет?"

He laughed.

He tossed my fake boob to me. It landed on page 327 with a splat. I stared at it. He said, "Nice cannonball. By the way." He smiled. Such good teeth.

And then he walked away.

"What did you say to him?" Bethany asked out of the side of her mouth. "It sounded hot."

I put my sunglasses on and tried to look as cool as a lopsided girl in a discount-bin bikini can look. "I asked him where the bathroom is."

She looked momentarily stricken, and then she laughed and so did I. I said, "You're lucky I philia you so much."

"I philia you, too," Bethany said. Then, pointing at the cookie, she added, "So are you going to put it back in or what?"

I picked it up, letting it dangle between my thumb and forefinger as if it really were a jellyfish I'd found in the pool. It was kind of gummy and awful. I looked down at my chest. I said, "Sorry, girls." And then I shouted, "HEY, COOPER!" and when he looked up, I thwacked him in the nose with my boob. He grabbed it, whooped, and went off to play catch with his friends.

Excerpt copyright © 2019 by Ariel Kaplan.
Cover art copyright © 2019 by Christine Blackburne.
Published by Alfred A. Knopf, an imprint of Random House Children's Books,
a division of Penguin Random House LLC, New York.

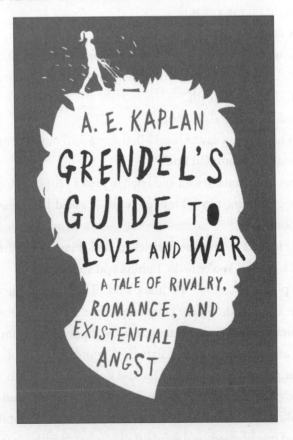